SS SHADOW EMPIRE
Canon II
Abalon

Palais Cêlesta

author　Tycoon SAITO
translator　Yoshie HIYAMA
publisher　Yasushi ITO
ISBN978-4-7876-0109-4
English Edition Dec.2019

SS SHADOW EMPIRE

Palais Cēlesta

Author Tycoon SAITO

Those worthy of reading this works
Les Centuries the hundred psalms 2-78

1行目　バブル経済の崩壊で海底に沈む景気の海神（＝アメリカ）。
2行目　アフリカの遺伝子にフランス系の混血者が為政者に
3行目　救援の遅れで（カリブ海？の）島々の住民は流血のままに放置されるだろう。
4行目　この事実のほうが下手に隠されたスキャンダルよりも失脚の原因となる

英語訳

　　The grand Neptune: USA, under collapsed bubble economy
　　African gene mixed French blood to act statesman's role
　　Way too late to rescue so people of (Caribbean?) Islands shall be left in blood shed
　　This fact will damage him more than the badly hidden scandal will

Middle French (Moyen Francais)
　　Le grand Neptune du profond de la mer
　　De gent Punique & sang Gauloys mesle

Les Isles a sang, pour le tardif ramer
Plus luy nuira que l'occult mal cele

The first line can be translated as a great Neptune sank deep in the bottom of the sea, but this literal translation woul sound nonsensical so the writer paraphrased it as American in the depression after the fall of bubble economy.

The second line would mean a dual heritage of Aflican and French genes and is telling such person will appear in America. The first statesman that satisfies this condition is President Obama.

The word Isles on the third line means islands. In the middle ages, this word Isles was often used to call the islands in the Caribbean Sea. If the relationship of this word with the first hald of this statement is tgaken into consideration, England and Japan are also called as islands, however, the wroter dee,s ot pre reaspman;e tp deco@jer tjos wprd os;es as os;amds om the Caribbean Sea. In this assumption, this line is taken as expressing the chaos caused by natural desasters and civil wars and so on.

Then, the forth line can be taken as that, the fact that he left the problems on the Caribbena Islands unattended later led to drive his political life into a corner.

The above translation is of that part of the psalms written by Michel Nostradamvs in 1555. This psalm exactly means the end of the Obama Administration! Whoever understands the writer's writing so far in this way, this book would become worthwhile for him to read. The ancient Latin spells present U as V so the writer is following this way here.

What the writer wishes to state here is to tell you the readers that in the contents of Les Centuries matters that cannot be taken as what already happened in the past are the ones that are for sure to happen in the future. Nostradamvs who penetrated the future was an issuer of cryptograph so he must have naturally seen through that cryptograph beakers would appear in the later times. Cryptograph does come to have its meaning oonly when breakers of the cryptograph exist. Most of the cryptograph breakers come to realize the true meaning of the cryptograph after the reactor event comes tro he apparent. Therefore, to those who lack ability of deciphering the cryptograph, it remains for ever to be totally meaningless. To show an actual example of reaction of those people who do not have any such ability, when the writer's acquaintance took this cryptanalysis to one major publishing company, he was questioned if he could clearly state what had not happened was going to happen in coming days for srue. The writer is talking about one completed work which was taken to this pulishing company in early Octoebr, 2008.

As an overall flow of this work, what the writer is intending to aim at is to pile up the fictional stories without losing the direction to have the work help leading the readers to follow the basis of the writer's deciphering of the flow of the story so that this work is not a simple fiction but an implication of natural disasters and damages of wars that will arise in the future. His prime intention is to present a clue to the readers to survive the coming future offering his readers to read his work in this understanding. To those readers that come to realize such writer's intention this work should be able to offer them a significantly great value.

■ Introduction

Uncontrolable desire will lead the world to ruin and destraction. There is no victory.

The human race experienced worldwide wars as many as twice in the 20th century. Despite this fact and the disastrous results caused by the two wars, war is repeated under the name of Justice. This can be called the destiny that humans who are unable to learn from the past are to face. Now, countries are showing the limit of being the countries in the frame of definition of the term of country and losing the original meaning of the word country and have totally deviated from peoples' happiness. Victims of former WW are now no longer victims. They underwent a transfiguration at the point they themselves came to obtain the power of the state.

For the purpose of benefiting one's own happiness, to sacrifice other's happiness with no argument is an unforgiven deed in front of the supreme existence of what we call God. Now that countries cannot guarantee their people's happiness, it is no wonder if such group that handles countries at its will beyhond the border of what countries ought to be.

Is what this group aims at creation of the tide of time securing the power which supersedes the power of countries and which could never be achieved in the previous century? We tend to believe what cannot be seen by the human eyes does not exist. This is wrong. What cannot be seen can only be seen by those who try to see as God does.

Now, the gate of Hell is open. For wide is the gate and broad is the way that leads to destruction. When power arbitrarily starts dashing to get another power, people must know what will be waiting for then. This work is to show where an organization which exceeds a countery which is not a county is to end up. This country does not own its territory but own all the territories. Such organization will not easily show its existence. All what we can see is to see it in its shadow and just to feel its being there.

Provided truth exists in this world, uncontrollable desire will lead the world to ruin and destruction.

There exists no victory.

CONTENTS

TABLE OF CONTENTS

SS SHADOW EMPIRE

Those who are qualified to read this book

Introduction ···6

CANON Ⅱ. Abalon ·· 11

  1. Alternative Fundraising Plan ······························· 13

  2. Robert's order and Simon's information················· 30

  3. First meeting with Indian Connection ·················· 51

  4. Maria's Room ·· 69

  5. China Connection·· 79

  6. Report from Robert and Simon ·························· 97

  7. The Official Check added on Hell Computer ··········105

  8. Person unbefitting a Researcher·······················121

  9. Transferring Check and Women Trouble ···············132

  10. The First Remittance ·······································144

  11. Deposit of Down Payment································151

  12. First Portion of Share ······································165

13. Remittance Preparation of Second Share·············179

14. Occurrence of Difficulty in making Remittance·······188

15. Departure for Abalone ·····································198

16. Night before the Third Remittance························209

17. Mafia's hunch ···231

18. Berthing Cargo Ship Cossak ····························239

19. Chasing by Santa Rosaria·······························245

20. Double Cross···250

21. Reloading on the Ocean ·································268

22. The Waves on Indian Ocean are High ···············281

23. Hunting for Escapees ····································299

24. Funeral and New Beginning····························319

25. Another Destruction ······································327

THE END of canon Ⅱ. Abalon ·····························338

SS SHADOW EMPIRE

CANON
II. Abalon

We often hear the word Love. There has been no other such age as this contemporary age when this many people are this badly in need of Love. However, fact that a number of crimes have been committed under the name of Love is also not denied. Women of extreme beauty giving free reign to their desires have been destroying a number of men. In other cases, power which Love is equipped with results in being transformed into a gush and in destroying a huge iron-walled organization. Love itself is opening a gulf waiting for those people to fall in who pursue only love which in fact leads to perishment.

Wickedness often times hides itself in love and is making a pit fall in your life. And strangely, that fact is frequently apt to be sealed. Here the writer will unseal that seal. Come and look, how all living things, great or small, are tossing about in what is called Love.

1. Alternative Fund Raising plan

A few weeks passed since Show Taro came back to Japan, in the early afternoon of some Saturday, he was in his office as usual waiting for visitors who may or may not come. Since he did not have any work to do, he browsed the English version news column on internet, and his eyes caught the EP news issued from Italy reporting a car which was carrying Bernard Gambino and his group exploded on the way from the court back to the prison and the defendants Bernard and his men successfully escaped.

This happening was not reported at all on Japanese newspapers or TV. It usually happens quite frequently that such cases which are assessed by Japanese news media as giving no influence to the politics and the economy of Japan are often ignored and are not reported in Japan.

The problem is such news which will influence Japanese investors tend to be disregarded by Japanese reporters. In the past in America an employee of a Japanese large-scale trading firm made a big loss through the transaction of copper forward trading, the tone of the report differs much between Japan and America. In America the size of the loss was precisely reported while on the other hand in Japan the Japanese trading firm concerned refrained from issuing its official comments with an excuse of short information and as a consequence this incident was not immediately reported in Japan. This caused a great loss to stock price crash to Japanese investors since they came to realize this occurrence after American investors' clearing of accounts. To win or to lose depends on enough information or short information which is not only taking place in the war front.

At the war front, such operation that lures the enemy's main troops to come out to the front using military damy is oftentimes practiced. For an actual example, during WW2 Japanese Imperial Navy lured American Task Force at the naval battle off the Engano Cape of Phillipines on October 5, 1944 using an airborn military unit without loading aircrafts on board.

It was not to mention that the decoy itself was not the real purpose of this strategy but the true object of this strategy was to delute the enemy to lead another fleet to plunge into Leyte Gulf, but after all, that fleet turned back for some totally unknown mysterious reasons. However, even if the fleet had successfully plunged into Leyte Gulf, the troops after landing would have faced a great difficulty due to lack of supplies and would not have been able to change the tide of the war in any significant way.

To add some more information, the Spanish word Engano which is meant for Cape Engano means 「deceive」 or 「flimflam」 but this must be a mere accidental coincidence. No one would know that the Spanish who named this cape as Engano may have had the ability of claiyavoyance of the naval battle that took place after several hundreds of years, however, it might have been the case that a religionist with a specialized training received some apocalypse or the like and named the pass as Enggano Pass.

Nostradamus wrote down in 「Le Centurise」 after WW1 soon coming WW2 that of naval battle would bigger than before.

2-40

First Line A little afterwards without much interval

— 14 —

Second Line A great fuss will take place on the sea and on the land

Third Line And that fuss develops into an extremely large-scaled naval battle

Forth Line Fire and beastial humans will continue to make attacks which were growing more and more cruel.

When this battle takes place is not referred by Nostradamus, but supposedly it will be certain that the size of such battle will be of a world wide scale as same as the previous war. This can be understood by the second line of the above psalm. It is admitted that at WW1 the air power was so insignificant that it was not good enough to influence the consequence of the war. However, naval battle of the WW2 was fought in a fairly large scale and at the last stage of the war, humans who are alike animals spread the devastation to no end with inhumanity, cruelty and atrocity.

American soldiers burnt jungles out with flamethrowers while Japanese soldiers flew airplane with fuel just enough for the one-way flight and stormed into American warships. It was reported that with this one-way airplane attack several of such huge warships as aircraft carriers were made sink deep in the sea in a moment. Analysis made by American troops of the record which had long been sealed since after the end of the war is now made open which is revealing the fact that the accuracy of the hitting rate of Kamikaze suicide corps was over 50%.

Contrary to this report, at the Japan side, some researchers were publicizing such propaganda that stated the hitting rate of Kamikaze was almost nil which however included planes with faulty maintenance and consequently crash landed before they reached the targeted warship. But what was truly happening must be the scene that American warship was floating on the sea presenting itself as a huge size target of attack by the Kamikaze planes which were able to have gone through the barrage and made a successful approach to the targeted warship.

In this modern world of economy lots of camouflage are being devised as a desparate endeavor to make corporations survive.

What is frequently exercised in Japan is that the management people who are struggling with worsened financial conditions of their corporations are taking the method of exchanging accommodation bills which means they issue post-dated bills or checks.

Taking this method, they take such bills or checks to their banks to get these accepted with a discounted rate and complete collection of bad debts within a few months time, or else, to try get more orders in an endeavor to let their corporations survice. In case these countermeasures work well, they can escape from the crisis, but if don't, these may possibly develop into a flaud case. Even if they dare to camouflage the case as a commercial transaction, unless that action causes any trouble to other unrelated people it won't be treated as a crime…

Now, Show Taro seemed to have a visit after a long while so went to the doorway to receive the visitor and found there the president Minoru Suzuki of Suzuki Shoten standing. He was the person who failed to change the fake of Rembrandt painting to cash in the past.

Show Taro [Welcome. Long time no see.]

— 16 —

Suzuki　　[Can you spare just about half an hour for me?]

Show Taro [Yes, of course. Please take it easy.]

Suzuki was looking around in Show Taro's office and made it sure that there was no one there, and sank himself in the sofa as was offered.

As suggested by Show Taro, Suzuki took Wasanbon (refined Japanese sugar) into the mouth. Putting the tea whisk aside Show Taro placed a Tenmoku tea bowl in front of the sofa, Suzuki took up the tea bowl from the Tenmoku stand. He slightly turned the front of the bowl and bowed once and took the tea. Then he again gazed that Tenmoku stand.

In the first place, Suzuki noticed that the Tenmoku stand was of vermilion colored Taimai painting. He thought it might have been made during the era of Song over to that of Yuan in China. Such products are called Karamono. Careful observation would find that a metal fitting called Fukurin was attached to enforce the edge of the Tenmoku stand to protect the rim of the stand. He noticed this edging was not made of tin alloy which meant that Tenmoku stand had not been made in Japan.

His findings of these facts were telling that this Tenmoku stand had been shipped out from China during the era of Sung over to that of Yuan.

Suzuki　　[I did not expect I could meet with such an old Tenmoku stand at a store selling European antiques.]

Show Taro [Antiques of the era of Yuan are obtainable in Europe. Those are the 13th century products. Originally it may have been a set of ten pieces.]

Suzuki　　[Well, at that age, Japanese overseas trading must have been booming.]

Lightly nodding, Suzuki put the Tenmoku stand down and put the tea bowl on it.

Suzuki [By the way, purpose of my visit today is that I wish to consult with you in secret about a task that came to my hand. Regarding 『The Man of the Golden Helmet』 which you kindly worked for me I failed to sell it successfully, but this new request was also the sort of the task that only art related professionals could deal with. What about your schedule today? Can you give me time today?]

Show Taro [As you will see, I do not expect many visitors, so please take time with me.]

Suzuki [I often visit Vietnam or Singapore for my import business of gardening bricks. This case is brought to me from my male acquaintance whom I came to be associated in Singapore. He wishes me to purchase paintings.]

Show Taro [Is what your Singapore acquaintance is talking about, such paintings of contemporary arts?]

Suzuki [Do you have any such good buys?]

Show Taro [Last month, a solicitor whom I know was seeking buyers for the paintings that are for liquidation due to bankruptcy of the owner and in those paintings I noticed some contemporary arts were mixed.]

Suzuki [Are those arts the ones painted before the artist's painting style has been perfected⋯]

Show Taro [You sound like not too keen about these. Besides those, there seem to be paintings of Late Impressionists of sizes from 10 to 20…what do you think?]

Suzuki   [Well, they will prefer the paintings that are readily exchangeable with cash as that sort of deal can be carried on in secret.]

Show Taro [I have another information which is a collector wishing to dispose modern art painted by Chinese artists. Those paintings were collected before such Chinese modern art fakes landed in Japan so there is a possibility those are authentic.]

Suzuki   [I see. You can make such kind of offers, too…]

Usual visitors will talk about some specific demand clearly pointing out such and such are what they want, but Suzuki's attitude looked like that his request was not based on his own interest but is for a task of someone else.

Show Taro [Sorry but I'm not really with you. To start with, art collectors have their own taste of art or the genre of preference, don't they?]

Suzuki   [They need paintings.]

Show Taro [Then, what genre of paintings? Oil paintings or Japanese paintings or else?]

Suzuki   [Well, frankly, this is not the matter of paintings.]

Show Taro returned his question giving him a little dubious look.

Show Taro [Won't you explain your proposal a little more in detail?]

Suzuki   [Should you not feel my proposal which I am now explaining unacceptable, promise me to wholely forget it. Can you keep this talk in absolute confidence?]

To Show Taro who was about to bent himself forward to Suzuki in curiosity, Suzuki said the above in a low but strong voice and rolled his eyes and staired at Show Taro. Confirming Show Taro's nodding, he started to continue talking.

Suzuki [Last month I went to Vietnum to purchase bricks and on the way home I dropped at Singapore where I was approached by a business person by the name of Genta Shiaku who is engazed in shrimp aquaculturing business in Indonesia. Before then, I had met him several times. What he proposed for me to deal was something in relation to the method of remittance, but as a form of business it is an art product trade.]

Show Taro [Remittance···and art objects? What is it all about?]

Suzuki [I wish you to receive orders for several times from now on.]

Show Taro [Sorry I am totally not with you. Won't you tell me more in detail of what you wish me to do.]

Suzuki [To be in short, it is business to make the flow of money untraceable using the trade of art objects as a cloak of invisibility.]

Show Taro [What at all do you want me to handle?]

Suzuki [In the first place you receive a purchase instruction of art products and you will receive the fund for such purchase. Next, you will be contacted and will learn cancellation of the deal due to their reasons. On receiving such cancellation notice, you are to make remittance of the 85% of the fund with the 15% as cancellation penalty. The fund won't be channeled through Japan. It goes to an overseas art dealer who is your trustworthy partner.]

Show Taro [Who is the original funder?]

Suzuki [Hell Computer of America.]

Show Taro [Where is the final receiver of the remittance?]

Suzuki [It will be either Dubai or Europe. The main thing is the fund must be channeled through places other than Japan. Reward to the practitioner is 12% and 3% is for the agents. If you have possible connection, we wish the fund to pass through any place other than Japan. Then if this can be done, we can share the 3% for each 1.5%.]

Show Taro [Is that one only deal?]

Suzuki [No, If we make the first try successful, we are to do the same exercise at least for several times.]

Show Taro [Are there any other conditions?]

Suzuki [The fund cannot go through Singapore. What I heard is at the previous time they wanted to try Vietnam, however, the branch manager of the bank accepted the processing of the fund only with presentation of export letter of credit.]

Show Taro posed to think over this offer and the face of Simon came up in his mind. As Show Taro understands Simon's cousin is in New York, it may be possible to investigate the trustworthiness of this story from the side of America. Thinking that just to make an investigation won't cost much, Show Taro opened his mouth.

Show Taro [Can you allow me for about a week or so? I will talk to my acquaintance overseas.]

Suzuki [I will appreciate it.]

Bowing lightly, Suzuki wiped cold sweat on his forehead.

Show Taro [By the way, what sort of amount will the first remittance be ?]

Suzuki [According to what Mr. Shiaku told me, an Indian jewelry dealer is to advise the amount of fund at the American side.]

Show Taro [One other question. For what purpose do they make remittance?]

Suzuki [It could be the wealthy person's diversified investment. In fact, I have not heard of the true purpose.]

Show Taro [At time of transaction is anyone coming to keep watching the deal?]

Suzuki [I understand so.]

Show Taro [Give me time. I will consult with my companion.]

Suzuki [Please be careful not to have this information leaked out.]

Hearing the contents of Suzuki's request, the word Money Laundering came up to his mind. But the characteristic point of this offer is that it is not the request to Show Taro himself receives the remittance and transfer it by establishing Show Taro's own private account at a bank. Also, this story is based on the trading style to pass the remittance through countries other than Japan which may somehow lessen Show Taro's stress. To Show Taro who has various overseas art business connections this offer is somewhat scary and at the same time pretty interesting.

Here, the writer must add some more explanation about money laundering. Money laundering is the flow of money earned by criminal deeds such as gambling, drug transaction, prostitution, and fraud which oftentimes amount to a great deal of sum and because the amount comes to be so big that the yielding source of such sum of money becomes difficult to be sort out. For this reason, such fund can form a route for political fund contribution and this criminal act is being committed beyond the border of countries in order to pull the wool over investigation authorities' eyes.

And, of course, such action can be taken simply to help make the globally acting businessmen's attempt to escape from payment of a large sum of income tax or inheritance tax successful. Wealthy people also often take such actions as to purchase gold or pratinum ingots or the Impressionists' paintings which they hung on the wall of their son's dining room as means to avoid the risk coming from inflation or foreign currency exchange losses as dealing records of such assets are quite difficult to be traced.

And suppose this sort of action is applied to a jewelry dealer, he will take the action of starting off with purchase of a brilliant-cut diamond of a size of more than one carat. What the writer means here is when some one tries money-laundering, he won't take the means of buying real estate as such a deal needs official documentations which won't suit to the purpose of "erasing the footprint" (=to hide the money shifting route).

And in many cases, such fund will usually be transferred to a bank account of a third country where that fund was not earned nor where the person's present address exists. However, needless to add, if such person originally lives in a country where no income tax is assessed called 'tax heaven', he is exempted from most of such worries.

The important point there was that he should not form such a deal alone by himself. Reason why is if the deal develops into smokescreen, he will surely be caught in a trouble. Therefore, he has to form up a syndicate with several companions and together with them to face the negotiation with his opposite. To speak the least of the situation of the opposite side there should exist a cerain organization to share the earnings of the deal, and if it is a fraud, such large organization shall not exist behind the deal. What the writer wishes to mean is behind a big deal there must exist the back shade without exception so this existance can work as supporting evidence of the deal's credibility.

Talking that far, Suzuki left Show Taro's office showing a relieved look. Not losing time, Show Taro sent an e-mail to Robert Grant who was said to be working as an investigator for a U.K. insurance company. He did not forget to add to that e-mail asking Robert if he might have heard such a fraud case from any one of his contact.

What he did next was to check his business card holder and take out the card of Simon Zamir who was doing in Kobe a wholesale business of America-made sundrygoods. He came out of his office to the point of the place where the wiring condition is smoothly working and phoned him while walking. According to Romano Sfolza, Simon seemed to be related to Mosad, the Israelian special service agency, so Show Taro expected that he would be the first to come back to him with results of his investigation inside the

— 24 —

country of America.

Show Taro told Simon Suzuki's talk and got Simon's assurance that he would ask his cousin in New York about the matter Show Taro raised, though Simon told on that phone that if such a story comes with a request for Show Taro to pay for a guarantee money for his promise to enforce practice of this promise, such story is almost no doubt a flaud. Simon's reasoning for his saying so is quite simple and obvious. Person who takes the biggest risk is the practitioner himself whose name and account details are made open, therefore, that such person who bears the highest risk is to be demanded a guarantee deposit is completely absurd. In case the practioner betrays, if he belongs to a registered corporeal organization, a follow-up survey can be possible, therefore, such organization can be accused for commitment of the crime of flaud.

In order to help Show Taro, Simon tendered a request to Show Taro to dig out such information of the name of the opposite side organization of the Indian jewelers for example. Hearing Simon's request, Show Taro was convinced that Simon as the person concerned about foreign trading business had an expert knowledge of the full range of such laws.

The next person Show Taro made a contact with was naturally Akemi Kitsuregawa, as he had heard before that she was using a sewig factory in Hong Kong for production of her less expensive range of garments. Ginza is the area where since 6 o'clock in the early evening pretty night butterflies start flying about appearing from nowhere. Amongst those butterflies Show Taro visited Akemi reaching her store on foot just about the time when she was making her ready to close the store and to go home. As she was in

— 25 —

her business suits since she was working till that moment, but already changed the earrings and the ring to more leisureful bold designed ones. She had just worn some perfume as well.

Akemi　　　　[Hi, my seldom visitor. That 「Oda-Musashi」 concert was quite enjoyable. Next time I really wish to go to his concert with you, so won't you try to match your availability?]

Show Taro　[Apologies. There was a late hour appointment with my customer last week who was insisting to see an oil painting of my possession. I will make it up next time for sure.]

Akemi　　　　[His last week concert was his 3,000th memorable concert borrowing out the whole site of Odaiba Seaside Park. His concert is popular with his talks and not only with the singing performance. The surprise guest of that time was Kyuzo Wakayama who was in pure white clothes aboard his yatcht which he parked alongside the harvour and joined the concert.]

Show Taro　[You mean he was wearing a captain's uniform?]

Akemi　　　　[Did you know that already?]

Show Taro　[I saw him in that costume on the internet news video.]

Akemi　　　　[The red color bouquet was overfloaded with flowers.]

Show Taro　[Of which roses were seizing just about one third.]

Akemi　　　　[From my seat, I could not distinguish the species of flowers.]

Show Taro　[Roses and some orchids.]

Akemi　　　　[He then continued and talked 「If I had seen this

— 26 —

scene when I was a child, I would have thought it was a dream of mine in which Mr. Wakayama ran me over by his car and came for apologies with flowers.』 and at this comment the whole hall burst into big laughter.]

Show Taro [Then? He didn't disappear as is?]

Akemi [Then he sang 『All The Time For You』 and went away.]

Show Taro [By the way didn't Oda Musashi sing 『Declaration of Clean Sweep』 ?]

Akemi [He did, perhaps 20 minutes past the opening of the show time. That 『Declaration of Clean Sweep』 became a hit song taken up by TV but I think the other song of 『Spirits Acting Shady』 is more becoming to his entity as that song is telling human life.]

Show Taro [I promise I will make time for sure at next chance.]

Akemi [I won't trust your 'next', so you must come with me tonight.]

Saying so, she took the key of her car from her bag and casually handed it over to Show Taro. This means she was proposing to spend the whole night that night with him at the Tokyo Bay area. Walking across the parking area, they discussed whereto they should go. They finally agreed to go and visit The China Town in Yokohama. While driving her car, Show Taro explained to her about the business that Suziki in that daytime asked him to take up. She was listening to him with her eyes rolling and seemed to have thought the story interesting.

Akemi   [As I know a woman president of an apparel company in Hong Kong, I will introduce you to her. She studied abroad in Japan and I understand she hired a financial advisor as her exlusive assistant.]

Show Taro [I am trying to locate art dealers.]

Akemi   [I think there should be some among her acquaintances as in her salon several authentic antiques are being decorated. She has a power to be able to collect that many authentics in her generation. But promise one thing. You are never to get involved in her three principles.]

Show Taro [What are those all about?]

Akemi   [If you promise, I will tell you.]

Show Taro [Sure, sure I do.]

Akemi   [Her three principles are whenever, wherever and whoever. She says men exist just for the purpose of serving her.]

Show Taro [That's interesting. Auch.ch.ch⋯]

As Akemi twisted Show Taro's cheek abruptly, he was just about losing control of the steering wheel.

Akemi   [She may be beautiful, but is a nasty woman as regards men.]

Show Taro [I can understand that.]

Akemi   [Men who did not have relationship with her are gays and this news will spread over Hong Kong on the following day.]

Show Taro [That's absurd. I can no way believe such rumor.]

Akemi   [You will see I am right if only you meet her.]

And this time she is leaning against his arm so again the car started swinging about on the highway.

Show Taro [Does she come to Japan often?]

Akemi   [She stays in Japan at least one week per month.]

Show Taro [Do you think if I meet her I can recognize she is the person.]

Akemi   [I shall never let you two be alone.]

Show Taro [As you please.]

To Show Taro, it seemed Akemi's usual jerousy started coming up, but soon after then her reasoning turned to show up as a well-founded fact.

2. Instruction from Robert and Information from Simon

One week afterwards, an e-mail reply from Robert came back to Show Taro with the following contents

TO TOM BOE

FM ROBERT GRANT

This is to acknowledge receipt of your e-mail. As a similar case that happened in the past, there is an instance of a case concerning the development of a personal computer software at Hell Computer. The procedure of this case is as follows. Hell Computer place the order with a certain dealer and open a letter of credit.

Then, the dealer who receives the order of this software from Hell Computer transfers part of this order to Hell Computer's designated dealer. In this manner, funds which are drawn out of America are remitted to Hell Computer's account that is provided in Dubay or Europe via a certain third country. Among such deals it sometimes happens that some will become the case of a demand of reimbursement using the insurance coverage for reasons as lost cargoes en route during the shipment. The characteristic point of such occurance is when such loss of cargoes is reported, the dealer without exception has been lost and untraceable. Therefore, to deal with such transactions we the insurance company must be most cautious. Therefore, we urge you to exert your utmost care to deal with this case.

To add more, once a lost DVD disk could be found later, the container which should contain such DVD disk was always empty. Hell Computer is insisting that they use a special system in which

— 30 —

the program is made to disappear for protection purposes once such gas injected container is opened up, but we are still pursuing the credibility of their insistence. When you obtain any supportive information, please advise us all such in detail.

As regards your question about the nature of such fund, I regret to tell you nothing has been clarified yet. However, what is sure about it is that it is also unthinkable that Hell Computer is simply trying to hide the fund for assess mamangement purposes. Please don't fail to report to us all information you will obtain of the related Indian jewelers or any other names of relations.

Good Luck !

Show Taro, reading Robert's e-mail this far, came to be able to understand that Robert has written this e-mail nonchalantly to show Show Taro that he is engaging himself in this tracing business as an insurance inspector. What puzzled Show Taro was his insurance company itself has not yet been able to make any definite clarification about for what purpose this programmed flow of fund is being fabricated, as there presented absolutely no answer to the question as to what is moving on the backward flow to this fund flow. However, Robert's insurance company seems to have grasped some evidence with which they can say positively that Hell Computer is not hiding the fund for the purpose of asset management.

That day, differently from usual exercise, he used a city hotel for meeting Simon who came from Kobe. He was eager to take Sushi of Tsukiji. As usual, Akemi accompanied with him. Different from Maria, Simon was not feeling weired of Akemi.

Simon comes to Tokyo often for jewelry trading, but he spends most of time while he is in Tokyo at Okachimachi where is the jewelry wholesale trading place. This time, he specially asked Show Taro to take him to a good Sushi house or restaurant, therefore, Show Taro scheduled to take him to Ginza but to not too conspicuous Sushi place. Should he take him to a famous and outstanding Sushi house, he would have to keep feeling uneasy not knowing who may happen to take the next table and also it is important that he chooses a place where will not be overcrowded in the evening of a weekday which is an important condition for a dinner where they talk business. Customer stratum is also another important factor to choose the restaurant. If such public security people as policemen or Yakuza members who belong to a big Yakuza group are sitting at the next table or nearby, it will certainly make them feel uncomfortable.

That Sushi House is hidden down on the basement floor of a multi tenant building facing a side street in Ginza showing the atmosphere of shelter in the crowded Ginza and has its own enthusiastic customers. As it was an early evening time, the daytime was getting faint but was still there so the gate lump was not really standing out. A tall stone lantern which was sprinkled with water was giving the visitors a sort of sense of relief and relaxation. Going through the restaurant curtain Noren with letters written in white Kanji charactors on the fabric of indigo blue color as [Tai-Hei-Raku(=Happy-go-Lucky)], fresh smell of the cedar sliding door which was replaced half a year ago was pleasantly felt. They posed a moment there and opened the cedar door.

Sushi chef　[Welcome.]

Show Taro　[Good evening. I'm Hayashi. I booked three seats tonight.]

Simon   [Hello, good evening. I am Simon.]

Simon was planning to make this place his perch in Tokyo thereafter, so he remembered chef's face and tried to let the chef remember Simon, too.

Proprietress [Will you please come this way.]

The eldery proprietress opened the Shoji door which was connected to the Tatami matress room behind the Shoji door.

Not taking time, Show Taro alerted Akemi to sit at the wall side end corner of the room and he sat next to her.

Following them, Simon sat at the opposite side of the table. Then the proprietress asked them while handing small dump towels to each of them.

Proprietress [Please allow me to reconfirm your reserved order···
                those which are not probihited for a Judaist are squid,
                octopus and conger eel, is my understanding correct?]

Simon   [Sorry I can't take shrimps, either. Fish without scapes
                are all not allowed.]

Proprietress [Oh, I see. I understand. Is the course of chef's choice
                'Fuku'(Happiness) as reserved acceptable?]

Simon   [Tonight's dinner is Mr. Hayashi's reservation, but this
                is on me as a reciprocation dinnder for him.]

So Simon told the proprietress and asked her to have the bill delivered to him.

Proprietress [You are our first guest here, aren't you?]

Simon   [You're right, as I come from Kobe···But as I am
                seeking a good restaurant that is not for sightseeing
                visitors and can be used for entertaining my business

contacts so I asked Mr. Hayashi to make reservation and take me such a place as here.]

Proprietress [Oh, I see. Thank you for your coming. Please use us whenever you will be in Tokyo.]

Simon [And, regarding the menu, how different are Fuku, Roku and Ju to each other?]

Proprietress [Fuku means 'sometimes lee is better than the wine' so the dish consists of the cut-out leftover of the Sushi fish so the kinds of fish differ at times. Fuku consists of 9 kinds of fish served with a soup. Ryoku is of eleven fish and the soup and Ju thirteen and soup.]

Simon [I see⋯..then three servings of Ju⋯.and two bottles of the vintage press beer please. And put a good amount of wasabi.]

Proprietress [Yes.]

The proprietress went away quickly and returned in less than 30 seconds and placed in front of each guest a small Kiseto Mukozuke container which contained a few pieces of green soybeans. Following this, well cooled glass goblet of French made was placed and skillfully whipping beer into bubbling state she filled the glasses with it. After placing each glass at each guest, the proprietress bowed and went out closing the Shoji door. Until Sushi is ready, they kept idle chatting to kill time. Toasting to each other, the banquet started.

Simon [Taking this opportunity, let me thank you again for all your care to me while in Italy. This is just a sigh of my gratitude so please take another glass of beer.]

Show Taro [Tableware used here are the chef's special selection.

Even with a single piece of glass for beer his commitment is reflected.]

Akemi [He will never allow to serve beer with a glass printed the logo of the beer brewer. Am I correct?]

Simon [Surface of this glass is not flatly smooth like sheet glass used before the war.]

Show Taro [This glass has such surface as the ice in the half way of melting and it looks that is what the chef likes it.]

Simon [Well said. I do agree.]

Akemi [What about this container of soybeans?]

Show Taro [This looks like a piece of Kiseto created by a ceramic artist who belongs to a young generation. Seemingly, he must have well considered the color matching of the green of soybeans.]

Simon [I now understand Japanese eats by eyes, too.]

Show Taro [When the proprietress was here she did not dare to explain but as the rank of the food goes up from Fuku then to Ryoku and to Ju, most naturally the tableware is also grading up. This is the charactor of this restaurant.]

Simon [And that is exactly Fuku means the leftover fortune. Taking good food with good tableware will prolong your life to 100 years. The longest we can live from now on will be 30 years, so why not enjoy today's life.]

Show Taro [Such viewpoint depends humans' concept of values. As regards tableware, people will know its value only after they use it.]

Akemi [While they are stored in cupboard, the essential

— 35 —

condition that they must satisfy is how well they can be layed. Also, at time of being washed, they must satisfy to be of handy shape for being washed.]

Simon [Rosanjin, the giant of food lover, was consistent with his choice of tableware that can raise the importance of seasonal presentation or of tableware that draw out the delicious presentation of served foods.]

Akemi [And that must be the reason why Rosanjin was selling tableware of his choice.]

Simon [But he was originally an antique dealer. He then developed himself into good tableware dealer and then to good foods.]

Akemi [He built Kiln at Yamazaki in Kamakura.]

Simon [There, he had young bamboo color tiles baked for his bathroom and decorated it to suite his taste.]

Akemi [He must have been so-to-speak a Japanese version of Antonio Gaudi.]

Simon [Construction and foods belong to different categories but the ultimate end of the philosophy must be the same.]

Show Taro [What can be said for sure is as regards contribution to Japanese culture, the influence Rosanjin created lasted beyond his lifetime.]

Akemi [What you mean is⋯]

Simon [What I mean is, for instance, handling either Seto or Mino-yaki, the potter Toyozo Arakawa who at a later date became a living national treasure used to be a helper of Rosanjin as a live-in pupil at his studio. While

	working for Rosanjin, he happened to find a piece of ceramic in Ohgayaof Mino which had the same pattern as on a broken piece found in Shino.]

Akemi	[Does that mean a rediscovery?]
Simon	[Can be so concluded. It is a famous story in the academic research field of Japanese ceramics.]
Show Taro	[But that rediscovery had no chance to be recognized as rediscovery unless he had not seen the piece of old Shino-yaki ceramic at the Rosanjin's studio.]
Simon	[His rediscovery led Toyozo Arakawa to a right track he ought to trace and finally he succeeded in reproducing the authentic Shino ceramics. In one's life, no one will be able to tell the other the right track he ought to pass through. Only God will show it often in an unexpectable way. Few humans can find that pass.]
Show Taro	[I see, you're quoting the words of the Bible···Jesus Christ aptly told the public 『Those who do not know where they are from and whereto they are going are not worth to be feared.』].
Simon	[Such people do not hold any strong intentionality. By the way, where is Show going?]
Show Taro	[I have come from the past and am walking towards future. And all living creatures will die with absolutely no exception. What is allowed for us to do is to ask ourselves what ought to be done by the time death will be due.]
Simon	[You're quite right. I believe humans live to die a good death.]

Then the conversation was made stopped with the voice of the proprietress.

Proprietress [Excuse me, please.]

Then the paper screen was opened and three cutting board style plates called Manaita-zara were brought in and each of these was placed in front of the three guests. Because of the big size of the plate which almost equals to the size of a cutting board it is called a Manaita-zara and the design of this big plate was also what Rosanjin created. Those cutting board plates were once dipped in water before Sushi is put on them. Such plates as of Bizen-yaki and Iga-Oribe were placed in front of the two men.

The cutting-board plate of Bizen-yaki was showing the chocolate color surface which was mixed with tiny stones of 2 to 3 mm which was forming the basic expression of the plate. The first step that a creator of Bizen-yaki takes in his creation of it is to reform quality of soil. And his work after his close check of the used soil condition is to be placed between the place near the furnace opening where flames are turning into red color with oxidative flames hitting there and the place at the bottom of the furnace where reducing flames are showing blue light. Then on top of these places such as sake bottle or flower container are placed wrapped by straws to prevent them from sticking to each other. Those places where such things have been placed leave round shape marks as flames do not reach there. Dilettantes love these marks calling these by the name of peony shaped rice dumplings. The works indeed looked like those by an artist who was half way to the veteran artists.

The cutting-board place of Iga has a pattern which shows white feldspar on the base of skin color melting into a round shape and in

— 38 —

addition to the part where ash glaze is added, about one third of the whole plate was applied by green color copper glaze. Both Iga and Shigaraki are using the same mountain soil taken from each side of the mountain respectively it is hard to distinguish which is which. The baking style called Oribe nowadays which is using a green color glaze was firstly unearthed at the ruins of an old mansion equipped with a climbing kiln which is considered as started in 1607.

This asymmetrical design is taken as Baroque style design which is not available from kilns in other countries.

The used color green represents the tradition of the people in the South Islands who used big leafs of banana plants to put their food on them. This habit of using banana leafs has been carried through from the primitive human era which certainly makes the food look more delicious with Sushi which means cut pieces of fresh fish.

Different from those plates placed for the two men, in front of Akemi the same cutting-board plate but of different design with faintly crimson color that is developing towards the edge of the plate. According to the unearthing researches of the ruins of Osaka Castle Shino-yaki was started to be produced around 1597. The grazing of Shino is a thick and sloppy grazing wrapping the ceramic body showing soft color coupling. Shino is liked by women and has a lot of female fans.

Here, let the writer go a little off the track. There may be some people who might like to put a question mark on those antique shops which always judge Shino or Oribe are products in the Momoyama era without exception. The writer is of opinion that those unearthed ceramics should be taken as the ones that belong to the category of Baroque culture such as Toshogu. Regretfully, the writer has to admit there are quite a number of antique shops even talking about the Tokyo area alone, which falsely appraise all Shino and Oribe they hold in their stock as the products in the Momoyama era just as an easy means of selling purposes, or those dealers who are lazy enough to have skipped studying the result of the research of excavation of ceramics during such a long time of the past ten or more years. Suppose the notice of authenticity on a box might read 'the era of Momoyama', how many of those dealers would be honest enough to tell that the result of the excavation had proven it was a product made in the first quarter of the 17th century? This is the point at issue which the current antique dealing world is facing. The writer strongly hopes that the more the shops are first class, the more sincere efforts they must make to study the results of professional researches.

Sushi pieces which were served to Akemi presented on a cutting-board plate were with balls of vinegared rice which were smaller than normal for about 20%. The chef who took good notice of her physique when she passed by him at the counter cooked her dish with smaller rice balls having noted she was wearing a fitting suit. That was hospitality of the chef. He knew difference of guests' stomach capacity between those who are casually dressed and who are wearing business suits.

Truly professional cooks in the meaning of corresponding to any part of the world have the established habit to watch the day's outdoor temperature and observe the state of the guests when they are coming into the restaurant and decide to use a bit more salt to help guests supplement the lost salt due to swetting during the daytime or watch their physique to adjust the size of the rice balls. Those cooks who do not have this power of observation of their guests are not able to make himself a professional cook. Just to refrain from smoking not to lose the sensibility of the tongue is far from enough to make him a successful cook.

What the writer is stating here is not to deny the fact of the nourishiments being contained in the seasonal food materials. The writer says here, to draw the best effect of the good nourishiment out of the materials the cook needs a keen observation ability of the guests' conditions. For instance, like this dinner gathering, when a variety of Sushi being served on one cutting-board plate, it comes totally to chef's discretion to ascertain the difference of food preference of the guests and also to pay delicate attention to female guests and serve foods of nice presentation to meet women's taste. Also. such ability of judgement is required by the proprietress who sits by the table and serves such dishes. In France, this sort of judging capability is also demanded from waiters. This ability is an important service factor both in the east and in the west of the world.

At the preparation stage of such cutting-board plates, such non-glazed ceramics are once dipped in water for about fifteen minutes before Sushi pieces are put on these. By adding this extra step of treatment, the pattern of the ceramics can come out more vividly and at the same time it comes to be labor saving at the washing basin because sticky leavings are lessened on the plates. The problem of sticky leavings won't happen with glazed plates, though. However, talking about the subtle atmosphere of the ceramics, there are plural kinds of ceramics producing such atmosphere like

Shino which has subtle crimson color over the white base or like Hagiyaki which shows slightly pinkish color produced by fire changing.

Which to choose depends on the selection of the variety of fish. To show some examples of different qualities of plates, there is Shino-yaki which shows traces of tiny air bubbles without air, or like Hagi-yaki which still has bubbles on the surface but not as much as Shino-yaki and as regards Oribe, its surface is almost smooth and has no bubbles. As a matter of course, when those used plates are washed in the basin sometime after the dinner is finished the smoother the surface of plates are the easier the washing work becomes. However, for the feast for the eyes, such bubbly plates are said to present more primitive feeling and therefore present a fresher appearance. Having served cutting boards, she additionally served small Teshio-zara (salt pat) of the size of about ten centimeters diameter.

At the dinner which Simon hosted, each plate used showed different patterns and pleased the eyes of all guests there.

Simon   [So this is antique Ko-Imari .]

Proprietress [We cannot afford to use antiques only like the top-class Japanese restaurant, so, please enjoy this plate as the only antique available here. Talking about antiques, those small size ceramics such as Soba Choko noodle dipping sauce cups are authentic antiques used at this restaurant.]

Simon   [Is that your avocational selection?]

Proprietress [You're right. Such small antiques do not cost a great deal of money. Other than those antiques, we purchase newly made ceramics by potters ranging from young to middle stage potters as we are hoping to encourage and help increase their work efforts. But the small plates are antiques which we purchase for use here in the hope of educating our potters to learn the wisdom of the olden time people. We are hoping among those contemporary potters some may be able to do a winning work.]

Simon   [You are trying to grow up potters, aren't you.]

Proprietress [Dishes in the old times are, for instance, easy to be stored as they can be piled up as a set of five dishes, or there is a size discrimination of which plate for what use, or dishes are used to match the tray or the tray with legs. Nowadays, nucrealization of families have progressed losing granpa or granma who can teach such old times wisdom to their heirs. Fortunately, my family has grandparents and because we are lucky to have them with us, I do wish to have such wisdom succeeded to young generations, at least those young people who gather here, since I have no child.]

Simon   [I see that is the reason why such strange shaped tableware of difficult handling are being shown at the exhibition.]

Akemi   [Also at the art department of the leading department stores.]

Proprietress [Both of you are quite right. Therefore, to grow potters does not mean to just buy from the potters

— 43 —

with no question.]

Simon [Honey, I have come to like this restaurant more and more.]

Proprietress [Please stay with us in future as well.]

Then Simon took up the bottle of the specially squeezed beer and in a casual way poured the beer into glasses of Show Taro and Akemi. Seeing the proprietress retiring from the room, they changed the topic.

Show Taro [I understand your companions rescued Bernard Gambino last week.]

Simon [They are his companions and not mine. My cousin is the wife of my cousin living in New York.]

Akemi [But you must be interested in Alois?]

Simon [He is surely the enemy of my grandfather, but in any case, he won't live long.]

Simon answered in the way that he would no longer wish to get concerned about such a matter, in addition to showing himself as not too keen to work with Mafias.

Show Taro [Changing the subject, regarding the case of Hell Computer I referred to the other day…]

Simon [It seems certain that an Indian organization is having the remittance made.]

Simon looked feeling thirsty so he took a sip of beer and continued.

Simon [Who is the Japanese that is involved in this case?]

Show Taro [The Japanese involved sounds like a person by the name of Genta Shiaku who is culturing shrimps in Indonesia. Mr. Shiaku approached Mr. Suzuki with this

— 44 —

transaction.]

Simon   [When you find out the name of the Indian jeweler, please inform me. I will make an investigation at my side, too.]

Show Taro   [As I am scheduled to meet him during next week, I am hopeful I will be able to get more information at that time.]

Simon   [Has the route of remittance for this time been fixed?]

Akemi   [According to a fax message from Jinlian Pan, my Hong Kong Chinese friend, Mr. Chen Jing Ji is now checking art dealers and regarding remittance, Mr. ZeDeng Mao is also thinking about it.]

Saying so, Akemi spread the fax paper that came from Hong kong and showed it to Simon. He looked into that fax and looked at Akemi and grinned.

Simon   [Your Hong Kongnese friend looks to be connected with the mistery men to whom even the Chinese Government dares not touch. I remember I have seen their names on some documents regarding the jewelry trading in Hong Kong. I understand they are rumored to have some blood relationship with the clan of Mao Zedong but nothing more about them is known.]

Akemi   [Both of them are known as difficult to be contacted.]

Simon   [Have you yourself met them?]

Akemi replied in the mood of boasting a bit of her having met such big men.

Akemi   [When I went to Hong Kong I continued on to visit Macao by vessel from Hong Kong guided by Ms. Pan

— 45 —

and in Macao I met Mr. Chen Jing Ji. As I remember it, Mr. Chen Jing Ji owns a casino there.]

Simon   [Nicola or Bernard may be familiar with that sort of business.]

Show Taro [Please tell me if you can get information from them, as I guess Robert will also be curious.]

Mumbling his mouth with brow fish Sashimi finished chewing and finally opened his mouth.

Simon   [What about information from Robert?]

Show Taro [What I understand is that Hell Computer till now has been making remittance to the second subcontractor treating him as Hell's designated contractor,]

Simon   [Do you know the reason why Hell did such switch-over of its remittees?]

Simon   [As Hell's agent disappeared, there must have been some troubles.]

Simon   [Did Hell make remittance for at least several times before it changed to a new remittee?]

Show Taro [I understand so.]

As their conversation developed into a direction of somewhat obscure end, Akemi cut into them.

Akemi   [Is this a dangerous deal?]

Show Taro [We only play the role of introducing some agents for making remittance stationing overseas and I myself have not even met Mr. Shiaku as yet. In other words, I have no hint of their own secret at this moment. So, the present state we are involved in is still on the safe stage.]

Akemi   [Is there any risk of this deal conflicting with Japanese laws?]

Show Taro [What we are supposed to do is to introduce them to a dealer who does overseas trading and in return are given the introduction fee. This is no way to violate either Japanese laws and foreign countries' laws, is it? For instance, if someone makes a shrine visit at dead of night to put a curse of death on a person and strikes a neil on a straw doll, if on the following day such targeted person dies in China due to heart attack, can you lawfully punish such someone?]

Akemi   [Ms. Abe Maria is different! She may probably be able to make it.]

Simon   [In the light of common sense, I also see no problem though Miss Maria looks a bit weird to me. In Japan in the Heian era there was a time when cursing someone was deemed as a crime, but in this world governed by modern laws, such causal relationship is not lawfully accepted.]

Swallowing a fatty tuna nigirizushi, Simon tried to help Show Taro out for the pursuit of Akemi but, in any case, he looked like denying Maria for physiological reasons. Remembering that Maria's father was killed while he was trace-investigating the case of the painting owned by a Sicilian church and stolen by Mafia, it is quite understandable that Maria herself would not be able to accept Simon for physiological reasons as well.

Simon   [Hi, Chef, About time for sake. Two cold sake bottles please!]

Chef　　　　[Yes, sir.]

After some time, a couple of sake bottles each of which contained a little more than two-Go sake (more than 360 ml) were brought about. When that 2-Go bottles were placed in front of them, before they started filling their large sake cups with the sake, both Simon and Show Taro checked one cup each by grasping them, checking the thickness of the ceramic with their fingers or putting them upside down, using their five senses for making a value judgement of the cups. This value judgement ceremony was finished in less than thirty seconds, then Show Taro spoke out.

Show Taro [This place is serving good quality large sake cups as well.]

Simon　　　[This kind of cups comes too heavy if made by an amateur potter, and potters of the plain level tend to make the overall surface of the cup too thin.]

Akemi　　　[What is the point that decides good or bad?]

Show Taro [The Maestro work makes some part of the cup thicker than the other part so extra hot sake can be contained without problem.]

Simon　　　[For instance, this one has a thick part under the outside surface of the cup. The other one looks to have a virtical outside but the middle part of the inside is made thicker to prevent the holder of the cup from a heat-burn.]

Show Taro [Mr. Simon belongs to the professional level ceramic appraiser.]

Simon　　　[No, no, I'm not that good. Only I have my own

obsessiveness on ceramics as Rosanjin also said he had. Have you heard a story of curry and rice dished up on a piece of newspaper which was cooked by the first-class chef against the same recepe cooked by a common housewife being put on a plain but clean looking plate?]

Akemi [I have read that story. As I remember it, normal people will take the one on the white plate.]

Simon [And that is the very reason why I decided to come to Japan. As I have learnt about Rosanjin during my student time and also came to learn that the Japanese ceramic tableware has authentic reasons hidden deep in it.]

Show Taro [I see. Then you mean the purpose of your visit to Japan is to study Japanese cooking?]

Simon [Not exactly. I majored literatue at school. The first book I happened to come to read was a book written by Rosanjin which is the start of my studying this person Rosanjin. As I continued to study about this person, I came to find that I myself had become a mania of cooking and tableware.]

Show Taro [Well, interesting. Anyway, have this cup from me.]

Simon [Oh, thank you⋯This Bizen bottle is of high shoulder.]

Show Taro [You know if this bottle of this size were of an Imonoko tuber style without shoulder, such could never contain two-Go sake.]

Simon [Absolutely⋯Does this candle shape Oribe sake bottle have to be necessarily this particular shape to contain a minimum of two-Go sake?]

Show Taro [Probably, after the determined manners were systemized in the world of tea ceremony, these shapes were admitted to be the best for use.]

Simon [As you say, Bizen at this restaurant is made from good and sticky soil.]

Show Taro [Quality of Bizen baking depends on quality of soil in the first place.]

Akemi [So are these worth being called as exhibition work of art?]

Show Taro [Especially for the contemporary potters.]

Simon [And those artists put their works in the middle of the conflict of reduction flames and oxidation flames.]

Show Taro [And color variation comes to happen for a certain percentage.]

Akemi [Do they primarily put more sake bottles than other items in that particular position of the kiln?]

Simon [That depends on the situation. But they cannot afford to waste the space, so they put flower vases and sake bottles together on top of a big plate. such variations produced in that conflicting position between the two kinds of flames show the independent characteristics of each school of artist groups.]

Akemi [Knowledge that Mr. Simon possesses may be beyond the level of professional potters.]

On that day, Show Taro and Akemi saw Simon off at his hotel. Both could and did enjoyed the sushi dinner fully as they did not have such food restriction as Simon had.

3. First meeting with Indian Connection

On that day, Show Taro was going to meet with the Indian connection at a hotel by Suzuki's arrangement. Distance to the hotel from the station where Show Taro and Suzuki gathered took only a few minutes on foot. It was Hotel Santa Lucia which was a stylish foreign-owned hotel. This group of hotels under the name of Santa Lucia was configured by multi-national share holders but the interior decorations were uniformed with Italian orientated designs.

Greeted by the doorman there, they entered through the entrance door and found the front desk in front of a huge size Boccicelli style mural painting. There was a Japanese man sitting on a chair next to a pillar at the opposite side of the front desk. That man and Suzuki exchanged nods. Next to this man there was another figure who looked like of Indian origin.

Genta   [Mr. Suzuki, The other side is impatiently waiting for you.]

Suzuki   [Where are we supposed to go?]

Genta   [Mr. Kubera is showing us to their penthouse.]

Following this India-origin man, they rode onto an elevator. When the elevator door is open, Kubera pushed the button of the destination floor. In a minute they arrived at the top floor.

Kubera   [This way, please.]

They were shown into Penthouse Capri. At the entrance door, two young men were assigned to stand. Kubera lifted his right hand and they promptly opened the door. The special room on the top floor of this hotel which was called penthouse in that hotel group, it looked like that name of the one of holiday resorts in Italy. It was meant for hotel's hospitality wishing their guests using this space on the top floor as a place for them to get relaxed like they would do at their own holiday house.

Inside the penthouse, half of the space was made as a bedroom and the balance of the space was made as a saloon where a sofa of Rococo revival style was placed and a dining set was seizing the light hot house side of the saloon.

In addition to those equipments, there were flowering plants such as large potted plants of orange tree which were altogether showing reproduction of paradise on the earth. All lamps were decorated with Venetian glass and the wall was of pink color marble pitching and the floor was covered with salmon pink color carpet to make the ambience of the whole saloon of the penthouse perfect.

On the mantelpiece, a clock made of white color marble and gold braiding was elegantly marking the passage of time. Marble of Italian origin was used for the furnace and the marble was adjusted with a half polished state to make it look not as conspicuous as the wall and that color adjustment was accentuating that white clock even more effectively.

On the table welcome fruits were decorated on a comport. A man who was at that table side waiting for the arrival of Show Taro's group walked toward the sofa at the side of the hothouse and exchange of business cards was started. Firstly, Suzuki introduced Genta Shiaku to Show Taro. Then Genta Shiaku introduced Show Taro to Kubera Prima, the jeweler, who could be known by a glance of the Indian origin, and to another business man named

Indrajit Divija. As was his usual habit, Show Taro placed the given business cards in the order of the sitting position of each of them and made a comparison with each of their faces against the cards given to him.

Titles on the business cards were as follows.

Nanyo Trading
President
Genta Shiaku

Kubera   Gem
Kubera Prima
Kubera Prima

Indy   Trading
CEO
Indrajit Divija

All three people were smiling. Shiaku was of his age of the sixties and a bit plump man with suntanned skin which showed he had been walking much in the strong sun. That observation might tell that he must be in shrimp aquaculture business. The person sitting next to him sounded to understand Japanese to some extent, but he was talking English with quite much Indian accent.

This man who had plentiful beard is also plump, wearing a big gold ring with ruby on his left ring finger. His business suit was of sort of rough make and he looked like the underling of the other man.

The last man called Indrajit was a tall man with well trained muscles on him and wore moustache. He seemed to be in his fortieth. He was making his questions in the American accent but the pronounciation sounded like that of Canadians. He was wearing a big, more than 10 carat Chrysoberyl Cat's Eye on his middle finger. When he talked with gestures, the beam line in the middle of the honey color displayed a mysterious glitter.

Since the olden times, not only in India but in everywhere, it is believed that jewelries are where magic creatures or spirits are dwelling. Among such jewelries, those which has chatoyancy effects, something like an eye is floating up onto the surface in the unpolished state of the back side of such jewelry, or otherwise some three light strings are triple crossed, or in some cases as many as six light streams are crossing on each other. Originally, people used to call Chrysoberyl Cat's Eye simply as Cat's Eye. In the recent years, among such as emerald which is the green beryl stone, some show such eye-look pattern on the surface. Also, in the same category of beryl stones, some light blue color aquamarines also have the eye which are now available on the market.

Taking this opportunity, one thing that needs to be known to the readers is there exist some jewelry dealers who sell red beryl calling these red emeralds. Suppose such misnaming can be accepted, it comes that aquamarine can be called as blue emerald. In consideration of the fact that emerald originally is meant for green color, you will see the above is unreasonable and not acceptable.

To add more instances, ruby and sapphire which are of aluminum oxidide also show the star, but as same as the explanation made about emerald, only red color stones are called ruby the original meaning of ruby being red, and all others are called sapphire. No one ever calls them blue ruby.

Sapphire other than blue color stones is called orange sapphire in accordance with the color, but among those sapphires some are of the color between yellow and orange which are called golden sapphire and the middle of pink and orange colors are called Pappalachia sapphire Pappalachia meaning the color of lotus flower. Those stones which show star marks have low transparency degree, so in most cases those stones are applied with a little rough cutting on the backside of the stone. Also, those are treated with so to called closed setting which means to shut out the light coming from the back side of the stone by having the light totally reflected in order to draw out the chatyansee effect to the fullest.

From the ancient times, spirits inside those gem stones have been sighting many business negotiations with those jewelries treated as talisman to sweep off the evil spirits. At this meeting from the viewpoint based on the life of the gem stones such human economical activity cannot be any more than just one ephemeral moment for the stones to watch. Chrysoberyl Cat's Eye set on a ring which was made from gold was producing such atmosphere as if the honey color of this gem were possessing on the ring rather than matching the ring and showing a harmonized coordination. And especially when silver alone without copper was included in gold bullion, yellow color would come out more strongly.

As copper content in Japanese 18 carat gold is pretty large, professional buyers usually detect the feel of red in gold used in Japan. In other words, the ring worn by Indrajit seemed to be a ring made in India and passed down from generation to generation.

In India, oftentimes 24 karats gold or such karats as extremely close to 24 gold is often used for jewerlies.

In a business meeting, to perceive in very short time the religious or cultural background that the other participants maintain is an important prerequisite to proceed an international negotiation successfully. For instance, action in your negotiation you have to take becomes different depending on wheather your negotiation partner is a person who acts on the basis of religiously established common sense or who never believes any bit of superstition. In case your negotiation partner is involved in a specific religion or political party or group, whether you can grasp that understanding or not before you start the negotiation will lead you to the crossroads of success or failure of the negotiation.

Genta   [People usually call me Genta, so please do so, Mr. Show Taro. Now, will you give us information regarding the execution route of this business in your mind.]

Show Taro [This time, I am planning to develop this business through my Hong Kong route connection.]

Genta   [Around when can I expect to receive from you information you are to obtain from your connection?]

Show Taro [Those of my connection are now working to get in touch with the financial authorities there to ascertain whether Hong Kong is now open for such deals or not.]

Genta [Do your people have good enough power to ascertain it and to deal with the financial authorities?]

Show Taro [I would not mind showing you the names only.]

To prove what he said, Show Taro handed over to Genta a copy of the cut-out part of the record of facsimile message. That cut-out piece of paper was only showing [Art dealer=Chen Jing Ji, Person concerned of remittance=ZeDeng Mao]. Genta showed that memo to Kubera, who looked a little surprised and turned against Indrajit and passed that information to him. This was proving this jewelry dealer could read Chinese charactors to some extent.

Kubera [Hong Kong Mafia related Mr. Chen Jing Ji and the name of a financial advisor who is rumored as a clan of Mao Zedong.]

Indrajit [What about their level of capability?]

Kubera [For us this is the first time to make a tie-in work with them but they are said never to meet foreigners.]

Indrajit [Where did you get that information?]

Kubera [I gathered this information from a man who was making frequent access to Singapore and Hong Kong. According to the information from him, Mr Chen Jing Ji sounds like an expert of human trafficking sending women from the farming area out to America or Europe besides operating a casino house. I heard that the reason why he had not been searched by the police was because he kept paying kickbacks to public security related government. Also, his wife is a daughter of the owner of Ximen Industries which is a pharmaceutical company. Through this route, Mr. Chen Jing Ji seems to sell copies of Bio Glow, an aphrodisiac and Harkenu Kureuz, hair growth agent, on internet.]

Indrajit [That must be inviting a lot of complaints?]

Kubera [Yes, Quite. Therefore, rumor says he is delivering genuine merchandise to the high officials of Chinese Government free of charge, making it an evidence of his importation being all of genuine merchandise.]

Indrajit [That story is quite disturbing to the sale of those merchandise of this hotel as here only genuine merchandise is being sold. By the way, what kind of person is the other Mr. Mao?]

Kubera [He is the financial advisor who is employed as advisor by the owner of a venture company over China and Hong Kong···and is a person who has such information as what cannot be obtained unless he is connected with the high officials of Chinese Government.]

Indrajit [And what is that information?]

Kubera [I heard he had known in one week advance the change of financial policies. Just to add, Hong Kong stationed Japanese seems to visit his office frequently.]

Indrajit [Is that because Japanese can be used?]

Kubera [No, It seems they are talking in Kantonese or English.]

Indrajit [Show Taro, Do you directly know both of these people?]

Show Taro [No, Through my acquaintances.]

Indrajit   [Okay. Do they have any request to you?]

Show Taro   [They request my reconfirmation of the 15% as incentive. As regards actual practice of this deal, due to high risk of fraud, in line with the widely practiced Hong Kong style transaction, we do this deal without deposit money, but if there are worries at your side, you can accompany us to the bank. One important point is we are not in a position to execute this deal if your identities are not clearly shown to me. I am not concerned about the nature of the fund and the purpose of it. These are all the conditions for this deal. If any lies or cheatings exist, all of this will be swept away, and I will not accept any future deals from you.]

Indrajit   [Do you have any past record of practice of remittance?]

Show Taro   [Mr. Ximen, the father-in-law of Chen Jing Ji, was working on remittance of the assistant to President of America as his exclusive assignment.]

Until then, the eyes which were not smiling till then in spite of his smiles on the face were seen smiling for the first time.

Indrajit   [I like your offer, Show Taro. I will give you our company pamphlet in duplicate per members of your execution unit, so, will you hand these over to each of them?]

Show Taro   [On receiving their final okay I will pass these to them.]

Indrajit   [The first fund is planned to be thee million dollars in the form of an official check.]

— 59 —

Official checks are to be issued only when the balance of the bank account from where the fund is drawn out in the form of a check signed by the branch manager of the bank. However, whether the absolute safety of such check is guaranteed or not is not always firm is another reality.

To explain why that can be said, with those fraud cases which took place some times in the past there were irreguralities of the addressee of the check and the amount of money. In such cases, commonly, the remmiter is as a matter of course a fictional company. What makes such cases more difficult in case the transaction is a case over the border is till such fictional official check comes to be ascertained as to whether it is negotiable or not is known only after about one month later.

If the presented check is an absolutely reliable check, it is not impossible that the cashing of the check be done by the third party on the condition of the third party deducting the interest for the period till the check is actually cashed, in other words, discounting the check. However, people concerned must keep in their mind that frauds are all the time seeking such victims who want an immediate cashing. If there is no good partner who can make a direct enquiry to the bank beyond the border from where the check has been issued, this kind of deal comes to be an extremely dangerous practicing game. This is of course referring to the risk rising at the side of accepting to do the remittance work.

Show Taro [As You are aware, Chinese Government often change their laws quite easily, therefore, at the point of time when the remittance is opened there is a need to acquire the Government's acceptance. What I also wish to ask is, is anyone going to stay in Hong Kong till collection of the official check is complete?]

Indrajit [Kubera and a few others. Incidentally, does Chinese Government frequently stop remittance?]

Show Taro [They don't stop inflow of foreign currencies, but outflow is often stopped by their own judgement.]

Indrajit [I do hope the border is open.]

Having said so, like many Americans do, Indrajit winked and crossed the middle finger and the ring finger.

Genta, who had been listening to the conversation exchanged in English, suddenly talked to Suzuki using Japanese.

Genta [Mr. Suzuki, your acute insight looks like having hit a big gold vein.]

Suzuki [No, no, Gen-san, Just a good luck. I regret my intuition should have worked this well at the time of the oil painting case.]

The two were laughing facing to each other. Then, the first meeting was over, so Show Taro dubbed two records in the IC recorder before he came back to his office.

On return to his office, there came Robert in the late afternoon of that day as he was dropping at his Japan branch office.

Robert [What kind of people were they?]

Show Taro took out copies of their business cards and passed these to him.

Show Taro [The shrimp aquafarmer is a Japanese by the name of Shiaku. Besides aquafarming this man seems to be doing lumber and South sea Pearl tradings commuting between Indonesia and Singapore. The next man is

Kubera a jewelry dealer who as you see it on his card seems to have a store each in India, Singapore and California. The last man is Indrajit who is above Kubera. He seems to be trading automotive materials and on the other hand dealing with personal computer related business. His business brand Indy looks like the naming when he was once eagerly wishing to race at Indy 500. He speaks American English like Canadian.]

Robert　　[On a different note, when are you to meet those who are sticking to you at the China Collection?]

Show Taro　[I am to fly to Hong Kong day after tomorrow and meet Jinlian Pan through introduction by Akemi.]

Robert grinned and gave Show Taro an advice.

Robert　　[So again you are going to be accompanied by Nine Tails⋯Jinlian Pan is also a notorious woman. She is called Belle Lotus, so you had better watch yourself.]

Show Taro　[What do you mean by Belle Lotus?]

Robert　　[In the era of la Belle Epoque among those courtesans there was one called La Belle Otero. Men who loved her were ruined by her dissipation and as a consequence, at least six men were driven to commit self suicide. She was a femme fatale. Among the hotels in South France, there is one which is known to have a roof which has similar shape of her breasts. She is also remembered as the first actress that played in the first silent film. She was a sample of evil woman and the source of lots of gaudy topics. During the time of la Belle Epoque, such courtesans were everywhere in abundance.]

Show Taro [And how were her last days?]

Robert [She retired when WW1 was over and bought an apartment house worth in present currency value 15million dollars and making it a seed capital she grew her property to about 25 million. But as she could not stop gambling at cashino and at last when she died at the age of 95, she was said to be penniless.]

He shrugged his shoulders and implicitly showed the fate of the unlucky businessmen who had relationship with Belle Lotus.

Show Taro [She was a lucky woman, wasn't she.]

Show Taro's reaction to Robert's story made Robert embarrassed.

Robert [How can you say that?]

Show Taro [Firstly, she was lucky to have had a beautiful face and a voluptuously curvy body despite no such surgical technology as cosmetic surgery was available in that age. Secondly, she safely survived such an era of WW1. And thirdly, her men may have killed themselves but did not involve and kill her.]

Robert [Doesn't that mean she was not loved by them?]

Show Taro [If she had been hated by those men, she should have been killed by them?]

Robert [So you can make such interpretation of the case⋯]

Show Taro [And when she retired, she owned a huge amount of property so she could freely commute to casino where she loved and lived a full life of 95 years.]

Robert [But the former Otero ended her life alone.]

Show Taro [In this contemporary world, there are many people who will not get married even though they are wealthy enough to start a family.]

Robert [In the urban areas, yes.]

Show Taro [In a sense, that era she lived could not cope up with her speed of running the top of the era. Therefore, the only unfortune she had to face was that she failed to meet a man whom she could be going for broke to get his love and also, she failed to be loved by that man.]

Robert [As you say, in that sense she must have overrun the foremost cutting edge of that era she lived.]

Show Taro [Do you know Gabrielle Coco Chanel?]

Robert [Do you mean that Chanel who made a great success in the brand business?]

Show Taro [Her men in the early times loved her just as mistress. She fell in love with an SS officer during WW2 and for that reason she was put in a state that was not much different from exile when after the war was over.]

Robert [But she made herself revived.]

Show Taro [But she did not get married after that so she did not have a chance to start a family and consequently she died alone in a flat of Hotel Ritz.]

Robert [Among her famous quotes, there is one which states in her expression 「women who are not loved by men have no existence value」.

Show Taro [In that logics, were lives of Gabrielle Coco Chanel or La Belle Otero valueless?]

Robert [I do understand what you want to say. That they were not loved by men will not change the fact that they led the culture of that era.]

Show Taro [If value of a man is measured by how much impact the man had on the history, the value will be equally the same for Caesar or Napoleon or Hitler. Apart from the results, no one will try their utmost from the first to destroy themselves.]

Robert [With what logics do you treat those three on the same line?]

Show Taro [Caesar led ancient Rome to the opposite direction of democracy. What is the historical evaluation of Caesar in the contemporary age?]

Robert [Hero.]

Show Taro [Napoleon tried to branch bourgeoisevolution and Napoleonic code to Europe and lost his battles and ended as war criminal and was exiled to Saint Helena but after his death the evaluation changed.]

Robert [His body was carried through Arch of Triumph, marched through Champ Elysees and has since been enshrined at les Invalides.]

Show Taro [Hitler had worries about colonial markets getting blocked by imperialistic politics and also about communism which led him to rise WW2 with support by the majority of the German nation. The world's evaluation of Hitler regarding the Jewish issue is worst ever, but on the other hand, he brought out the dead body of Napoleon II in a coffin from Austria and enshrined it in Les Invalides. I wonder if this performance of his by itself ought to be thanked by French people?]

Robert [Well, I can understand that if one is not allowed to be buried by one's mother's grave, then one may wish to be buried besides one's father or uncle. Especially, even though nominally and for the short term only, it is the case of Napoleon II, the emperor of French nation (Empire Francais).]

Before and after French Revolution, the title of rulers varied subtlely. Formally it was Emperor of France (Roi de France), which was later changed to King of French people (Roi de Francaise). This means a change from absolute monarchy to constitutional monarchy.

What has to be remembered in addition to the above is the brand name Napoleon used for cognac has a story which is, wine that was overproduced at time of the birth of Napoleon II celebrating his birth was distillated and as the means to add some value such cognac was named as Napoleon and started to be sold to the public. And French people at this contemporary age still keep selling the cognac Napoleon to the world and keep making profit, therefore for this reason, normally France could have accepted the coffin of Napoleon II at a much earlier date, but for the only reason that the mother was from the Hapsburg's, France had long been refusing to have him buried in France. As a matter of fact, Napoleon II was a disturbing existence to his mother for her remarriage after the death of Napoleon I. Such being the reason of his delayed return to France, Napoleon II from the personal viewpoint can be said to be a quite unhappy person.

Show Taro [NS, namely, Nazis Administration, well maintained outburn and created an automotive company and so far that administration was doing a good work, but if they take their action for rising a war in order to keep winning in elections, such administration can be called a monster produced by democracy. Unless every one is careful, democracy may go to extreme to grow up something that will destroy democracy itself.]

Robert [Your logic almost belongs to Zen dialogue.]

Show Taro [History cannot simply be evaluated. Values that is a justice at one age could turn to injustice at the other age.]

Robert [Do you know such history other than France?]

Show Taro [Taking an example in Japan, Ashikaga Takauji can be said to be a good example.]

Robert [Is that the man who was the first Barbarian-subduing General of Muromachi shogunate?]

Show Taro [His legal wife was a sister of the regent of Kamakura shogunate, but at time of Kenmu restration, he went to the side of Emperor Godaigo. Then at a later time when administration of Emperor Godaigo was centerized by court nobles of the Heian era who came to control the administrative power and to ignore the samurai members who had cooperated to knock down Kamakura shogunate, he caused a coup and made a member of imperial family the emperor who supported him at the coup and created an age when two emperors called the period of the northern and southern dynasties came to exist in Japan.]

Robert   [Oh, What you told me is difficult to evaluate.]

Show Taro [In the historical viewpoint that deems Imperial court or direct Imperial rule as the most important, Emperor Godaigo is to be supported, however, from the side of the warriors who knocked down Kamakura shogunate, to have court nobles rewarded and to left warriers unrewarded were not acceptable letting them believe that only court nobles are given fevolitism.]

Robert   [And that is the historical viewing from the side of the warriers, you mean?]

Show Taro [Before WW2, Ashikaga Takauji was not a hero but nothing but an arch villain and a rebel.]

Robert   [Well, this logic of yours is again a difficult one for me to comment. It is again alike a Zen dialogue.]

Show Taro [And, this is a copy of the recorded tape of today's meeting. Please make the information in the tape as a crue to find whatever lies behind the information.]

Show Taro quickly handed over to Robert one set of the copies of the tape that he had dubbed before Robert came to see Show Taro that day.

Robert   [See you again.]

That day was a busy day. Show Taro sent out by carrier White Pigeon another dubbed set of copied tape and copies of the business cards of the three men to Simon in Kobe and visited Abe Maria.

— 68 —

4. Maria's Room

Maria had a room for her fortune telling business in Ginza where Show Taro had an appointment to meet her at 4 o'clock. As her business was going well, it was rather difficult to get a reservation at the weekend, but it looked that the first half of the week days had some vacant time. Maria's fortune telling room was located in a small multi-tenant building facing the back street of Ginza. With the common image of the place Ginza, that area where her building was standing was a rather shabby corner of Ginza where many less busy small size clubs were jostling. This kind of location might be better suited for Maria to have her consulting room as that location is better suited for secret visit of such visitors as second rank bar mastresses called chie-mama (little mom), or else, as business women.

Show Taro went into the building by the side of an alley and found an elevator at the bottom of the collider. The building looked like about thirty years since it was built. He rode on a rather old fashion styled elevator and took a bit of time to locate the button to push which was to stop at Maria's floor. Buried in colorful mini-club signs, the sign 「Maria's Room」 could not be instantly found.

On that elevator button showing 「Medium of Love, Maria'a Room」 many women's life dramas were thickly sticked to.

That elevator itself looked not being cleaned carefully. Just a little dark light was being thrown inside the elevator.

Getting the elevator off on the floor where Maria's room was located, he felt the faint scent of stirred up incense. That scent is floating out from the room that was located at the bottom of the corridor. On the door, the words quoted from Gospel of Matthew of book of the Bible were written as 『Enter Ye from the Narrow Gate』. He opened that door and entered. Looking around the room, he saw a big household Shinto altar being placed in the front. He understood that the person enshrined was Seimei Abe. He would be the greatest shaman of her ancestors. A mirror which was placed in the middle of the altar was bluntly shining which looked like quietly emphacizing that it was an ancestral mirror inherited for generations.

Show Taro [Good evening.]

Maria   [Are you with Akemi today?]

Show Taro [No. As I will pay you with this card, I wish you to give me some advice.]

Show Taro made it clear with Maria that the expense she would demand would be paid from the investigation expenses in Robert's connection. She took a glance of that card and understood it would be a business that could be well paid for.

Maria   [Okay if that is the case. As Akemi is kind of neuvous.]

Maria got relaxed a little bit and suggested Show Taro to take a seat.

Maria   [Please be seated on that chair.]

As suggested Show Taro was sitting on one of the chairs at the side of the entrance door and talked to Maria.

Show Taro [As I thought, you are enshirining your ancestor.]

Maria   [Yes, as I am using the name of Ave Maria. But in addition, I am also enshrining Kaemon Takashima as called Master Donsho Takashima.]

Show Taro [I guess you may incidentally enshrine other fortune telling people as well?]

Maria [Those astrologists or shamen who did excellent performance in various places in the world in the past were also my objects of enshrinement.]

Show Taro [Regarding Taros Cards, are you also using ancient Card?]

Maria [When I divine some big thing, namely, future of the era or a war, I sometimes use Tarot Cards of the 19th century. But for most cases of private consultation, I just use the cards that I have been using for these ten years.]

Show Taro [Are investors also interested in your divining of how the war would develop or such matters?]

Maria [Secretaries of politicians are visiting me. Sometimes I tell fortune of future of Japan or matters concerning diplomatic tactics.]

Show Taro [So you receive alian people, too?]

Maria [May I ask you why you feel so?]

Show Taro [By the way, your aged set of Tarot Cards truly looks like of the early part of the 19th century and the memo written on the back of the cards looks like showing very old ink.]

Maria [As you rightfully said, that Tarot Cards placed there is a Marseilles made set produced around year 1804. What I gathered when I obtained that set, it seems to have been possessed by a diplomat's family of then French Government. In other words, that set may have been used for fortune telling Napoleon's future.]

Show Taro [Now I understand hearing your words why I thought these must be quite old cards.]

Maria [As you will understand just by looking around, this place is also the world of multi-number doctrine.]

Show Taro [Incidentally, is there any relationship between the cards unearthed in the ruins of ancient Egypt and Tarot Cards?]

Maria [Some schools of reseachers seem insisting that Ta of Tarot Cards should mean a road and Ro of Taro should equal to the French word roi or king in English based on the ancient Egypcian language. If this theory is taken up, Tarot Cards can be interpreted as the King's road where anyone can go through.]

Show Taro [Born, grown up, get old and sick⋯and die, Is it?]

Maria [Quite right.]

Show Taro [After all, what Tarot Cards will tell is salvation from old-sick-die which is no different from Buddhahood told by Shakyamuni.]

While Show Taro was sitting on the chair, she made a cup of tea and put it on the table. The scent of green tea was floating towards him. Show Taro was checking inside of his bag and found in a few seconds the business cards he was looking for.

Show Taro [What I wish you to tell the fortune of is the three men as per these calling cards. I confirmed their birth date details on their passports.]

Maria [How could you confirm such information?]

Show Taro [I told those of the side of China connection that I had been told to confirm at least birth date details. The side of India is demanding copies of company registration certificate from the side of China, so that the side of India must show something otherwise the business won't take place.]

Maria [I see. Then you already finished confirming that the names on the business cards and those on the passports do match.]

Show Taro [Here you see color copies of the information about each of them.]

Maria looked at those copies for a few seconds and write the birth dates on her notebook. Then she seemed to be doing some calculation, then put her hands on their business cards and closed eyes. Next, she joined her hands in player and murmured some words for a little while and opened her mouth.

Maria [Regarding Genta Shiaku, his performance of last year of shrimp trading was a sale of two containers to the fishery industry in Japan. He is also handling export of karaki lumbers. Karaki being shinny, it may be taken as pearls. In past, he had brought into Japan a story of remittance relating to similar business but that story was a fraud talk···he approached a man called Mr. Hide with this fraud story. I can see the sight where he was trying to persuade Mr. Hide to invest 15% of the fund under a name of deposit or cancellation fee··· Whether this approach is true or false is unseen. The present case also has even possibility of true and false. If he finds you do not have such organization power as to make remittance done, he will intend to extort at least several million yen out of you telling you that amount of money is indispensable to keep you safe, fabricating the fact that you heard this story as a cause of trouble you will have to face. I understand he is acting as a secretary of Lions Club but his character changes once he surpasses the border.]

Show Taro [Do you see if he was committing criminal transactions in past?]

Maria [There is high possibility of his judging his counter partner as no use, and if he determines that partner has no more value to him and if he so determines he swindles that partner. In any case, much caution does no harm.]

Show Taro [So he is a crafty old fox.]

Maria [You're about right.]

Show Taro [Then, what about the next person?]

Maria [As his name Kubera Prima means, he is a person who is fond of money to no end. He has got involved in any thing that could benefit him with money. He was involved in creating work of counterfeit checks in past. However, he is not a person who takes any action on his own will. I can see with this case, too, that he is being handled by another demonic being, motivated by money.]

Show Taro [A greedy miser⋯is he.]

Maria [The original meaning of Kubera is Treasure God.]

— 74 —

Show Taro [What does Prima mean?]

Maria [It could be Love.]

Show Tar [Could it be his family name?]

Maria [The practical meaning of it as a name would be 'very much in love with Treasue God'].

She spat out those words and showed a little complicated look.

Maria took a deep breath to control her breathing, and put her palm over the next business card.

Maria [I can't see this clearly. Just wait a moment.]

Saying so, she took out a rock crystal ball which he had seen before and put it at the side of the business card. She then held both of her hands over the rock crystal ball, started to cast a spell. Her half-closed eyes got thinner as time went and were finally closed completely. Fifteen seconds later, Maria slowly started talking. Lights in the room were adjusted to be rather dim so it was no exaggeration to describe that scene as producing a weird air.

Maria [This man is of the Brahmin family. The family name Divija means regeneration. He is protected by strong magical powers. Also, Indrajit means a person who can win over Indra God. This name Indrajit is the name of the prince of the inhabitants of the spirit of the world and he is immortal. In other words, he is given enough power to reincarnate as many times as he wishes and to take the lead of wrongdoing, however, he cannot be said as the true mastermind behind the scene. There yet exists a person called Raja.

Indrajit is trading export and import business of spear comporments of automobiles or motor bikes and once in the past he was arrested on a separate charge. Probably suspect of export to the direction of Pakistan. However, in that case, as arrangement of a container for replacement could be done in time, he replaced the barrel of an auto cannon with silencer of motor bikes, and also grew minor officials a sop, and successfully escaped from danger. The benefactor at that time was a man called Raja ⋯ the back business of this man seems to be arms dealer. One thing I wish to point out is, as Raja means king, I see him living in a castle. He looks like spending his life always being waited on by his chamberlains.]

Show Taro thought that Maria could see this much just by sighting a thing that the person in question had touched by his hands and had kept in his chest pocket, therefore, should there at his side exist such person as Maria and this thought made him feel weird. But at the same time, he came to have a feeling to wish to see the true character of Raja as his curiocity got the better of fear.

Show Taro [By the way, can you see any more about Raja?]

Maria   [It is next to impossible to see through the strongly guarded boundaries. Boundaries exist around Indrajit and that is the point which makes fundamental difference from Kubera. It is because he himself originally came from Baramon. He was sent to a university in Canada to study religion, but he became indulged in car racing and came to be disowned by his

— 76 —

parents.

When he was absorbed in car racing, he committed an error of skipping to ensure the tightness of the screws at time of tire exchange work and because of this overlook, the machine spinned during the racing and crashed into the car his friend was riding and consequently killed that friend of him. That was the time when he came to know Raja…is what I am now seeing.]

Show Taro [Did that accident happen in Indianapolis?]

Maria [That is difficult for me to perceive, but what I see looks like a circuit field in the oblong shape. Maize is waving in the wind.]

Show Taro [I see…What he said 'Indy500' in his talks the other day must be meant for this…]

Maria [Place where he met the founder of H・E・・・L・・L, Hell Computer was there, too. It means the sponsor of the machine which met that accident was Hell.]

Maria looks like seeing the image of crushed machine and the racer even though vaguely.

Maria [Can I tell you one other thing. This won't relate to the hearing fee but as this image comes up to me like automatically.]

Maria started to say hesitantly.

Show Taro [What is it?]

Maria [You have got the sort of face that suggests you might have trouble with women in near future. In an overseas country, you will get involved in exchange of being given a chance to meet someone who is believed to be a foreigner…]

Show Taro [I shall be in Hong Kong day after tomorrow, but you can see it now.]

Maria [I asked you today for the first thing about Miss Akemi, didn't I. Reason why I made that question is because her aura is stuck around you. She is also going to Hong Kong, isn't she?]

Show Taro [How do you know that···]

Maria [Last week Miss Akemi came to consult with me. What I saw then on her was naturally one of her Hong Kong business contacts. Also, she made a reservation to meet me again starting the day after tomorrow for one week. Therefore, I could make a guess though vaguely what is going to happen. I will come to meet you in Hong Kong again but please keep this meeting in secret to her.]

Show Taro [I understand. Then, let's meet again in Hong Kong.]

What he gathered was that Akemi was going to Hong Kong taking Maria with her. At any rate, that the fate of others comes to be seen is half way a very interesting experience, but the rest of the half is sort of scary.

5. China Connection

Weather in Hong Kong was still much sultrier than in Japan. What Show Taro felt at the first moment on arrival at the airport in Hong Kong was this mugginess. Sunshine in this southern country was still keeping its brightness. He rode on a car that came to pick him up at 10 o'clock on the following morning. On this car Show Taro and Akemi who had been with him since yesterday, and also Maria as an exclusive fortune teller to Akemi got together. At the high-level floor of a skyscraper from which all Hong Kong region can be overviewed Akemi's friend by the name of Pan had an office. Pan seemed to be somewhat occupied so her telephone conversation with her business contacts was prolonging exceeding the appointed time with Akemi and her group. Delaying for the appointment by ten minutes, they were to meet her shown to her office by her secretary.

In that room, crystal glass or Art Nouveau vases were decorated, but the most eye-catching decoration was an oddly shaped rock placed under the downlight. There are scarcely any traditional Chinese decorations. Even that mysterious rock was not Chinese as the paulownia wood box for that rock which was placed next to the rock was evidencing that it had been purchased not in China but in Japan. The overall impression of that room was a decoration using subdued colors which was not like the taste of common Chinese women.

They were shown to the next room and while they were sitting on the sofa there, Japanese Maccha tea was brought in.

The secretary bowed once in silence and served the tea to each person and went out. The served soft tea cakes were of Japanese made which looked like being ordered by air from Japan

Show Taro [Is she fond of Japanese tea?]

To this question, Akemi readily replied.

Akemi [According to her, it is Maccha that still keeps the Chinese traditional tea style which disappeared in Mongolian Dynasty and she wonders the way of taking Chinese tea at the present age was truly the correct way based on tradition or not.]

Maria [But···those tea cakes aren't from Japan?]

Akemi [I guess these are also what was cooked here by somebody here.]

Show Taro [Are those antiques also to her taste?]

Akemi [Yes, What she says is that there are too many fakes in Hong Kong so she is making it a rule to make her purchase when she visits Tokyo or Kyoto of such Chinese antiques in old paulownia wood or cedar wood only.]

Show Taro [Antiques of which era is she purchasing?]

Akemi [I understand she buys mainly those before the Edo era.]

Show Taro [Why is she concentrating on that particular period of the history?]

Akemi [In China, there are too many fakes so it is extremely difficult to ascertain which are authentic. Especially, the five clawd dragon which is the symbol of the

— 80 —

Emperor was abundantly reproduced and sold after Qing Dynasty was ruined. Therefore, there are scarcely any authentics on the market. Those which were taken into Japan before the Edo era were what specially distinguished families in Japan carefully selected and purchased. Therefore, among the antiques that belong to this junle, there is little chance for fakes mixed.]

Show Taro [That has a valid point.]

Akemi [In addition, those which were sent to Japan as gifts from Emperor Manchuria are considered to contain mostly authentic antiques. And in the following age of the Chinese Cultural Revolution, the treasured objects of men of letters flew out on the market in abundance. The supporting purchasers of those were Japanese. Those Japanese took such things out from boxes made of paper or fabric and repacked them into paulownia wood boxes. On the surface of such boxes the procuring history was recorded and the seal of owners was stamped which proves that such items were carefully treated and enjoyed by the Japanese old historical families]

Show Taro [So, is that the reason why Ms. Pan makes her purchase only in Japan?]

Akemi [And, many fakes of Chinese paintings, calligraphic works and chinawares are sold on the Chinese market so she makes it a rule never to buy such items on the Chinese market. As I have heard so directly from her before.]

Show Taro [That is a quite thoughtful decision. As she says, such cases that a painting which has been obtained by a winning bid for the bid price of ten million yen turns out to have a value of less than ten thousand yen do exist quite often, but price of calligraphic works is far less, so there still is a better chance to buy authentics at a cheap price. Doesn't this fact interest her at all?]

Akemi [But I think she is not really buying calligraphic works. What I understand is she cannot read what is written so that if she buys such work of unreadable letters, she might just as well choose to buy hierograph or cuneiform writing works.]

Maria [I'm puzzled to understand what she means.]

Akemi [Well, suppose she hungs such work on the wall and her visitors will ask 「how do you read it?」 and she cannot read it and feels ashamed. That is the reason.]

Show Taro [This tea bowl is a Japanese-made, isn't it.]

Saying so, Show Taro had a look of inside of the tea bowl foot.

Akemi [She was saying she realized in Japan that bowls made of pottery is better for use as pottery bowls won't become too hot to touch at time of taking tea. Therefore, she is collecting pottery tea bowls in wooden box from Japan.]

Show Taro [However, such pretty old and pretty good quality works cannot be obtained unless you pay pretty much money. She looks to be aware of this fact. This one, too, is not a very old one but is a decent work by a

— 82 —

potter with above the average level of skills.]

Akemi [In Japan, like in other countries the old-fashioned apprentice system is now falling down, which is leading to the decrease of potters who can select the ways to spin the pottery wheel differently at the part that needs to be lighter in weight and at the part that needs to be thicker to resist heat. Only those artists that have been able to acquire such technic will be first-class potters and can leave their names in the history.]

Akemi explained trying to show her knowledge of potteries, therefore, Show Taro pretended as if he were quite impressed.

Show Taro [Akemi does have good knowledge.]

Akemi [Such bowls that amateur potters produce are thick and too heavy, and just to make the whole surface of bowls thinner cannot be used for hot tea serving. This is a matter of course, isn't it.]

Show Taro [Such exquisite balance is obtainable only through inheritance of technics in the master and pupil relationship.]

Akemi [In our student days, she used to accompany me to her sightseeing trips along with tours of facilities so I had a lot of chance to get a bit of knowledge of various matters.]

Maria [Are you saying such visits include visits to potteries?]

Akemi [I've been to Arita and also to Seto, not to talk about Kyoto where I visited such workshops of Kyo-yaki, Yuzen dyeing, Japanese cake, lacquer art and

— 83 —

ornamental hair pin or every conceivable place of such.]

Maria [What at all was the reason why you did such wide range of visits?]

Akemi [In the Chinese mainland at the Chinese Cultural Revolution all maestros of traditional handcraft were massacred. Can you believe it? China concentrated its total efforts on wiping out its own culture.]

Show Taro [If a country is led by such leaders who can understand only theories, such outrageous cases often took place in the history. Chinese Cultural Revolution can be said as one of those.]

Akemi [The grandmother of Jinlian used to be a mistress of Entetsu merchant (dealing salt and iron) and for this reason she had a very hard time being persecuted as decadent bourgeois.]

Show Taro [And one other reason for persecution might have been jeorousy of her beauty. In addition, residence of such salt and iron merchant used to be a very broard mansion. I remember I heard such phrase as 「Eat in Guangzhou, wed in Suzhou, die in Hangzhou」. Probably in and around Suzhou, there must have been many beautiful young daughters of that beautiful mistress.]

Akemi [So that I heard the mistress ran away to Hong Kong staking her life.]

It came to be clear to Show Taro from the conversation so far with Akemi, that Jinlian and Akemi were companions for seeing

— 84 —

and studying many such observations they shared at their student days.

Akemi   [Looks like she finally finished her telephoning task.]

A business suits in strong pink color jumped into the visitors' eyes. There stood a woman with clear-cut features bearing long hair. She was not very tall but her neck-opening was showing the voluptuous look that was called bell lotus storing magical enchantment. Apparently, she knows how to uplight her appearance so that she concentrated all bright colours onto her clothes to have others eyes forcussed on her. Show Taro became aware she had a skin as white as snow.

Akemi   [Let me do introduction, this is Mr. Show Taro and
                that is Ms. Maria, then Miss Jinlian Pan.]

Finising exchange of calling cards, Jinlian hung her handbag on her arm and declared.

Jinlian   [From now on, I will take you all to Mr. Chen Jing Ji.]

Jinlian went on to show them to the prepared helicopter for them to ride on it. Apparently Jinlian is also of a character to wish to lead people so she appointed the seats of Akemi and Maria and let Show Taro sit next to her. Though Akemi did know this would be the case, she looked to be crossed, and was being soothed by Maria in a small voice.

Show Taro [Your Japanese is fluent.]

Jinlian   [As I learned at a college in Japan.]

Show Taro [Around when was it?]

Jinlian   [Just about twelve years ago.]

Into the eyes of ShowTaro, the jewelry Jinlian was wearing which he did not notice much till then. This could be the only subject of talk for this sudden first meeting.

Show Taro [As the cut on the other side of this can be seen as being doubled, this is a fairly large peridot, isn't it.]

In case the size reaches a certain level, regarding gemstone with double reflection, the ridge line of the boarder on the face called facet is seen doubly in the same theory as a hair being observed as double through rock crystal.

If one is accustomed to use this identifying method, in case double line is observed through a loope on a transparent gemstone, he can determine it as a ruby and if single line then that is a spinel. To add more information, time when the difference of double and single reflection of ruby and spinel could come to be determined by non- distructive inspection started in the 1880th

Jinlian [Seems you have good knowledge of gemstone. I am making it my habit to use reddish gems in the day time and greenish ones for the night time. Value of jewelry much depends on the color, doesn't it. That is the reason why I was wearing mandarin garnet in the orange colour group till a short time ago.]

Show Taro [I see. That was the reason why that accessory was not too standing up on your pinkish color clothes.]

Among the category of jewelries, garnet is a jewelry that has a variety of colours as same as sapphire. Most Japanese are misunderstanding that garnet is always of red pomegranate color. Talking about orange color family, such garnet in the color of mandarin orange is called mandarin garnet and of green color family, in addition to green garnet, there is demantoid garnet mainly from Russia which has an extremely strong brightness. Additinally, there is a color changing garnet which normally is of blue color but turns to be red under incandescent lamp. This color changing gem may work as talisman same as alexandrite.

Talking about jemstone of the green color family, if transparency and the largeness are required as an accessory, the large grain Peridot which Jinlian was wearing can be said as a good choice. If that were emerald in a similar color shade, cost would come to be too forbidable to be used casually. If sapphire, green color sapphire does not have enough clarity so its rank as a jewelry comes to be quite low. Lastly, talking about garnet in the green color family, and especially demantoid exceeding one carat, cost acceleratingly soars up, therefore use of this jewel plentifully is not quite recommendable from the cost viewpoint.

For this woman called by the code name of Bell Lotus, to call her wonderful lotus sounds like the most suitable name for her. But in Japan, since the ancient times they used to call maidservantas lotus leaves and the high-class prostitutes as lotus flowers. To Show Taro who had the above knowledge, this code for Jinlian sounded rather more pursuasive. The person whoever he was who created the name Bell Lotus getting the hint from La Bell Otero who is a well remembered courtesan may have been an intellectual person who knows this part of Japanese history.

Jinlian　　　[I don't believe in the value of birthday stones. they are Jeweler's creation solely meant for promotion of their sales. My selection is based on colors of stones to suit me which I believe will lead me to the magic world before the medieval period of the history. Do you understand?]

Show Taro [As you say, Color green has been cherished as a symbol color for keeping youth both in the East and the West ever since the ancient times, therefore, Caesar made a collection of emerald and Xi Taihou, Jade.]

In Japan, too, on the crown of Kannon of Sangatudo at Todaiji Temple, jade from Itoigawa was used as far as I remember. That must be of the collection of Emperor Shomu and Empress Komyo. As that jade was used on the crown, mining of jade at Itoigawa was since prohibited.]

Jinlian [Is Japanese jade a talisman of the shape of an unborn child?]

Show Taro [Well, I cannot readily anwer that question⋯ clarification of your question will take a lot more time. One thing which is known is when X.Taihou passed away, there was a big oriental melon shape jade pendant was placed on the chest of her dead body.]

Jinlian [Do you mean it can be obtained if I open the coffin?]

Eyes of Jinlian were rolling so Show Taro could get that she was interested in that story.

Show Taro [What I heard is that at a later date Revolutionry Government sent Millitary Police for opening the coffin for fund supplement purposes but the police failed to find the jade pendant.]

Jinlian   [Hmm⋯but from whom did Show hear such news?]

Show Taro [What I heard is the grandfather of a friend of my acquaintance was one of the military policemen that Military Police sent to the cemetery in the hope of recovering the jade.]

Jinlian   [I didn't expect such information could be obtained in Japan.]

Show Taro [The jade in question must have been taken away by one of the eunuchs.]

Jinlian   [Even an Emperor ends up as a mere substance if he is dead, right?]

Show Taro [As I haven't heard any Japanese possesses it, it may be in the hand of somebody somewhere in Europe such as U.K. or France.]

Jinlian   [Should you ever be able to obtain it, would you let me have it.]

Show Taro [Sure, I will do so.]

Jinlian   [Incidentally, when I visit Japan next time, could you be my sightseeing guide please?]

Show Taro [My pleasure, but I guess you already know Japan well, don't you?]

Jinlian   [While I was a student in Japan, I was tied up with Akemi to play with her⋯so I didn't have much chance to do what I myself like to do.]

Show Taro [I see. If that is the case, you can make a day trip to Kamamura from Tokyo.]

Jinlian   [Oh, I'm happy to hear that.]

Each time of the shake of helicopter he felt she was leaning on his shoulder. Also, she was casting a bewitching flirtatious glance to him all the time. He thought she was embodying the name Belle Lotus.

Show Taro [Your skin is as fare as can be for a person of Hong Kong.]

Jinlian [As I keep flying about on my business all the time, I cannot afford to stay in Hong Kong even half a time of my life. I spend rest of time in Japan or Europe.]

Show Taro [If you are in Cannes, you're Venus there.]

Jinlian [Oh, I'm flattered. How far have you gone with Akemi? I undertand you're a Don Juan. Mind you, I will let you turn to me even for one night. Akemi's type of men is my type of men. Got it?]

Show Taro [. . .]

Show Taro felt as if he were sitting on a chair of thorns while being wide aware of Akemi's accusing stare, being unable to escape from Jinlian who does not stop leaning on him.

They arrived at casino in a short while but that short trip was an extremely long time for Show Taro to bear with.

On the seat at the back of the that of Jinlian and Show Taro Akemi and Maria were seated but such conversation between Jinlian and Show Taro could not be overheard disturbed by the roaring sound of helicopter. But the scene of Jinlian leaning her body on Show Taro was enough for rubbing Akemi's nerves in the wrong way.

Akemi [Can you guarantee that you said Show Taro will not turn to her to be true?]

Maria who was observing Akemi's irritation replied.

Maria   [No. He will never be emortionally absorbed by her. But he will soon be going to establish relationship for some business collaporation with her.]

The medium Maria did see a shade of a woman which was not Julian's was secretly approaching Show Taro but Maria thought timing is wrong to talk about it to Akemi. However, this reply of Maria seemed to be incomprehensible to Akemi . 「Why and what for the business collaboration is?」 Akemi could not understand what Maria implied by only judging from the present scene developing in the helicopter.

They agreed to meet back at casino at night. Until then they spent time to unpack their luggage in the respective hotel rooms. When Show Taro was doing unpacking at his room, there came Akemi.

Akemi   [You, don't make eyes at Jinlian.]

Show Taro [Can I ask what talk did you have with Jinlian? She called me a Don Juan…]

Akemi   [Jinlian is a bind follower of Tokyo mode. Therefore, she wants to follow and copy whatever I like.]

Show Taro [How is tonight's arrangement set?]

Akemi   [This room of yours is a connecting suite with the room of Jinlian. She said if I do not allow her to stay at this connecting suite, she will not let you meet ZeDeng Mao.]

Show Taro could not find what to say about this clearly strange situation. Normally, connecting suite means the lock of the door between two separate rooms is kept open so users of both rooms

— 91 —

can visit each other without going out to the collider and in from the collider. In most cases such connecting suits are used by two relatives or such sort of visitors⋯

Show Taro [⋯]

At that time, from the connecting room Jinlian who had not yet changed her dress put out her face and cut in the conversation between Akemi and Shotaro.

Jinlian [Please change your clothes quickly. Your tuxedo is there in that case. Oh, Akemi is here⋯please dress yourself up.]

Apparently, Jinlian, too, now looks to be conscious of Akemi's existence there. While reluctantly Akemi went back to her room Jinlian called Show Taro in turn to come to her room.

Jinlian [Show, please put the zipper up.]

Apparently, she was fawning on him and turned around to show the backside of the rame-containing patterned dress. At her back black color underwear was showing where there was a naked body which was so luring that might as well give him an impulse to push her down to the bed if Akemi were not there. Female feramon was filling all around there but he just started to lift the zipper up when she turned around and tried to kiss him. Her red rouge sticked to his mouth and at that moment there was a knock and Akemi and Maria came in.

On finding the trace of rouge on Show Taro who opened the door, Akemi lost herself and flapped his face twice impulsively but Show Taro was just at a loss at what happened. Then Akemi declared Jinlian as follows.

Akemi [I will take my luggage here into this room.]

Jinlian [Oh, why didn't you say so earlier. I now see you like the match of the three. Let's play with him together.]

Akemi previously told Jinlian that Show Taro was a Don Juan in an intention to keep Jinlian away but obviously Jinlian took Akemi's words seriously. In such situation, Jinlian was still thinking it was a good opportunity to play a sex game together with Akemi and with this man of unbounded potency.

Akemi [I will never let you touch Show Taro.]

Jinlian [Are you a maniac of being looked?]

Akemi [I will never pass him to you all the more.]

At this word of her, Jinlian for the first time looks to understand that Akemi was very serious.

Jinlian [Okay, I bet you don't want to meet ZeDeng Mao. Remember he is the person to assume the remittance operation.]

As a result, this scene ended as a very noisy catfight but all through that time, Maria was there keeping silence.

As Maria was standing there without issuing one single word, the door was kept to be left open, when a man in tuxedo came in from the elevator. Seeing his figure, Jinlian's talking tone suddenly changed and became calm.

Jinlian [Let me do the introduction. This gentleman is the person who is arranging remittance. That is Mr. Show Taro and Ms. Akemi, and Ms. Maria.]

Jinlian did this introduction in Japanese. That man came near to Show Taro and gave one bow and greeted handing his business card to him.

Kezawa   [I am greeting to you in Japanese now. That I greet using Japanese is after quite a while since the last time. I am working as financial advisor for Jinlian Pan. My name is Noboru Kezawa.]

With Show Taro first, the rest of people except Jinlian were surprised at his introduction and in this surprise, they exchanged their business cards with Mr. Kezawa.

Show Taro   [I am Hayashi of Palais Flora].

Kezawa   [I have not used Japanese for more than the past ten years, so after this meeting, please refrain from telling others that I am a Japanese. This is one condition of my accepting this assignment. Is it clear with all of you?]

Show Taro   [Then how do you like us to call you from now on?]

Mao   [Please call me either Mao or 『ZeDeng Mao』. This has been my pen name since from ten years ago.]

Show Taro   [Okay, well understood.]

Mao   [However, the temptation by Jinlian is too good an opportunity to pass up, isn't it?]

Show Taro retorted this sudden question from ZeDeng Mau.

Show Taro   [What about you?]

Mao   [I have no interest in women. Moreover, all of those men who slept with Jinlian finished pouring all the profit they made from the money game into her and ended with self suiside. Chen Jing Ji will be no exception. By now at least eight are already dead.]

Hearing this, Jinlian cut in the abashed look.

Jinlian   [It is a big lie. Mr. Show Taro, don't take his words

— 94 —

seriously.]

Maria   [No, it is not. She let quite a few die.]

Akemi   [Ms. Maria can see it.]

Hearing Akemi, Mao reacted in return.

Mao   [Your prophecy is pretty significant. I am a petite fan
of you.

Your deciphering of holoscope as listed on the magazine 『Maria's
Room』 is quite something.]

Maria   [Are you a feng sui master geomancer fully employed
by Jinlian?]

Mao   [I repeat I am a financial advisor.]

He said it quietly but adamantly.

After a while, a room boy came and announced that the meeting
room was ready for their use, so they moved to the meeting room.

Then, there at the meeting room, Chen Jing Ji who also owned
the casino joined them for the first time.

Show Taro [Which company is Mr. Chen planning to use to
receive the official check issued by Hell Computer/]

Chen   [I am thinking about using 『Gallery Mandarin』 which
is listed on top of this list. As there are quie many
fraud cases using official checks, till the exchange to
cash is complete, a person who belongs to the other
side is schedulled to stay in this hotel.]

Show Taro [In other words, if any falsehood is found that person
shall be executed. Is this correct?]

Chen   [3% of the face value of the check shall be received by
Mr. Show Taro as a kickback and this 3% will have to
be collected by Mr. Show Taro from the 6% that is

— 95 —

	going to Jinlian Pan and Mr. Show Taro is to share this 3% by halves with Mr. Suzuki or so.]
Jinlian	[I will pay Ms. Akemi and Mr. Show Taro 1.5% and 3% respectively.]
Akemi	[Why not 4.5% to me and of this 4.5% 3% to Show Taro?]
Jinlian	[To decide which company's check to use is up to my decision.]
Show Taro	[What about the remittance method?]
Mao	[The first remittance will be sent to the designated account from Town Bank, Hong Kong but after that, we may use a different routing. Three times are the maximum to use one same routing. Also, in case more provisions for restricting remittance are issued, we will take a different means.]

At this place, though Maria kept silence, she felt Jinlian had not given Show Taro up as yet, and at the same time she was concerned about the characteristics of the fund. Or, more exactly saying, she had presentiment of something that was related to many corpes once remittance was completed. The meeting was over with a toast with champagne, but Maria got depressed worrying Jinlian might get beside herself over again with men as per the destiny that results from her previous life.

6. Report from Robert and Simon

Coming back to Japan, Show Taro proposed the condition presented by the Chinese connection and also faxed a copy of the legal personality registration of the remittee to Robert and Simon. During his absence, one each e-mail had been delivered to his office from both of them. Needless to say, Show Taro passed the information regarding Chen Jing Ji and ZeDeng Mao but kept the information of Mao being a Japanese in secret.

Mail from Robert was stating as below. What interested Show Taro was Robert's naming at Euro Pole was added to that e-mail. Show Taro had been aware Robert was Euro Pole related person but as Robert would not tell it to Show Taro, Show Taro kept treating him as an inspector of an insurance company.

Details of the person concerned

Genta Shiaku=Chirac

Last year's trading performance as shrimp aquafarmer was two containerful loads for export to Japan.

According to an unconfirmed information, he seems to be committing such criminal incidents as to let Japanese obtain duvious fake checks and to shake the Japanese down for deposit money.

Kubera Prima=Black Magna

He is a jewelry dealer but history of his activity in Europe could not be traced.

Indrajit Divija=Phoenix

This person is engaged in export-import trading of automotive and motor bike materials and PC parts and travels around in Europe at least for several times per year. He is also trading with Lebanon and Syria and is rumored that he handles component parts of weapons produced in Eastern Asia. He has a plural number of criminal records but every time he has been freed due to insufficient evidences before such cases of his were taken into the court. He has a background of studying overseas at a collage in Canada and stayed there for several years after graduation. Though this information is an unconfirmed one, his hobby will probably be restoration of hot rods.

Jinlian Pan＝Bell Lotus

Her name is wellknown in the apparel trading field in Hong Kong. She is a genious to destroy men and the more she destroys men the better her business is stepping up.

Chen Jing Ji＝Cinderella Boy

Starting his carrier with wholesale business of pharmaceutical products, married with the only daughter of Ximen Industries and currently managing a hotel and a casino.

He seems to be an orphan having flown into Hong Kong from the continent China. A lover of Belle Lotus.

ZeDeng Mao＝Shaman Rouge

Controlling underground money of Hong Kong. Suspicious person who grasps the news of change of policies of Chinese Government at lease a few days earlier than any body. For this reason, he is rumored as a grandson of Mao Zedong which however Chinese Government kept unconfirming.

The next e-mail that Show Taro opened was one from Simon. Some part of information contained in his e-mail was duplicating the news from Robert.

Simon himself had never revealed to Show Taro that he was in truth related to Mosad, therefore, Show Taro also kept pretending not to know such fact and under this unstable condition he was utilizing information tendered from Simon.

Genta Shiaku=Chirac

At the beginning he is marked by the police for his trading of cultured pearls in Indonesia, but later he is suspected to have dealt with black pearls that are burnt by radiative rays and is mistaken as a French person so he comes to be called by the name of Chirac. He makes blackmailing his business which he is practicing in and around Singapore using false checks under the name of American banks as issurers.

Kubera Prima=Black Magna

His name is notorious as regards wholesale of inferior quality large drop black pearls. His base office in California iss also being used as liaison office of Indians living in America. He is also marked in suspicion of industrial spy business in relation to computers.

Indrajit Divija=Phoenix

He is in an import/export business of automotive components but seems to be related to weapon smuggling deals internationally. At his back, power of him not to be arrested is working. He looks like to have a strong air supremacy.

Chen Jing Ji=Cinderella Boy

Major supply source of female dancers who smuggle into America, besides his business of operation of a hotel and a casino. He is in fact a trafficker, however, as he is exempralily dominating a big sum of money to the authorities in charge, he is always exempted from the regulation. He is also donating enough amount of bribe to the American industries who are buying from him so that to take any action contrary to his interest is deemed to be a taboo between Ameica and China.

ZeDeng Mao=Shaman Rouge

He is a controller of the Hong Kong underground money and there is an information that he is talking Chinese, English and French.

There is a report that he is foreseeing the change of policy of Chinese government one week before the Govermental officers in charge finalized the change. For that reason, there is the reasoning of him to be the grandson of Chairman Mao and also another reasoning of him as a psychic. Whichever may apply, he is said to be a mysterious man. He is sometimes seen playing at casino with roulette and is rumored that he bets at only one point for several times and earned several ten thousand dollars and vanishes away. But at the gambling spot where he plays, lots of gambers gather so his visit is always welcomed by the casio owner.

Jinlian Pan=Belle Lotus

All businessmen who love this business woman are sure to be

destroyed is a widely spreading rumor. Her beautiful features are one of the top of only few in Asia. Already she led six Chinese go broke and two Americans, too.

Hell Computer

Their products are developed targeting at such high technology which even huckers coming from the hell can not break. The founder of this company is boasting that whoever can break his technology will be nobody but the troops of God. The company holds many bank accounts all over America. There exist numerous trading accounts which even authorities can not get the whole picture and also there exist accounts under the same name accountee but which have absolutely no relation with his business. It is totally unknown why Hell Computer keeps silence regarding this matter of accounts. Those finance relation experts are regarding it a nonsence to bring a law suit for their use of similar name for those unknown accounts.

Reading and comparing the contents of both e-mails will help Show Taro to keep himself safe. He now understands that Shiaku played fairly gaudy trading using false checks. But with the deal this time, if the check is a fake he will be killed without fail so he won't dare to take such action. To let the India related personnel live there means such result.

In addition, Maria is pointing out existance of a person whom Indrajit is called Raja, however, this person is only described as the mastery of the air. In any case, even if Maria just says so, Simon may feel creepy but will not take it too seriously.

Having obtained this much information, Show Taro made a contact with Suzuki. Purpose of his contact with Suzuki is to ask him to make a full explanation to Shiaku that this deal will not allow him to use his usual swindling practice of using false check and of using deposit in name, or in some cases by blackmailing like such a way as forcing payment of money using the exposure of details of the deal as reason. Show Taro's intention in this case with this China connection is until the check can finally be cashed, he is to keep the Indian side people in the state of being invited, namely to keep them in hostage.

Unless the check can be cashed, it is impossible to make an escape alive from China as in China any commiter of economic crime of such a large amount of three million dollars will very possibly be gundowned in an open space.

Of a number of criminal offenders of foreign nationality, those who were carried out with death order in China must have had an easy thought which is in such a country like China, even they were arrested as criminal offenders, unless they were not murderers, the heaviest punishment would be not more than expulsion from the country. However, the original legal codes called Ritsuryo codes that were applied to Eastern Asian counties were the creation of the ancient international emirates, Tang Dynasty.

'Ritsu' of the Ritsuryo codes can be translated as 'Penal Code' in this modern world, which stipulates and indicates what crime would deserve what penalty for the purpose of establishing the public order. 'ryo' of the Ritsuryo codes means in today's terms Cabinet order to stipulate methods to determine policy-making process and bureaucratic procedures at each governmental office.

In other words, Ritsuryo codes can be interpreted as basic rules to help the emperor's and his cabinet's policy decision be proclaimed to all parts of China and administered without delay. Readers in this modern world who have read this part of the book so far will notice the law of the modern world is different from Roman law and Napoleon code at the point that the latter is referring to right and duty of the people while the former is not.

In other words, Tang or Japan at the past times did not include right and duty of individuals in the region where law was ruling. Suppose counterfeiting crime is committed, such case is taken as violation of right of coinage and the criminal was sentenced to death on a charge of national treason. On the other hand, in the modern Japan, such criminal was teated in the category of economical crime so death sentence cannot be thought about, but in China where the tradition since Ritsuryo code of the old era is continuing to be applicable, it is a matter of course that such criminal shall be gundowned in an open place.

Under such circumstances in China, such criminal as involved in the sale of drugs which can make many tens of people disabled or as economy criminal of fraud of the money value that exceeds average citizen's lifetime income are casually sentenced to death and are gundowned in an open place. The writer presumes that such rule may be taken into consideration as one direction of solution in the sense of antisocial nature. In Japan, many young people are easily getting involved themselves in fraud endlessly without trying to get their earnings by swetting labour. The writer considers that one of the reasons of this kind of crime never ceases in Japan is because of absence of death sentence to those frauders who obtain the frauded money that equals to several ten years of average wadge gained by citizens. Such instance will not be treated as the case of death sentence in European and American laws either, but in case the size of such fraud is just overwhelmingly large or continuously repeated involving over the world or used as means of terrorists' money laundering purposes consequently leading to death of a mass of innocent people, the writer thinks that in future rules for those crimes may have a chance to be reconsidered and changed.

Analizing the information that has been obtained to that stage Show Taro came to realize that if this case in his hands should be a fraud, he now stands the side of a snare of a large-scale economy crime that was being set against him. He now understands if what he suspects should turn out to be real it means he was made to join to grasp the tail of the crime of world scale money laundering and weapon trading, so, he will have no other choice but to have to confirm that he has already been involved in such situation as stated above.

7. The Official Check Added On Hell Computer

It was about two weeks later since Show Taro met for the first time with Genta Shiaku, when Show Taro was again contacted by Shiaku

That two weeks would mean that the Indian connection side also needed that long time for investigation. Suzuki also must have fully understood the meaning of the offer from the Chinese side. As long as this time the case started on the condition of no deposit, the explanation has already been made as to no false check can be used and if cashing of the check is unable to be done Indian side related people will be arrested in China. To Show Taro's narrow office, Suzuki also came accompanying Shiaku.

Show Taro [Considerably long time since then passed, so may I ask if preparation at the Indian side is now ready or not?]

Genta [Oh, yes, of course. But their side looks to spend time for a few different types of preparations.]

Show Taro [So, can the check be prepared as Mr. Chen desires?]

Genta [Check addressed to Gallery Mandarin has been prepared. Face value of the check is 3 million dollars. As we also prepared a letter of purchasing request of paintings from Hell, I wish you to convey it.]

Suzuki [Tell me we can still retreat from this deal.]

Show Taro [In view of the fact that no go-sign has yet been obtained from the Chinese side, it could be called as a

— 105 —

little bit of flying, Yes? Gen.]

Genta   [As Kubera is in Japan now, can we get the answer from him here?]

Show Taro [Okay, I will convey your message, but can I have a color copy of the check and copy of the letter of the Painting purchasing request addressed to Hell Computer now?]

Genta   [Here it is.]

Saying that, he took out from the bag a file and put it on the table once and took from the file the Hell Computer letterheads. Seeing this, Show Taro kept the papers on the table and without touching the papers so as not to leave his fingerprint on them and carefully viewed the papers. However, despite his careful check, what he saw were only the two papers of a color copy of the official check and the document regarding the order request.

Show Taro [Where is the copy of the request of cancellation of purchase?]

Genta   [Is such document needed at this point of time?]

Show Taro [If which bank account of what country is the remittance is to be made for is unknown, Zedeng Mao was saying he cannot make consideration of remittance.]

Genta   [What about having Kubera take such here?]

Show Taro [Gen, If we become watched by Chinese Government, there will be no way to make a come back to the free world. I did tell this to Mr. Suzuki⋯Didn't I, Mr. Suzuki?]

Suzuki   [Well⋯ya]

— 106 —

Judging from Suzuki's appearance, it looks like the request from the side of Show Taro was not fully conveyed to their side.]

Genta   [Mr. Suzuki, that is what I heard for the first time.]

Suzuki turned pale and became a shell. On the face of Genta anger and uneasiness were altogether came out. Show Taro instinctly felt that this check is false, so he told slowly and in an adamant way that this case could never be turned to be used for extortion to Genta Shiaku and his group.

Show Taro [Here, I am formally explaining to you. Even if remittance can be made to China, if remittance cannot be made from China to other countries, this business must be postponed. The Chinese side will offer hotel accommodations till the cashing is complete, but this offer of the accommodation is in a sense a hostage.

With false check, those people concerned will not be able to go out from China and for an economy criminal of the amount of 3 million dollars, all of the concerned people shall be put a triangle shape cap written Death Sentence on it and made parading around in the city on a truck and shall be gundowned in an open place.

Mr. Chen told me that in the past he had no experience to go successful tagging with Indians, but he mailed me saying in this case, he can get hostages so Indians will become serious about this deal. Please convey this message to Mr. Indrajit as well.]

Genta   [I do understand. Please give me another week.]

Show Taro [Who are going to be present in China at time of cashing the check? Please fix the people, too.]

These words of Show Taro included the meaning of the need for them to decide which ones are to die in case the check is false. Until

— 107 —

just then Genta was on the side of a hunter, but now he was put on the other side of being hunt so he was slightly trembling.

Genta [Show, I do understand, so anyway, I will go and meet Kubera.]

Saying so, Genta went out of Show Taro's office hurriedly. Suzuki wiped sweat on his forehead but kept looking down.

Show Taro [Mr. Suzuki, Weren't you at my side? If you should have been in China when the check of this time could not be cashed, you also would have been gundowned. By the way, what percentage is the incentive from Gen?]

Suzuki [⋯1.5% of the face value.]

Show Taro [Well, that could well be covered by what you will get. The planned share of you was 1.5% but I will now change it to the 0.5% of the face value. So your share comes to be 2%. Do you accept 2%?]

Suzuki [Well, that is⋯..a bit ⋯.]

Show Taro [Once China Connection comes to know this story, you will be arrested by China without fail, then what do you do?]

Suzuki [W..well, that is ⋯fine.]

Shiaku conveyed the message from Show Taro to Kubera who in turn relayed the message to Indrajit and Indrajit went to report it to the roots of air supremacy. Indrajit rode on his car and went through the crowded streets with slow paces and finally arrived at a castle wall of uncovered big sandstone. There was a plain and a bit expanded space where he parked his car. Then, from a corner like a hollow of sandstone a guard came to the side of the driver's

— 108 —

seat of his car.

Indrajit   [I need to meet Lord. Raja.]

Guard   [Oh, Mr. Indrajit⋯this way please ⋯]

The castle gate which weathered some hundreds of years opened squeaking. Going through the gate, there was the entrance of the castle. He parked his car at the carriage entrance. A doorman came and opened the rear door but as he saw no one on the rear seat, he hurriedly came around to the front seat door to open it.

Doorman   [Are you here today with some urgent business?]

Indrajit   [Correct. I hope Lord. Raja is available.]

Doorman   [He is having a guest at the moment but please come in anyway.]

In this way, Indrajit entered Raja Mitra's castle. He left his car with the key and the car was immediately transferred to a different place by a substitute driver. They kept no car at the carrage entrance which means the visitor's privacy could be safely guarded.

The outside temperature was 40 ℃ or thereabouts consecutively but the temperature inside of the castle was kept about 24℃ so it was pleasant being in there. The main collidor was made of marble stone mosaic tiles covered by red carpet. Big chandeliers were hung here and there and guards who looked alike doormen were standing. Marble stone wall of Passages for guests were rubbed up so guests did not have a chance to walk to different directions. Having walked through the long corridor, there was an open hall where a butler dressed in traditional Indian national costume was waiting.

Butler   [With no one in tow, are you here for some urgent matter?]

— 109 —

Indrajit   [Yes, indeed. Could I see him?]

Buter   [He is meeting a guest, but please come in. This way please.]

Then, from there, Indrajit was guided by a doorman whom the butler dressed in traditional Indian costume ordered at his beckoning to guide Indrajit. In the gallery made of marble stone of baroque revival style, a crystal glass chandelier with at least twenty lights attached was hunging and on the way to reach that gallery there decorated several oil paintings of successive castle lords and also a few landscape paintings of European sceneries. That scene was showing that the castle load here is of a family of successive generations.

Entering through a door which was guarded by the guards of the gallery, there was a room of about 100 square meters with off-white marble stone panels were pasted on the wall and the floor and on that floor, a few pieces of soft carpets were placed. From the window the outside landscape was observed. This room was functioning as the lord's audience room. As yet there was no sign of a person there behind the thin lace curtain, but Indrajit kept prostrating himself in the center of the guest carpet which was weaving out the pattern of a hunting scene. He was kept waiting in that posture on that guest carpet for about half an hour.

Indrajit overheard from around the door beyond the lace curtain, footsteps and a laughing voice. At the next moment, the door opened and Raja Mitra attended by the butler came into the room. Waiting for Raja to sit in the center of the seat which had the woven pattern of Tree of Life, Indrajit getting a bit nervous issued his voice

Indrajit   [Your highness Raja Mitra, I have two reports to make.]

Raja Mitra   [Indrajjit, Raise your head. You are permitted to report to me directly.]

Bulter   [You may raise your face and talk directly to him.]

So Indrajit was finally allowed to talk to Raja face to face. Raja had a beard and was putting a parrot on his shoulder.

Indrajit   [One is bad news but another one is good news. This time, false check will not work for this business. This is the bad part of the report. The good news is the connection we are to use does have capability to make remittance successfully which means it is worth waiting for the past several years.]

Raja Mitra   [So you mean Gorgon can be transported, don't you.]

Indrajit   [Please make arrangement for transportation, too.]

Raja Mitra   [Soldiers in Middle East will be pleased.]

Indrajit   [Please give me your permission for us to start making preparation work of a remittable check.]

Raja Mitra   [My permission is granted. Incidentally, who is the opposite side?]

Indrajit   [Zedeng Mao and Chen Jing Ji. According to the news from Wang Chao, they are professional handlers of underground money and gambling respectively.]

Raja Mitra   [Indrajit, your grandfather was a hero of Indian National Army which participated in Battle of Imphal. He cornered the U.K. army with his ingenuity and willpower.]

— 111 —

Indrajit [I have heared the grandfather of your highness also did great at SS Free Indian Corps.]

Raja Mitra [What I heard is in the first place he was studying in London when he was convened and suddenly taken to Cairo. And it was the Indian unit that was deserted in front of the advancing Rommel tank unit.]

Indrajit [However, for that fact, the destiny changed, didn't it?]

Raja Mitra [My grandfather who was an international student in U.K. offered coorperation to acquire independence of India and had a chance to meet Subhas Chandra Bose, the great leader (Netaji). My grandfather was deeply moved hearing Bose' words of 「Give me blood and I shall give you Freedom!」.]

Indrajit [Now I see. That is the reason why he got belonged to SS Free Indian Legion (Indische Freiwillinggenlegion der SS).]

Raja Mitra [On that D day when Normandy invasion was carried out, he happened to be out at the sea side due to communication equipment fault.]

Indrajit [And there he saw the hideous scene, I see.]

Raja Mitra [Look, The first unit that got riddled with bullets of the U.K. advance parties when they tried to make a landing was the colonial army, namely, Indian soldiers. And of the American landing units, those soldiers who fought bravely and whose corpes were stepped on by the units arriving next were Africans. Such facts were never recorded in video recording of America and U.K.]

Indrajit	[It must be a very painful experience to Your Highness' grandfather.]
Raja Mitra	[According to what my grandfather told me, as he was in Paris, besides SS high class officials he met a mysterious person.]
Indrajit	[Whom did he meet?]
Raja Mitra	[Luk Gauric who was a librarian at Natinal Archieves of France working for high officials of NSDAP.]
Indrajit	[I have a feeling that I met a person of that name···]
Raja Mitra	[He is the grandfather of the medician who came here several times. They are using the same name over their generations. Especially when astrology is related, they make it a rule to call themselves Lucas Gauricus in Latin.]
Indrajit	[Did that Luc Gauric talk any thing special?]
Raja Mitra	[What my grandfather told me is the reason why Luc was consulted by the NSDAP high officials was because Luc already knew that the fate of NS high officials or generals was going to face a great difficulty in 1945.]
Indrajit	[Before the war of Germany versus Soviet with Barbarossa as the start took place?]
Raja Mitra	[Hess seemed to be exercising a simplified astrology by himself. Therefore, he already understood the fate of Adolf Hitler as early as when he joined the NS party given the member number of 555. But as Hess was not very confident of what he saw in his own astrology, he applied for the holoscope telling by

	Elsbeth Evertin on the newspaper at that time.]

Indrajit [I see. That is the reason why many NS high class officers like Himmler or Goebbels in addition to Hess were admirers of Nostradums 「Les Centuries (Hundred Psalms)」].

Raja Mitra [They already knew Nostradamus had written about them in his Les Centuries. But apart from Nostradamus, it was also a fact that Mussolini of Fascist Party did know his fate of at least half of it.]

Indrajit [Still, was what he could know only half of his fate?]

Raja Mitra [That is the difficult point of deciphering Nostradums' prophecy. He made his book unable to be deciphered especially by governmental administrators, hiding keys which are time-locked till a certain time arrives. And when the time comes only some specific persons can get the crue to open the lock. Only those specific persons who were not the high rank government officials then···that is what Maestro Lucas Gauricus told my grand father.]

Indrajit [So, Does that mean Himmler or Goebbels were dashing forward even though they know only half of their fates?]

Raja Mitra [Yes, That was the reason why they could organize the attack squad (SS) and rely on it despite the fact the storm troop (SA) already existed.]

Indrajit [Did Hess know the best where the NS military government was going?]

Raja Mitra [According to Luc, there are psalms which are difficult

— 114 —

to decipher and the reason why those are difficult is dual decipherings are possible and both of such deciphering can be taken as right.]

Indrajit   [Does that both decipherings can be right mean that time goes as it will be, or else, there will be a switchback once and then the history can shift to the next time dimension?]

Raja Mitrea [Yes, you are right.]

Indrajit   [Suppose this dual meaning was hidden since from the first edition, could you please teach me an example?]

Raja Mitra [The first edition of 「Les Centuries」 which Nostradamus wrote is stored at National Archieves of France in Paris of which the forth line of 7-14 states [Black taking over White, New idea superseding the Outdated..this statement could be deciphered in two ways.

The ethnic movement radicalists using black color as their image leader will take place of liberalism symborized in white.

This can be read as the fresh ideology will take place of the out-of-date ideology, while on the other hand it can also be read such as when the ethnic radicalism changes from the old structure to a new one, liberalism will change to ethnic radicalism.]

Indrajit   [Which meaning was Hess thinking is Nostradum's true motive?]

Raja Mitra [In the beginning Hess seemed to simply taking it as Black will rise up as a new power but as he continued his investigation of holoscope, he at last became aware that Black to rise up once and to retreat and to be

— 115 —

recomposed into a new form over again and then for the first time it would take place of liberalism. This is what I heard.]

Indrajit [And it is not the age of Adolf Hitler, is his conclusion?]

Raja Mitra [Hess may have been wondering thinking it could be his age.]

Indrajit [Will that be the reason why U.K. Government did not release Rudolf Hess even when he became extremely aged in spite of the clear fact that he had absolutely no relation to the war crimes committed by NS since after June, 1940?]

Raja Mitra [I guess U.K.Government did not want to let the man free who could decipher the future. Hess should have been able to foresee the movement of Soviet as well⋯ By the way, didn't you hear from your grandfather anything about Subhas Chandra Bose?]

Indrajit [I heard that he always ended his speech with 「Chalo Delhi!」 , namely On to Delhi!]

Raja Mitra [That is my favorite phrase, too. Indrajit, Continue to work faithfully for me.]

Indrajit [Yes, Sir, Your highness.]

Raja Mitra [Chalo Delhi!]

Reflexively, all that were at that place, in other words, Raja Mitra, Indrajit, the butler and guards, were altogether saluted with Roman salute. In a moment the air changed to tense atmosphere. After the salutation, Indrajit politely bowed once and turned around and made his exit.

Raja Mitra [Report this meeting to Alois.]

— 116 —

Butler   [Yes, sir, I will make an arrangement immediately.]

Perhaps his last talk to Suzuki in a pretty adamant tone may have worked. Within one week's time since that last meeting, he was again visited by Suzuki and Shiaku. This time unlike from last time they presented copy of check, purchase instruction sheet and request for cancellation in writing in one batch. As regards hostage arrangement details, in addition to Kubera, it was set that Shiaku and Suzuki shall be in China at that hotel on a shift on weekly basis and at time of remittance being made, Indrajit will witness the actual remitting action by Mao.

As Show Taro could feel sure checking all those prepared documents that there would be no chance for fraud to be played, he made copies of all those documents and finished preparation to hand over these copies to Jinlian via Akemi. He at the same time sent such copies to Robert and Simon. Needless to say, the American side was to do the confirmation work as to the credibility of the contents of that check, and Robert would also be interested as one of the accounts that is to receive the remittance was a bank in London. Eventually, bank to receive the remittance was to be one of the three accounts that came to be ascertained this time.

The official check to be used at that time was such as below according to a copy.

```
OFFICIAL CHECK
                                        C# 72160086
                ISSUING  BRANCH  Nabalon Main

PAY TO THE ORDER OF
Gallery Mandarin Ltd.     $3,000,000 DOLS 00CTS
Last Bank of America

PURCHASER    HELL COMPUTERS INC.
```

Furthermore, the purchase request document was showing no defect and so as the document of cancellation request. The remittance was planned to be made to one of those three of Dubai, London and Zurich. The issuer was in America and the receiver's banks of the remittance include banks in two cities in Europe. Though the color copies do not clearly show the details but writing pad with Hell Computer's official name printed looked to be used. If the pad was embossed, Show Taro thought the set could probably be perfectly acceptable.

Show Taro arrived in Ginza in the late afternoon. Akemi had contacted him telling him she had prepared by telephone all countermeajures against Jinlian so he could deliver the document to her. Akemi looked to be putting up guards against Jinlian. Wednesdays are the days for many stores to be closed but Akemi was closing her office on Sundays. Entering the entrance, her secretary came out. It looked like that Jinlian was already present in the president's room. Trying not to face her in the president's room, he turned back and there he found Maria standing.

Maria   [Let's go back.]

She took Show Taro's arm asking for an escort. He wondered why, so asked her. She replied in a small voice.

Maria [This is a request from Ms. Akemi. She wants me to work for having Ms. Jinlian give you up.]

Show Taro [⋯]

They waited for elevator to come. When they went into the elevator there sounded Jinlian's voice. On the spur of the moment Maria put her lips on his and thickly entangled her tongue with his. When the elevator door closed, Maria thrust him away and said.

Maria [I just felt Ms Jinlian would not believe if she did not see that we entangled our tongues.]

Show Taro [Was that really all?]

Maria [My assignment.]

Show Taro [⋯]

Some perplexing time flew till Show Taro sent Maria to 「Maria's Room」, then on Maria's cell phone, booing voice flew out.

Akemi [Didn't we conclude the contract that is to have Jinlian give Show up? Jinlian told me she kissed Show even entangling their tongues. How could you do that? I will never pay you the balance of the payment!]

Maria [But didn't Miss Jinlian give in without a fight, did she?]

Akemi [Well⋯That was what it was⋯]

Maria [I could see her mind. I am awfully sorry.]

Akemi [I put my flag on Show Taro. You must promise not to toutch him again.]

Maria [I know.]

It looked like that the other one was still there nearby Akemi, so

— 119 —

her voice was faintly heard.

Jinlian   [Look, Akemi! Show will be tired with Maria without fail.]

Akemi   [She has come back so I will hang up.]

Telephone was arbitrarily cut. Show Taro gradually came to understand what sort of secret promise was built up between the two women.

Show Taro   [Difficult time for you, Ms. Maria. You are being swung about by Akemi.]

Maria   [I wouldn't care.]

Show Taro   [I won't forget.]

Maria   [Forget what?]

Show Taro   [Your kiss.]

Suddenly Maria's tone of voice changed.

Maria   [Suit yourself!]

While elevator was just arriving, she ran up the stairs at the side of the elevator. Till then, she did not have him feel she was a woman but that day to Show Taro, Maria was like a completely different person.

8. Person unbeffiting an Researcher

One week afterwards, Simon and Robert came together to see Show Taro. Needless to say, they ought to have the information about the contents of the check. That time, the three met in the room at Hotel Labyrinth in Tokyo where Robert was staying. Putting the afternoon tea set in his room the room service stuff exited and then the meeting of this time started.

Simon [I could make sure that in this official check 3 million dollars are surely deposited.]

Show Taro [So it is not a false check.]

Simon [You can be rest assured.]

Robert [It was also confirmed that at the account to which this remittance is to be made, sometimes a large sum of money has been deposited or drawn out.]

Simon [By the way, I wish to take with me one of my acquaintances at time of this transaction being made. Will you accept this request of mine?]

Show Taro [Okay, but for what reason is your request?]

Simon [Reason is this account has not been used for normal transactions of Hell Computer.]

Show Taro [Do you mean this account is an account of some one other than Hell Computer?]

Simon [It looks like an account that CFO of Hell opened but was not used for about three years, which has now revived for use. We wish to grasp the purpose of the money in this account.]

— 121 —

Show Taro [So you mean to get that knowledge is an important work for an insurance company.]

Simon [You are right. As this remittance is in the form of 3milion dollar worth painting transaction.]

Show Taro [Is the person coming with you a British person?]

Simon [No, An American.]

Show Taro [Understood. I will create a reason for that person to come with you.]

Simon rang the room next to Robert's, and then soon after the call, a rather small woman came in. She was a brunette hair woman and looked bright, wearing a Venetian Tombow-Dama (glass beads) necklace and a large Keshi baroque ring. She did not look like a researcher and had a charm which is disarming people who invite her to enter their room.

Simon [Let me introduce Nancy Franchetti.]

Nancy [Call me Nancy.]

Robert [She is a researcher of an American insurance company. As her home town is Chicago, Indrajit may have seen her somewhere there.]

Show Taro was aware that the business backround of Nancy would be helpful but was also aware her participation in this deal would give an opposite effect to Akemi. However, Robert seems to be considering the existance of Nancy could be an effective means to prevent Akemi from asserting herself excessively.

Show Taro [What type of deal are you thinking about?]

Robert [She is regularly visiting Eastern Asian countries for the art objects insurance research works. She is working on a full percentage payment system. She is

— 122 —

an owner of rental buildings in Chicago, New York and Italy.]

Her assignment sounds like a rather high-handed approach, but Show Taro remembered her family name was the one that he had surely heared in Italy before.

Show Taro [Are you afraid this transaction may spill into Europe?]

Robert [Look before you leap···that is what I mean.]

Show Taro [What I am afraid is that her beauty may cause a certain kind of problem.]

And at Show Taro's words, Robert reacted simultaneously and spoke out.

Robert [Unless we control Nine Tails and Belle Lotus, this transaction will face a risk of getting broken down with an unexpecting starting point.

We can fabricate a story that while you were in America you coincidentally came to work with her. She can speak broken Japanese and can understand Italian, too. You can accompany her to Europe as well.

Tell them she is your old friend and keep close contact with her. I don't wish such a case of Vienna to happen again where leaving two women you became untraceable.]

Show Taro [I understand what you say.]

The short but goodlooking Nancy came near to Show Taro to shake hands with him so he shook her hands. He thought she must already have a business partner to work together, but she looked not to wish to tell him who the person was. On that day he discussed with Nancy as his work partner in order to make up a story in detail of the fabricated past between them. But to Show

— 123 —

Taro, this work of fabricating the past story beween the two at the dinner meeting with a public security related person, Nancy, was felt like something similar to a background survey. That Robert made Nancy as Show Taro's partner could be Robert's conspiracy. After dinner was finished the two continued to talk at the lounge of the hotel.

Nancy   [You, too, were in Mid West for your automotive work, weren't you.]

Show Taro [Yes, I was working at Suzume Indiana Automotive for a few years. For the damage procedures of the container transportation, I had a chance to meet insurance people for several times.]

Nancy   [Let's take that time when we came to be acquainted. That organization was the one that was producing Tsubame under the Messerschumitt licence during WW2, wasn't it.]

Out of Show Taro's knowledge, she looked to have made some examination beforehand. As she said, that automotive company was producing an air fighter called Tsubame and with this connection, after WW2 they are producing light aircrafts called Suzume.

Show Taro [By the way I think I have heard the word Franchetti before.]

Nancy   [Have you ever been to Venice?]

Show Taro [Yes, several times.]

Nancy   [My relative is living near there.]

Show Taro [Those mansions that are built facing Canal Grande are all Palazzoes of the successful families in overseas

— 124 —

trading business.]

Nancy [At the back side of the fondamenta alongside the narrow stream, a fair number of parazettos are hidden.]

Show Taro [As cars are not running, that streets are somewhat quiet and comfortable, especially the narrow stream area.]

Nancy [Well, but sometimes that place was covred by water at time of acqua alta (high tide).]

Show Taro [Cafes facing Piazza San Marco also suffer acqua alta··· in the calle from that square through to Academia Art Museum I remember there was a shop that was dealing with antique Venetian weaving merchandise. Those merchants who handle such merchandise which must be guarded against wet must have a hard time.]

Nancy [They have to put all their merchandise on the shelves or sometimes have to carry those upstairs, so the work is very hard.]

Show Taro [That they have to do such exercise may be contributing to body shape-up and health.]

Nancy [That could help them to shapeup their bodies depending on the type of business they are handling, but could be the cause of their headache. I mean for such business that is depending on sightseeing tourists. There are shops for tourists and those shops will have to face no visitor therefore no gain.]

Show Taro [Besides Venetian weavings, Murano glass is the local speciality of Venice, isn't it.]

| Nancy | [Strictly speaking, Murano glass is a product which is produced at workshops on the Murano Island, therefore Murano glass is a Murano Island's local speciality being sold in the neighborhood of that area of production. But besides Murano glass, Venice is known as its lace products. Such Venetian lace is used to be placed under an antique pot to decorate a table. By placing the lace, the pot will stay safely on furnitures made before the 17th century which are not plane finished.] |

Nancy [Strictly speaking, Murano glass is a product which is produced at workshops on the Murano Island, therefore Murano glass is a Murano Island's local speciality being sold in the neighborhood of that area of production. But besides Murano glass, Venice is known as its lace products. Such Venetian lace is used to be placed under an antique pot to decorate a table. By placing the lace, the pot will stay safely on furnitures made before the 17th century which are not plane finished.]

Show Taro [As you say, furnitures of ancient age were not plane finished.]

Nancy [In addition, plywood technology was firstly developed in Netherlands and perfected in U.K.]

Show Taro [Amazing you know so well.]

Nancy [If you come and visit my house, I can show you the 17th century furniture without plane finish and also the 18th century plywood made furnitures. Regarding plywood furniture, in Netherlands, two plywood sheets are simply pasted together making the direction of the grain at right angle, but in U.K., material wood was rolled to be peeled spirally, then was pasted together. By this method, fairly large wood material came to become available and such heaviness at the times when natural wood was used was gone and the wood material became a lot lighter.]

Show Taro [Is light weight furniture a lot easier to handle?]

Nancy [Indeed. Light furniture is easy to be handled at time

of cleaning the room. With heavy furniture, if we try
to seriously use a vaccum cleaner all over the room,
we will be ended up exhausted.]

Show Taro [What time of furniture do you like?]

Nancy [Such completely lifted up furniture as with lion's paw
so that underneath of the furniture can be easily
vaccum cleaned, or otherwise such furniture as
completely attaching the floor so no dust can pile up
underneath of it.]

Show Taro [That means you can get the same handy cleaning
with cat's paw furniture.]

Nancy [Cat's paw came after Rococo. In Italy, from
Reneissance after Rococo to Baroque, most were lion's
paw. That's why we have to fight with vaccum cleaner
as all such furniture are bulky as well as easy to keep
dust.]

Show Taro [When dust remains as you fail to completely vacuum
dust, will frustration pile up?]

Nancy [Yes, indeed. It piles up together with dust.]

Both of them looked each other and laughed.

Show Taro [By the way, of Toscan furniture many are with row
wood but those ones of Venice are painted.]

Nancy [Differently from inland area, in Venice, sea wind
blows. Into furnitures made of row wood, sea salt
which becomes into grains will enter in the hollows
among the grains of the wood which makes such
joining parts as nails get rusted and come to get rot.
Such furniture won't last long. You see?]

Show Taro [That's why they painted their furniture like in moss green.]

Nancy [Not really. Fashinable Venetians draw such pictures as bouquet.]

Show Taro [I see. Moss green background is becoming to floral pattern.]

Nancy [At some nobles' mansions they have their furniture in red.]

Show Taro [In other areas in Italy, to paint in red of the side of the furniture that face walls so that side of furniture comes to be unvisible is called red finish which is only permitted to nobles who have the right of succession to the throne, am I right?]

Nancy [Surely, I don't see such style of painting at the mansions owned by row class nobles.]

Talking this far, Show Taro became aware that Nancy may not necessarily be irrerevant to Venice.

Show Taro [No wonder. By the way, why do you say you may have met Indrajit before.]

Nancy [Indrajit is a name of Genie, but it means one that wins over Indra God. But I have a memory that I heard ten or more years ago someone was saying Indrajit means 「one that wins over Indy 500」.]

This story of hers attracted Show Taro's interest quite much.

Show Taro [Where did you hear that?]

Nancy [A long time ago, the boyfriend of my room mate who was working as a campaign girl in Chicago was telling it⋯may be twelve to thirteen years ago, I guess.]

— 128 —

Show Taro [I see. That is why Indrajit came again this time.]

Nancy [This is too good for taken as coincidence, but it is one of the reasons why I was chosen this time.]

Show Taro [jit would mean a winner in India, I see. Then, do you know what it means in the automotive industry?]

Nancy [Well, well, Just in Time, isn't it?]

Show Taro [Correct answer. But grammatically, to be in time is expressed as just on time.]

Nancy [You tried my knowledge of automotive industry.]

Show Taro [As it will become a problem if the firstly set introduction details so easily differ.]

Nancy [As long as any one that lives in mid west, it will not happen that the person has no neighborer who is related to automotive industry, except in such case that the place is a typical local town and all the town residents are leading Armish like lives, those residents can have no knowledge of automotive industry.]

As Show Taro came to hear that much of what she knew, he became to wish to dig out Nancy's level of knowledge of art objects even more.

Show Taro [Taking about the person in charge of Art Insurance, Do you love Italian art as well?]

Nancy [Such divine skill of Michelangelo's curving out from marble stone makes us feel that he took out what was inside the marble stone that was eager to go out from there.]

Show Taro [The name Michelangelo was made from combining Archangel Micael and angel.]

— 129 —

Nancy	[Then what?]

Show Taro [When both are together it comes to be God's army against Satan. That was why Pope wished to almost compulsorily let him work. That is why his Pieta at Vatican was so very percect yet it is not possessed by any evil spirits.]

Nancy [In the eastern world, they say anything that is perfect cannot escape from being possessed by evil spirits.]

Show Taro [In the western world, it is said all wrong deeds are human deeds, so, perfection will be only made either by god or demon?]

Nancy [Is there any wrong deed as regards this time's remittance?]

Show Taro [It is said that one can cheat many people once but cannot continue to cheat them. If cheating is repeated for several times, without fail some open seams come out. However, it is also important to be patient and wait till a definite evidence can be obtained.]

Nancy [Unless our aim is to find out the purpose of obtaining the money, the meaning to work on this remittance will be lost.

If the destination where the remittance is going can be defined, such account can be frozen at any time after remittance is completed. It is far more difficult to draw the money out of the account than just to make remittance to that account.]

Show Taro [If the real purpose of this assignment is to find out what exists behind this flow of money, the first remmitance of 3 million dollars is just a meaninglessly small money so we must keep patient till we grasp the whole scheme of this plot.]

Nancy　　　[You're right⋯]

Seeing Nancy who stifled a yawn Show Taro understood she had not yet adjusted herself to the present situation she was put in.

Show Taro [You must be suffering from jet lag. You had better retire now.]

Having heard from her so far, Show Taro now sees the matching point of interest between him and Nancy. He also felt he then could understand why Robert selected Nancy who had good knowledge of art.

9. Transferring Check and Women's Trouble

Finally, the day came when the delivery of the check of Hell Computer was to be made. Kubera and Shiaku taking Indrajit showed up at the heliport and by the car which Jinlian had arranged, firstly Suzuki, then Show Taro and Akemi also stepped up into the helicopter. They altogether rode onto a large-size helicopter which had been made ready and waiting for those people, then they started to fly directly to Macao. On arrival of the helicopter on the rooftop of casino, Chen Jing Ji came out to receive them. This casino was in a different hotel from previous.

This whole action was done out of the knowledge of Robert and his people, so if they could find and confirm the departure of helicopter, Show Taro hoped they would automatically understand the situation.

Show Taro went to the bathroom and using his cellphone rang Nancy and told her the name of casino just to make sure. When he came back to the meeting room, there had already been ZeDeng Mao. He was dressed in Chinese clothings with sunglasses, which was apparently showing he would not use Japanese that day.

Chen Jing Ji [Thank you for your coming all the way today.]

Jinlian [We wish to compare the real check and the color copy at once.]

Indrajit made eye contact with Kubera, who took the official check out. In silence, he placed the check in front to Chen Jing Ji. Mao who was sitting next to him took the check up with hands

— 132 —

covered by white gloves and peered through it to confirm it as genuine. He then read the confirmation of order.

Mao   [Please prepare the cancelling document ready to be made for all addressees by the time when cashing comes to be completed.]

Indrajit made an eye contact, then Kubera took back the official check in silence.

Indrajit   [Why is your request?]

Mao   [If the address to which remittance cannot be made is on the list at the time of cancelling document is completed, I will contact you.]

Chen   [By the way, till then, who is going to stay at the casino of our company?]

Genta   [Kubera. The other one will be shifted by myself and Suzuki on the each other week basis.]

Chen   [A special room has been ready. Later I will show you there. We will guard the room on a 24- hour basis.]

Genta   [Can we go out?]

Chen   [We will make a guard attend.]

Genta   [I understand.]

Chen   [Let us toast.]

Waiters poured champagne into glasses and all of them toasted. After that, Chen Jing Ji came near to Shiaku and Kubera and whisphered into their ears.

Chen   [Do you like to spend tonight at casino, or if needs be, we can arrange women in which case please tell the front desk the number of the room on the photo.]

— 133 —

The scene of Kubera and Shiaku looked each other and smirked took place.

Kubera [Seriously···I am scared if my wife comes to know it.]

Chen [Don't worry, It is on me for tonight as an expression of esteem to get acquainted with you. To guard your usual life, we will put the expebse on the debit note under the category of expenditure of for the purchase of necessities.]

Genta [Mr. Suzuki, I will take this previllage before you.]

Suzuki [That offer has no connection with me.]

Genta [Mr. Suzuki is pretty weak with his wife.]

Chen [Okay, then, tell me later.]

Kubera [Mr. Chen is awfully thorough in his preparations.]

Genta [Indeed.]

With Jinlian first, those who are not to stay there took helicopter again after about three hours and returned to Hong Kong. On the helicopter, Show Taro could gain the seat where he could talk with Indrajit.

Show Taro [Your way of taking is just like a Canadian, Mr. Indrajjit.]

Indrajit [Call me Indie, Show.]

Show Taro [Okay.]

Indrajit [I spent my collage days in Toronto as an overseas student. During that time, I was a member of the auto club there. I had to try hard to be a member so had little chance to study at the college.]

Indrajit [Show, you got the midwest accent, too. Where were you there?]

— 134 —

Show Taro [Indiana. I went to view Indy500 several times. The Hot rod show in autumm was also good.]

Indrajit [I miss Hot rod show much.]

Show Taro [Several hundred cars were gathering, so in the morning of that day, the time in Indianapolis was winded back for some ten years. I particularly like the elegance of 1931 year Packerd.]

Indrajit [Were you riding on some Hot rod?]

Show Taro [My neighborer, Kevin Smith who was a retired military veteran often rode with me on his Roadster. As I remember it, it was an aqua color Chevrolet Bel Air 4.6L. Though such old cars were not equipped with resin parts, they could be beautifully revived if rust could be removed and then paint-sprayed. Removing the silver-plating layers and electroplate them, they could be well recovered.]

Indrajit [Bel Air, that is a car with a beautiful press line, isn't it.]

Show Taro [That is the car of the age when air conditioner was not yet available, but cars manufactured in the age of 1958 could be said cars of the best age of American car production.]

Indrajit [My friend who was an overseas student coming from India was using an old Cadillac.]

Show Taro [Was that the one with tealphins?]

Indrajit [Yes, it was.]

Show Taro [The broard space was just like a bed.]

Indrajit [That car cannot bear winding roads not like European cars, but with that bounding suspension it can run straight forward so even running on poorly maintained free way you can drink Cola or eat hamberger without problem.]

Show Taro [Indie, you were also taken aboard that car.]

Indrajit [Yes, and I was also allowed to do the maintainance. I used to disassemble the engine and tune it up.]

Show Taro [How?]

Indrajit [Disassembling the cilindar block and removing the casting fin. Piston ring was to be replaced with new one. Casting fin of the cylinderhead to get a smoother gas flow. Then, remove the protruding parts inside the exhaust pipe.]

Show Taro [Didn't you adjust the fuel injection quantity?]

Indrajit [Yes, but just a little. If you wish to get more power, imcomplete combustion can easily take place. In addition, the owner of the car was estimating the fuel expense in consideration of the running distance, so he did not want to race the extravagant power.]

Show Taro [American web of roads surely have quite long distances.]

Indrajit [I understood how broard the road network was in America well when I was driving towards west. I ran to the west for quite a few days and when I was running through the road in the area called Badlands which is a wild land even without any single farm house for as long as 70 miles which I crossed with only two cars in an hour. In that broad land if your car went down, you could not do anything but to pray for God regretting your own fault of leaving the car with poor maintainance.]

Show Taro [But as you are here alive, your car didn't break down?]

Indrajit [As I did full restoration work by myself. Then I ran my car on the long slope up to the end, then all of sudden the Rocky Mountains crowned with snow were jumping into my eyes. The pioneers on covered wagons aiming at the frontier of America may have been greatly impressed as well looking at that view.]

Show Taro [In that era of the pioneers, they couldn't afford to enjoy that speed as you did.]

Indrajit [No, indeed. That overwhelming excitement I tasted could only be gained as I was driving my car like the wind.]

Show Taro [How far did you run at that time?]

Indrajit [I ran to Yellow Stone to the hot spring. Then I continued to run further to the east till Toronto in Canada. By the way, haven't you ever run a long way?]

Show Taro [In Christmas holiday season I ran down to the south every year. Winter in Indiana is long. So that I make an escape from that long winter to Florida or New Orleans. In Indiana, roads are all flat but going into Kentucky, roads there are as straight as in Indiana but change into a big wave with lots of ups and downs. Then roads are coming down to Tennessee. Passing by Tennessee, entering Georgia where the plant species suddenly change to a lot more pine trees. Going down to the south from Chattanooga, roads come to be flat. From there for a long, long while, we run on flat roads and somewhere past Atlanta I am to stay overnight. I can have a sound sleep with fatigue gained from the broad land America. I start to run on the following morning and coming into Florida I stop over at the first information center and am given many kinds of coupon tickets and a cup of orange juice. Taking that glass of orange juice in one gulp I can have a feeling that I have finally escaped from the coldness and I can feel coming back to life in every corner of my body.]

Indrajit [I have been to Orland in Florida several times. What did you do in there?]

Show Taro [Staying at a hotel located in the area from Key Largo to Key West and leisurely enjoyed sea kayaking. As I do not do auto-fidding by myself I won't go to west. I spent the rest of time to visit the fortress created by Spanish people. Incidentally, returning to your story, Indie seems to like mechanical work but you didn't visit Indy500, did you? Haven't you ever heard that loud cheers and the stir at the corner into which the car is crashing?]

Indrajit [I have been to Indy500 for several times for mechanic works. Outrageous experience to hear that sound of the machine, excited cheering and that enjoyable job-

— 138 —

well-done party…talking about the party, I wonder how Emily will be now.]

Show Taro [Your ex?]

Indrajit [Yah, Unless that accident happened, the racing team could obtain green card following the racer.]

Show Taro [So the driver was killed?]

Indrajit [That was a terrible accident. My dreams were all gone and I retuned to India.]

Show Taro [What about Emily?]

Indrajit [Emily Brown. She continued to write to me for about half a year after that.]

Show Taro [Memory of the spring time of the life…]

Indrajit [On your hand, Show, Is there any one in Indiana?]

Show Taro [I used to meet on business a woman Nancy who came back having been assigned to our group in relation to art insurance part of the job.]

Indrajit [So did you reopen the relationship with her?]

Indrajit loudly raised his voice in spite of himself, but as he felt cold gazing of Jinlian and Akemi, he became silent.

That these two women and Show Taro were in a strangled relationship was already grasped by Indrajit while on the way here.

Show Taro [Indy, by the way where that lacing team belongs to?]

Indrajit [Well, That was Hell Computer.]

Show Taro [And since then have you been working on the Hell related works?]

Indrajjit [As CFO of Hell and I became friends, I can use their account.]

Show Taro [Well done.]

Indrajit   [Yah, I guess.]

Show Taro [Are you getting lots of work from Hell?]

Indrajit   [Well, so-so many.]

To Show Taro, it sounded like the account was of Hell Computer but the money floating was of a different character. However, as Indrajit suddenly became silent, Show Taro felt he might have made such question too hastely.

On that night, hosted by Jinlian, a Chinese dinner party was held. That Jinlian and Akemi sitting both sides of Show Taro and getting themselves to contain each other was sensed by Suzuki and Indrajit. As they were staying at different hotels, they parted with Suzuki and Indrajit at the party place.

Coming back to the hotel room, Show Taro took his cell phone and contacted Nancy.

Show Taro [Nancy? This is Tom. I got the name of Phoenix' woman at his time in America.]

Nancy   [Who is she, Tom?]

Show Taro [Emily Brown.]

After silence for a few seconds, her voice raised suddenly.

Nancy   [Is it true!]

Show Taro [No mistake. He did say so.]

Nancy   [She was my room mate.]

Show Taro [Then, I may have said an unnecessary thing.]

Nancy   [What did you say?]

Show Taro [I said Nancy with whom I was communicating in line with damage insurance works in Indiana became in charge of this case and so I incidentally met her again.]

Nancy   [So I must pretend to behave as your ex-woman. Okay. But the Indian group is supposed to leave here by the first flight tomorrow morning , isn't it right?]

Show Taro [Correct.]

And there came knocking at the door laudly.

Show Taro [Some one came, so let me cut the line.]

Getting sick from overdrinking, Jinlian and Akemi were flowing into the room.

Akemi   [I did hear on the return helicopter. What kind of woman is Nancy! Sit and explain fully.]

Jinlian   [Akemi, can you hear me! Show is not yours.]

Akemi   [I am the first!]

Jinlian   [If you say that, Nancy is the first! Look, Listen carefully! The most charming one is to get him is a natural matter of course.]

Those two drunken tigers slipped into Show Taro's bed getting rid of the clothes and fell asleep.

Well, really was what he felt. He then had a room boy bring a towel-like blanket and slept on the sofa. He thought what Maria was saying as women's trouble then involved him, but that was just the beginning of the women's trouble that he had to face.

At 7 o'clock on the following morning, there was a knock at the door. Answering the knock Jinlian who was half asleep and all but nude opened the door.

Nancy   [Oh, S-sorry.]

She apologized reflectively, but looking at the room number again, she confirmed that was the room of Show Taro. As she recognized that a substance that was curling up on the sofa was

— 141 —

Show Taro, she decided to playact according to what she gathered from Show Taro the day before, namely to behave as his ex-girlfriend.

Nancy   [Hey, Tom, Darling, Getup.]

Talking in a sweet voice Nany suddenly showered her kisses on Show Taro. Show Taro opened one of his eyes and saw Nancy and all but nude Jinlian. Before Show Taro could say anything, Akemi grasping the edge of the pillow was striking Nancy.

Akemi   [Screw it! You came to take him back, as far as to Hong Kong!]

Nancy   [Who are you?]

As Nancy had heard of detailed information of these two women from Robert, she was acting trying to look composed as much as she could.

Jinlian   [It's clear as you can· see it? Two women and one man.]

Nancy   [I just see two naked women and that's all.]

Then, by that time Show Taro's blood pressure finally starts to work and to come up, he opened his mouth.

Show Taro [Nancy, Let's go to the launge downstairs.]

Leaving the two women behind, they came out of the room. The nearly naked two women did not follow them.

Nancy   [What the hell is that scene?]

Show Taro [Well, that may be my star. Then, what for are you here?]

Nancy   [What I heard from you yesterday was only about the woman of Phoenix.]

Show Taro [When he was in the racing team, he said he made

— 142 —

friends with Hell's CFO and since then he has been borrowing the Hell account and practicing his remittance business, though the monies he handled at that account have no relation to Hell Computer…]

Nancy [Then, anything else?]

Show Taro [As a result that those two restrained each other, Phoenix came to keep silence. Their next meeting will be when the check is cashed and remitted.]

They saw the two women wearing jackets were coming down in the lobby from the elevator. Nancy felt danger but not forgetting to make her play to the bitter end, she did not forget to kiss Show Taro, but after she kissed him, she dashed out of the hotel. It goes without saying that Show Taro was beaten up by the two women.

10. The First Remmitance

Time flew and when the cashing of the check became able to be done any time, all the members concerned again gathered at a hotel in Macao on the day before the cashing day. From the side of Indian connection all of Indrajit, Kubera, Shiaku and Suzuki were present and at the China connecton side Jinlian Pan, ZeDeng Mao and Chen Jing Ji were ready. From the Japan side, Akemi was present taking Maria, which seemed to look like her preventive measures. Looking over those faces, Show Taro was convinced that the deal of remittance this time was not fraud to say the least of it. That night a dinner party with all these ten people was planned to be held.

Show Taro asked Akemi to prepare a seat next to Indrajit for him. Next to the seat of Show Taro, Jinlian and Akemi was letting Maria sit. Show Taro wondered if the two women were planning to have Maria look at through fluoroscopy something of their interst. Indrajit, who seemed not to care about such scene, talked to Show Taro.

Indrajit　　[Show, When will you let me see Nancy?]

Show Taro　[Indy, I will take her next time for sure. She is working on a commission system, but is also busy with the work as a building owner so when she gets tied up with negotiation with tenants she cannot really move.]

Indrajit　　[I am wondering if I may have heard the name Nancy or may not.]

Shaw Taro　[What do you mean by that?]

— 144 —

Indrajit	[I myself am not sure, but if I see her, I may remember her.]
Show Taro	[I see. By the way, are you, Indy, a married man?]
Indrajit	[No. Except Emiry, women are all the same to me. My father is very noisy telling me to choose one from Brahmins.]
Show Taro	[Suppose you can find Emiry what will you do?]
Indrajit	[I wish to have even a glance.]
Show Taro	[If she is single, what will you do?]
Indrajit	[Do you know anything about whereabouts her?]
Show Taro	[It's just a supposition.]
Indrajit	[I'm not interested in 'if' or 'suppose' talk.]
Chen	[This time, what about Mr. Indrajit stay in China on a week based shifting. Mr. Kubera fully enjoyed his stay.]
Indrajit	[Yah, I understand you treated Kubera every night. It was a very special treatment, wasn't it.]
Jinlian	[He may no longer be wishing to return to his wife.]
Kubera	[I do with to see my children's faces.]
Genta	[As Kubera has five children.]
Suzuki	[I envy Mr. Genta as he has not to worry about his wife.]
Chen	[Chinese Government welcome money being dropped in China.]
Mao	[To which country are you planning to make remmitance tomorrow?]
Indrait	[Dubai will be the country.]
Mao	[No worries about remmitance.]

— 145 —

Indrajit   [That is good. If it goes wrong, I shall come to infuriate Raja Mitra.]

Chen   [With this as a start if we can establish such business as to enable continuous remmitance to happen, Mr. Mitra will appreciate it. Please spread such news of success among your group. By so doing all concerned shall be able to be profited.]

Indrajit   [But for that much, production in China, or North Korea or Russia will have to be made possible.]

Chen   [So, are you saying export from China will become necessary?]

Indrajit   [Well, I will talk about this subject sometime later.]

The night of that day passed with such chat going on.

The next day came. Chen Jing Ji and Kubera went into a certain bank and confirmed that the remittance had been put into the account. Confirming this, they shifted the money to their accounts at the bank located next to that bank. When these procedures are completed, Mao and Indrajit came out of the car.

And Mao and Indrajit completed remittance procedures to send 2.55 million dollars to the nominated account in a bank in Dubai according to the prescription on the cancellation instruction document and handed a copy of the remittance to Indrajit. Chen Jing Ji handed a check to Jinlian as well and she declared that she would go to Japan together with Show Taro and Akemi and would pass them a check issued by a Japanese bank. Akemi told her ordering cost was always remitted to Jinlian's bank account which she held in Japan.

Akemi hated Jinlian's plot for her to meet Show Taro in Japan, but she regreted she couldn't mention it at that place.

After that day till the news that the remittance arrived safely in Dubai came into the cell phone of Indrajit, days waiting for the news were spent with continuous sumptuous feasts. All that time, Akemi used Maria to watch out if Nancy might appear and she felt relieved at Maria's assurance that no shade of Nancy was seen. Talking about Jinlian, not caring about Nancy at all, while she was having an affair with Chen Jing Ji, she bluntly kept casting amorous glances to Show Taro. Jinlian was a woman filled with such power which was so plentiful that it made people concerned wonder where that power came from.

In such circumstances, Show Taro was contacting Nancy and gathering the information about whereabout Emily Brown. Of course, Nancy had already grasped the information as to whereaoutts Emily and was waiting the best timing to use Emily as a trump card.

So far, all what Nancy told Show Taro was Emily having waited for contact from Indrajit for one full year after Indrajit went back to India after that accident but that she wrote back to Indrajit only in the first half of the one year.

Show Taro [According to what Indrajit told me, Emily wrote him only for half a year after they parted.]

Nancy [Does it mean his parents forced him to marry some one?]

Show Taro [That would well be the case. Ever since then, he kept to be single up to now.]

Nancy [Shall I contact Emily?]

Show Taro [Emily could be a tramp to have Indrajit secede from

Raja Mitra. I guess this is worth doing···Let's set up this honey trap.]

He hung the cell phone up and turned around where Maria was standing.

Show Taro [····..]

Maria [So Ms. Nancy is in fact not your woman. Still, you must have been secretly enjoying the mysterious turn of the fortune's wheel.　Who gave you such idea?]

Show Taro [It was a-horse-comes-from-a-gourd like happening. I just told at random such a story as my past with Nancy···he came to be in. Please keep this just between us.]

Maria [I think you better not get too much involved with Nancy though of course it is not my business.]

Show Taro [What do you see on Nancy?]

Maria [From her previous life till a little further into her future.]

Show Taro [I am adamant to say that she must have been in Vennice in past.]

Maria [I think so, too.]

Show Taro [She is intelligent and also does not give me much stress being together.]

Maria [I guess so, too.]

Show Taro [Mind you, don't tell this to Akemi.]

Maria [Of course not.]

Show Taro [I do hope this case will go well.]

Maria [You can rest assured that the remittance will be done smoothly.]

Show Taro [What about my 'seeming' of ill fortune with women?]

Maria [Unfortunately, I am under employment of Ms. Akemi, so cannot answer this question of yours.]

Show Taro [I am thinking if this present case can be finished safely, I might change my occupation…]

Maria [Probably that will not be necessary, as you have not entered that stage.]

Show Taro [Whatever it goes, please don't tell anything to Akemi.]

Maria [I fully understand.]

Thus, Show Taro put a muzzle on Maria, however, how she would move was unpredictable. Leaving those words in a meaningful manner, she turned her heels and went out.

After this, Show Taro did not overlook Indrajit who was getting some air exhausted with casino gambling.

Show Taro [Indy, Did you win?]

Indrajit [I lost 3,000 dollars tonight so I decided to give up for today.]

Show Taro [Wise decision. By the way, I rang Nancy who said she might be able to contact Emily. What will you do?]

Indrajit [Is that really true?...Stop joking. She stopped writing me only after six months. No way to expect she still remembers me.]

Show Taro [I have an idea, so, what about leaving it to me?]

Indrajit [Okay, but I can't afford to expect even half of such possibility.]

Show Taro [We will meet again possibly at the next chance of this remmitance work. At that time, I will introduce Nancy Franchetti to you.]

Indrajit   [Nancy WHO!]

Show Taro [Franchetti!]

Indrajit   [Now, I remembered! Your woman and Mine were room mates!]

Show Taro [Don't tell this to other people. She wrote you once per month for at least one year. It sounds like you did not write her only for the first six months.]

Indrajit   [Does it mean that her letters were quashed by my father?]

Show Taro [As this, too, is your fate so don't hate your father.]

Indrajit   [I know, I know.]

As Show Taro observed that Kubera was walking toward them, padding the shoulder of Indrajit lightly, he left him there.

On the following day, they received from Dubai a report confirming the money was successfully cashed. Hearing this news, they parted to return to each country. On that day of departure, Show Taro heard from Indrajit that the next remittance would be 7 million dollars.

11. Deposit of Down Payment

Information that 2.25million dollars as down payment were deposited was enigmatized and sent to Alois Brunner. The same information was also forwarded in just about real time to Heinrich Hizinger.

After receiving this deposit, arrangements for manufacturing was progressed. To place orders, request of catalogue submission to respective ordnance manufacturing companies or ordnance dealing companies was started to be sent. Those people were to gather material information to determine whether they can satisfy the demand of orderers and to make comparison and make careful review of all such relevant information gathered.

Among ordnance trading companies, there are some that have manufacturing process, but in some cases, there are such that are concentrating on selling through illegal channels those deteriorated and disposed ordnance. As a quick and dirty means, such that some dealers put on black market ordnance that was taken out directly from the army ammunition depo in exchange of narcotic drugs has been normalized.

Even troops of countries which are called powerful nations are not exceptions. Those ordnance that ran out due to the drill, even if number juggling was being exercised, such armories owned by the nation's armed forces in the area where SS was transfused were left untouched. Countries near to SS armories also existed. In the object projects, in addition to submarines or neuclear warheads, even chemical weapons were included.

Even though such cases were going on, the applicable military organization tried to hide the disorder of the military rules so that the real situation was hard to be revealed. Military organization under the no-war situation was nothing but a beurocratic organization embracing a bomb called corruption. In a war, continuous metabolism is going on, if war fighting power comes under the military power as listed on the book, such wrong deed can be easily found out. As long as defeat means death, number juggling comes to be seriously examined and done. When no war is going on, though the number of weapons may decrease due to military exercises, suppose 10% has been gone, it is quite natural that this fact is not being picked up. At the check done at the end of the fiscal year, there surely arises a shortage due to expendable articles and no longer exists in the ammunition depo, so all's fit.

If staff officers or commanders say okay, it means okay of all subordinates. This is what armed forces are.

Josef Brunner flew to the castle in India under the suggestion from Heinrich. Outside of this castle was made of slightly reddish sandstone so that the castle was blending into the surrounding hilly terrain, however, the inside of the castle was constructed gathering the best Isram construction technologies like Alhambra Palace in Spain and all gold color parts of the inside of the castle was made from genuine pure gold films pasted on white marble stone.

At the ceiling of nearly 4 meters high, a ceiling fan was spinning round and round. At the outside of the door leading to the study two Indian guards were attending and watching survants who were passing the collider. Making it inconspicuous at both sides of inside the door two SS members wearing black uniforms were guarding. In that southern country, as black color clothings were noticiable in the daytime, they were trying not to be noticed and wondered about what they were. On the sofa besides the window from where the courtyard was overlooked, several men were chatting drinking chai tea.

Josef   [I guess preparation of transport of Gorgon is progressing.]

With a parrot on his shoulder, Raja Mitra started to talk while giving the parrot seeds of sunflower.

Raja Mitra [Remittance just made is the first remittance, so all depends on the result of the other two remittances.]

Josef   [The first remittance can produce at lease one dozen, can't it.]

Raja Mitra [Yes. By the way, where do you want us to deliver them?]

Josef   [At Abalon we plan to transship between two cargo vessels but two lots shall be landed and stored there.]

Raja Mitra [Shall we inform the leaders of Indian Government.]

Josef   [Please start the ground work after the second remittance is completed.]

Raja Mitra [But why is that sea area called Abalon?]

Josef   [Haven't you heard the reason from your father?]

Raja Mitra [I think I heard from Mr. Heinrich but am not sure. I'm sorry I was intoxicated then.]

Josef   [During WW2, Japanese Imperial Navy got the sea control around there and afterwards their aircraft carrier task force attacked Colombo and Madagascar.

At that time, a destroyer which was attending the task force came to drift away due to engine troubles. While waiting for rescue, the crew dived into the sea and found a crowd of abalones. Since then the codename of that sea area became Abalon. And the Japanese avy provided U-boat which was used to connect Europe and Japan with that sea area.

As it was said that the original inhabitants of Andaman Sea would never communicate with the indigenous black persons, those with exceptional talent were selected and about one hundred families of such soldiers were made settled down at a fortress. This is the origin of Abalon. Japanese Navy insisted that the sea area was originally theirs so they used Navalon as their code name. N of Navalon seems to be N of Nippon. However, JN21 as a code had already been broken so that in the Allied Forces the name of Navalon diffused. When it was cinematized, as the place was unknown, they made the place as Mediterranean Sea for the convenience sake.]

Raja Mitra [Then, why B came to be V as Navalon?]

Josef [Most of Japanese do not distinguish the pronounciation difference of B and V or R and L. According to Mr. Kato of Midori Manji, as the ancient Latin pronounced AVE of the current age as A-We, there seems to exist such an explanation as that the language in Europe underwent changes, but I don't agree to this explanation.]

Raja Mitra [I see. That's why when the movie was firstly released
          …]

Josef [Alois, too, was worried if the secret was leaked so he
       visited the road show. I heard he was relieved to learn
       that the place was Mediterranean Sea.]

Raja Mitra [Still now, the original inhabitants are not aware there
          are SS African Troops there.]

Josef [As they scarcely wear clothes during the day time.]

Raja Mitra [As that place is in the tropics, suppose they were
          wearing military uniforms the original inhabitants
          would have easily found them. In the Indian troops
          there are two lineages of that of remnants of SS Indian
          Troops and of remnants of Indian National Army. Of
          those who own castles were educated in Europe and
          became SS. Sons of Indian people joined Indian
          National Army. Both Kubera and Indrajit are such
          remnants. That is the reason why Indian Army would
          not touch the three nautical miles of the sea near
          Abalon.]

Josef [I agree. By the way, from where will the principal
       body of Gorgon be coming?]

Raja Mitra [I will let it be confirmed.]

At Raja Mitra's beckoning, the butler held out a silver tray on
which a cell phone was placed. He took it up with an air of
consequence and rang with just one touch.

Raja Mitra [Hello, This is Mitra. Indy, with whom are you making
          arrangements to get the principal body of Gorgon?]

Different from when he was in his palace, it seemed that he did not need to care about the social status on telephone talks, so Mitra was talking in a quite frank way.

Indrajit [I decided to take the offer from a Chinese called Wang Chao as his quotation was the cheapest.]

Raja Mitra [Approximately from when can it be delivered? The customer is impatient.]

Indrajit [Three months after the remmitance of down payment is completed.]

Raja Mitra [Can it be a bit earlier?]

Indrajit [It might be possible if we could let them sell to us the portion stored in the army warehouse⋯but this will be an expensive exercise.]

Raja Mitra [Okay, understood. Good effort.]

When Raja Mitra hung up the telephone, the butler who was attending to him held forth a silver tray so he put the telephone on it.

Raja Mitra [As you have just heard, extra charge will be incurred anyway on either illegally getting from the army's armory or taking off the production line.]

Josef [Sounds like a good business to them.]

Raja Mitra [Level of completion of warhead cannot compete with Russian products but as regards propulse section of the gun, products from China or North Korea can be good enough. Is the end user this time an Afghan?]

Josef [You promised not to be curious about the enduser.]

To Josef whose tone of voice was a bit raised, Raja respectfully gave a light bowing.

Raja Mitra [Forgive me for being rude.]

— 156 —

Another business of SS was arms dealing. While doing this business, they used to save some quantity for themselves to make a reservation stock. Needless to say, their main end users were extremists in the regional conflicts but in some cases the governmental army of independent countries could be their object of selling their secondhand weapons. In such case it often happened that when many governmental army soldiers were captured, the prisoners' small arms flew out to the secondhand market and made a back flow.

Josef [Remittance this time will be 7 million dollars so hurry up to make arrangements.]

Raja Mitra [The remittance system this time is so far moving well.]

Josef, too, needed to learn what size this business would become for maneuvering Indian political circles.

Raja Mitra [And what size of remittance will be after this time?]

Josef [Fax me the amount of surcharge in case we choose to expedite this deal.]

Raja Mitra [Do you mean that the remittance amount will change depending on the size of the surcharge?]

Josef [Who will decide the amount is the end user and not us.]

Raja Mitra [You are quite right.]

Josef [Incidentally, Chen of China Connection seems to run casino and export of women as his business. My question is if he might be involved in drug business or not.]

Raja Mitra [What you mean is?]

Josef [The selling route of drug is overwrapping that of Mafia's, therefore, however well the ongoing business goes, we will make the third remittance the last one. Reason why we could develop our power this much is because we do not touch drug business. In Europe alone, we have some countries which political power is about to be grasped in our hands.]

Raja Mitra [SS will not assume political power, won't it.]

Josef [We have an agreement with NSAP about the range of each other's handling zone.]

Raja Mitra [What reason was it for at the beginning?]

Josef [Originally, as it is called the third empire, the first is Holy Roman Empire, then German Empire and the next comes NSDAP in which what was established as successor of Teutonic Order is SS (Nazi SS troops). Therefore, what is admitted by Teutonic Order is automatically admitted by SS. Knights' Territory or castles used as defence facility and the greatest right that was admitted by Holly Roman Emperor is the right to conquer Russia.]

Raja Mitra [Therefore the occupation of Ukraine was an absolute must, I see.]

Josef [Blackening Russia was also a top priority. During the time of WW2, Starlin was extending his influence inside the Moscow Administration as they were targeting at reddening the whole world. However, we

— 158 —

SS are thinking the best plan is to help only our sympathizers amongst those who aim at seizure of regime without biding their time for seizure of regime.]

Raja Mitra [Is that because there will be no obligation to support the people there unless the administration is forming the shape of a country?]

Josef [When to extend the country border came to be impossible as happened with global industries was in the latter part of the 20th century. In the contemporary age, neuclear weapons are aiming toward each other of great power nations. Without shifting the border line of countries, economical rights and interests can be enjoyed. This fact is obvious if you observe economical prosperity of Japan or Germany after WW2. On the contrary, in Soviet or China where men of power were showing off their military might, a handful of just a few may be wealthy but the people in general were left in poor lives. Therefore, clever Russians joined the civil liberties. There may have been some confusion at first, but as a result the country prospered. With our blackening policies we are making a success as well. You must be aware at the end of 2009, several thousands of Black Shirts greeted with Roman salute in Moscow.]

Raja Mitra [Yes, as you say, it was reported here on mass media in a small space.]

Josef [This kind of actitivies of ours is now difficult to be

	hidden from the public due to regulation of freedom of speech by anti-Nazi movement.]
Raja Mitra	[The actual number of Black Shirts must have been more than what was reported.]
Josef	[If those who could not partiticate in that meeting for some special reasons are included, the number of Black Shirts was at least five times of that several thousands.]
Raja Mitra	[I am amazed to learn even with such large number of participants, NS are able to escape from being arrested.]
Josef	[The political party with the black image color which is composed by the ethnic radicals is behaving itself carefully. That is the reason why the party will not handle drugs which will cause a head-on confrontation with the police authority.]
Raja Mitra	[So SS is doing well with the police authority.]
Josef	[You can see it if you see how Italy is doing. Drug business is a monoporized business to Mafias. Therefore, the counter power came to take the political power. At the side of that political power the old fascists exist. Mussorini did have a bad fascet but had a good fascet as well. Even such nation that has that much self-assurtion, at the point of the anti-mafia we can coordinate them to some good extent. That is the reason why we keep distance from those drug related groups.]
Raja Mitra	[I will let my men to do investigation on this matter

asap.]

Talking this way Raja Mitra sent a signal by raising his hand, his attendant came by and poured more chai tea into their cups and bowed once and retired.

Raja Mitra [By the way, I reckon those SS members are all vegetalians. Is vegetarian dinner acceptable for tonight?]

Josef [To SS members since from the age of Heinrich Himmler, guidance for members to keep the habit of no smoking and no alcopholic drinks and taking the least amount of meat dishes. Whether to keep this regulation or not is up to the individual, but of those regulations, no smoking has gained American citizenship.]

Raja Mitra [Nevertheless, not all Americans are supporting SS and this is regretful.]

Josef [The temperance system was abolished by the interference of Mafias.]

Raja Mitra [That the government abolished the law of Prohibition was in reflection of the fact that the reason why Alfonso Capone had gained a power was because of his smuggling business of alchohol. That governmental decision was like putting the cart before the horse. Suppose they had continued Prohibition, America might have been able to display leadership over Isram countries.]

Josef [The provision with which SS recommend no smoking, no alchoholic drinks, more vegetarian food and fish eating must match the long life conditions in the Asian monsoon region. In actual fact, the area where people are enjoying long average life span is where fish cooking is popular like in Italy or Scandinavia. But as an exception, Christians take a small amount of wine as the blood of Jesus Christ so this practice cannot be prohibited.]

Raja Mitra [They can change wine to reddish color tea, can't they?]

Josef [Vatican will not accept that idea.]

To the requests of SS which are in the swelling tendency, Raja Mitra was obediently obaying. SS itself is a mishmash of various ethnic radical groups. At that moment, the voice of Hienrich Hizinger or Romano Sforza was still influential so that Russians and Indians including himself decided to be patient and wait for the old generation getting less powerful. The highest point of time of Indian power will come only in a long time ahead. But in preparation for when that time comes, such organization that does not possess its people or its land could fully manage the world, to lay the foundations for such time was Raja Mitra's concern.

The origin of the name Raja Mitra came from the meaning of Raja which means 'king'. Maha of Maharaja has a meaning of 'great'. Originaly 'Raja' is meant for a raja as a fudal load to govern respective areas since the age when India was called Mughal and was meant for the highest rank of secularism though such rajas were expected to show respect to brahmins of the religious circles. And 'mitra' is meant for a god for the sun and light which faith is originated in ancient Persia. 'Mitra' was pronounced either as mitra

— 162 —

or mithra and in the west in ancient Rome this god was professed by men. It was defined that women were not allowed to profess this god.

The secred beast was a bull. They offered blood of bull as a sacrifice to god sitting on the weapons that Romans took by force from their enemy and part of this religious habit was used at Ara Pacis (alter of peace) in ancient Rome. Romans prayed peace to the goddness Rome curved in relief, and dedicated blood of bull. This was the national ritual that was carried out on January 30 of Julian Calender day every year starting 8AD till West Rome was ruined. Mitra was an undefeated war god. When the battle at the coloseum came to be abolished by Emperor Nero for cruetity as the reason, not only those gladiators became malcontent but to have antagonized citizens who admired God Mitra must have been the cause of downfall of Nero, though this idea is a pure supposition as research of Mitra piety has not reached that level of Christianism at the moment.

That Raja Mitra started to use this name was not irrelevant to the history of ancient Mitra piety expanded via Persia to Rome. Mitra predicted the Indian economy would surpass that of China in the second quarter (2025 ~ 2050) of the 21st century. China may lead the world as the worldly manufacturing factory but it does not have that much capability as India as regards mathematics.

In consideration of this circumstance, it can be said that the Indian computer technology is in a much advantageous situation than that of China. Should China wrongly stir up their ethnic nationalism, English may be boycotted and such situation may accordingly badly affect the quality of Chinese computer programmers. When that time comes Raja Mitra will come to be recognized and will gain the honor rightful as Raja Mitra. He has that prospect of future in his mind but on the other hand he understood that some more time would be needed till that time as India could become to play the main role in the world will come.

12. First Portion of Share

Ginza in Tokyo was a town where in the Edo era guild of craftworkers manufacturing silver coins was stationed. This is the reason why that area came to be called as Ginza (Silver craft station). This name Ginza therefore has specific charm to attract business handling various branded goods. For instance, the base of jewelry manufacture is gold and silver work but in the meaning of silver work, the name which is associated with silversmith is just exactly Ginza.

As among famous French brands, there exist such brands that started from processing silver, there in Japan as well, several brands that started from precious metal processing exist. As the Ginza area has that kind of classy image, the world welknown brand businesses are developing their retail stores with Namiki street as the main place.

Namiki Street in Ginza is a street with trees lining the street and has footpath on both sides of a narrow roadway. The width of the roadway is just about equal to the first rank military army road in ancient Roma. The traffic on the roadway of this confortably narrow width is suited to people leisurely walking on the footpath safely and peacefully enjoying window shoppings which environment was displaying classy atmosphere around there.

Near that classy Namiki Street, Akemi managed to own her head office building. To possess in Ginza the whole building is a proof of a successful business. On the basement floor, a parking space where several cars can be parked of her car and of the executives'. It is

— 165 —

convenient for Akemi to have this underground parking space as it saves her trouble to park her car in a crowded public car park. On the whole, her success started when her merchandise became to be well evaluated in western countries, but as same as most people who made a big success in their business Akemi had to spend strugging years before she became 30 years old.

Change to the success came when Akemi who was an illegitimate child could meet her father Kato in person much oftener after Kato's legal wife passed away. Those days Midori Manji was planning to build a plant in Europe. Therefore, Kato went there frequently for that purpose. This incidentally gave a chance to Akemi to develop her business. She accompanied him to Europe as his interpreter and got acquainted with a sister of Romano's wife who was a well-known actress in the cinema world. She started to use accessories Akemi was handling in one scene of a film in which she acted, which became a start of a success story of Akemi's merchandise on the accessory retailing market.

Day after day, small goods to which orders were onslaughtingly coming in, and also the merchandise line of that series of the small goods powerfully dragged her business forward. Later, such fortunre as some popular actresses chose and use the goods at Akemi's bourtiques in several movies, there came in Akemi's brand business a chance to develop the line to apparels and to jewelries which means she got a chance to deal with a much wider range of merchandise.

To Akemi in such situation, it was an important thing that she makes the whole builing of her office as an advertising sign to spread out the special image of her business.

— 166 —

The street crossing Namiki Street was not exactly keeping the same image as when it had been built, but could still fully choleograph a prime image. The building was made of heavy steel but around the showwindow on the first floor pure white marble stone was featured. At the entrance, a slim doorman whom Akemi hired in Italy was dressed in black and was standing. Inside the entrance at the side of the office area had a well polished marble stone wall and soft carpet was placed wall to wall.

Color of the carpet was what is called as Rikyu Nezumi, which had the color tone of slightly greeny grey but if one sees it carefully a pattern of Edo Komon was noticed to be woven in. Though the pattern was not so obviously noticiable from the distance as apparels made in America, designing which did not give a feeling of pressure even in narrow Japanese rooms and that pleased the visitors' eyes. In this performance Akemi's eagerness in her studies was shown and that was the reason why her merchandise was branded as Kyubi, the Perfect Beauty.

That day was the day when the members who broke up in Hong Kong were to gather again at Kyubi. Show Taro visited there as well wearing a jacket which was unusual for Show Taro. He opened the door leading to the office by himself and took an elevator. The interior decoration of the elevator looked like as if natural opals were pasted. Show Taro wondered if Akemi again changed the interior so he poked the wall and thought the wall was pasted by printed sheet. He took another look from a different angle and found that the sheet had an effect of play of color changing colors seven times just like genuine opal. Show Taro was quite impressed thinking the interior decoration material at the temporary age made a great progress.

The appearance of the wall looked like nothing but thinly sliced genuine jewel stone in about 10cm square and pasted and in addition at the height of the eyes the part of the wall looked exactly like black opal with comparably much red fire. Suppose this decoration were made of sliced boulder opal, the cost would have been formidable and what's more was such decoration would be far too heavy for an elevator to bear mechanically.

The finding and using exercise of new materials became dominantly notable after art deco, which took place since after 1930's. However, Akemi was also quite courageous to use those new materials that could be industrialized. Show Taro thought that enterprising attitude would be a necessary talent in order to acquire a position to seize a corner of image leader in the fashion industry.

The push buttons equipped at the elevator were also such as similar to mother of pearl appearance. These buttons also had translucency to show at which level the elevator was stopping. In the era of art noubeau of the 1890s and also in 1920s, use of mother of pearls was applied on atomizers or righters, but this use has since been ceased due the synergistic effect of uprising processing cost and also getting difficult to obtain natural materials.

However, the materials that Show Taro was viewing right in front of him could be taken as artificial materials considering the point of optical transmission. In addition, on the floor of the elevator, there was a pattern which at a glance might look like Incarose. This, too, was renovated to meet her choice. As there was no co-

— 168 —

rider on the elevator, he crouched down and touched the floor. He found it a printed sheet and not stone material. That Akemi was the type of person who always made challenges to things new was shown clearly on all these decorations.

Elevator stopped at the top floor where executive offices were located. The door opened and there a floor of a pattern which was similar to Roman mosaic was spreading. She might have got this idea from ruins of ancient Rome.

Trade ports in the Roman era used to have black and white mosaic floor like the flooring of Osteria, the ancient ruins, that was being unearthed at the mouth of River Tevera that flew through the middle of Rome. There spread sailing ships in the sea and the figures of mysterious fish on the floor which looked like the mosaic pattern used on the doorway of the bath. Walls there were covered by the same white marble panels which were the same as when he visited here in past so he somewhat felt at ease. The artdeco style pendant light equipped on the ceiling of the lobby was producing a well-fitting relaxed atmosphere. Show Taro rang the secretariet at the front counter, and the electronic lock at the entrance door started to make a sound to open, so he entered there. Inside the room her secretary was waiting and showed him to the adjoining room. After a while Jinlian and Akemi showed up and respectively took their seats.

Jinlian   [Thanks for your time the other day.]

Akemi   [Then, please make allotment using this morning's exchange rate.]

Jinlian   [May I use the telegraphic transfer middle rate of this morning?]

Suzuki	[Yes, you may.]
Show Taro	[No objection.]
Akemi	[Alright. Please adjust accounts of the dividend.]
Jinlian	[For Akemi, 45,000 dollars come to \5,265,000 and for Show, 90,000 dollars equals to \1,053,000. I will issue bank checks for those amounts of Yotsuba Bank, Ginza Branch.]

She handed one each check which she calculated using telegraphic transter middle rate in an efficient manner over to Akemi and Show Taro.

Jinlian	[This is Akemi's and this is Show's.]

As the first check that Suzuki had brought over was a false check, Show Taro had changed the share of Suzuki to 0.5% of the face value. In silence Show Taro used his calculator putting the figure of 1,755,000 to show Suzuki that 0.5% of 3 million dollars came to be that figure in yen and secretly showed that figure to Suzuki who was sitting next to him. Suzuki nodded in silence and took memo of that figure. Finishing the work, Jinlian and Akemi invited Show Taro for dinner.

Jinlian	[Look, Show, to commemorate this reunion, let's go out for dinner? My friend recently opened a sushi bar in Ginza though it is a reverse landing of sushi from China to Japan.]
Akemi	[My friend studied cooking in Italy for ten years and opened a restaurant at the end of last month. A nice place to view the night scene of Tokyo.]
Jinlian	[Wait, Akemi..Show is my business partner···especially today.]

— 170 —

Akemi   [Tokyo is my place, isn't it?]

Suzuki   [Please excuse me now, as I have another business appointment.]

Suzuki felt out of place to be there. As he had no reason to stay over there other than learning how much amout of money was going to be remitted to him, he stood up. Just at that time Show Taro's cell phone started playing ringtone melody. He checked the cell phone and noted that Nancy was calling.

Show Taro [Hello, Nancy, I am now going to pick you up. Okay.]

He felt maricous glare of the two women, but adamantly stood up in such a way to drive them away.

Show Taro [I, too, have another appointment, so excuse me now.]

With his words, the meeting ended.

Show Taro took the given check to the Ginza branch of the bank correspondent and cashed the check and finished remittance procedures of the portion of the check of Suzuki to him.

Finishing both tasks, he came out to the street and stop a taxicab and went to Hotel All Seasons where Nancy was waiting.

Jinlian was tracing him. She rang Akemi by her cell phone and joined Akemi riding on her car and started to chase Show Taro together. When Show Taro came into the lobby of the hotel where Nancy was waiting for him. Nancy did not overlook Jinlian coming off Akemi's red color car. That was the difference between an investigator and an amateur.

Nancy hugged Show Taro with dramatic gestures and kissed him. Show Taro was quite surprised but stopping kissing she whispered into his ear.

— 171 —

Nancy   [You are followed by Bell Lotus.]

Having said that, she kissed him over again. He could feel her breath on his cheek and also felt the amorous touch of her tongue and he also was piggybacking on her such coquettish behaviors unconsciously. As he has such impression on her that she and he were together in the long past, he kept ignoring Jinlian there. Following the hugging and the kissing Nancy took Show Taro's arm and the two rode on the elevator. Jinlian firmly confirmed at which level Nancy and Show Taro got the elevator off.

Coming back to her room with Show Taro, she rang room service and ordered dinner to be brought there, then started talking to Show Taro.

Nancy   [How much did you talk to Phoenix?]

Show Taro [He did not recognize your name right away but at the second time or so he said 「my woman and yours are room mates」.]

Nancy   [So, I am to play the role of your woman.]

Show Taro [I said so to him and he talked about his story about the past. The parents of Phoenix tried to let him wed to a brahmin and that was why they didn't show him letters that arrived since after six months.]

Nancy   [If that's the story, her whereabouts is known to me. To be short, she has been leading a single life during the past ten years.]

Show Taro [You mean she has kept to be unmarried?]

Nancy   [She got divorced for about twice.]

Show Taro [As I told him to let him meet Nancy, why not you to approach him and hear out how he is feeling about

— 172 —

her?]

Nancy [Okay, but I will have her understood that you are my man.]

Show Taro [Understood.]

Nancy [When is the meeting for the next remittance?]

Show Taro [We will get contacted about the second remittance very soon, as this time Phoenix knows my telephone number.]

Nancy [The bigger problem is those two women. If they find out what we are doing, we shall fail to get Phoenix on our side.]

Show Taro [By the way, in what you told her about your man in the fast, is there any thing which may lead him to detect our lie?]

For sometime Nancy's eyes were restless and then she came to get blushed and said.

Nancy [I frequently told her that as I let him strip me kissing a mole on my back, he knew well where on my back the mole was.]

Show Taro [Then, what about my taking a photo of the mole on your back.]

Looking at Show Taro who quickly took his digital camera out from his bag, though she was blushing, she took her clothes off and showed her back to Sho Taro. And at that very moment there was a knock at the door.

Show Taro [Who is it.]

Waitless [Room service.]

It was a woman's voice. He thought dinner which Nancy ordered

— 173 —

came pretty early, and so, he opened the door.

Then all of sudden slipping by the waitness, two women jumped into the room and changed there to be a slaughterhouse with screams and angry voices whirling.

Jinlian [You are such a bitch as to try to make off with my man!]

Nancy [You, the third wheel! You haven't slept with him, have you?]

Akemi [This whole situation is Maria's boss shot!]

Nancy [Don't boast just because you slept with him only for a few times!]

Akemi [Screw it!]

Akemi went out crying, and Jinlian followed her. The waitress just kept standing abashed.

Show Taro [Thank you for the delivery.]

Waitress [E···excuse me.]

Having getting her off quickly, Show Taro feeling better to see them off in any way returned to the sofa and sat on it. Using this lead time, Nancy had dressed herself up. When Show Taro started to place the dinner dishes on the table, Nancy came to help him and spoke to him.

Nancy [Whatever comes later may give us a hard time.]

Show Taro [In fooling the enemy, first you deceive your allies.]

Nancy [Don't forget where on my back the mole is.]

Show Taro [Incidentally, did you find out any information about Raja Mitra, the boss of Phoenix?]

Nancy [He is the commander-in-chief of arms dealers in South Asia called Lucifer. Mitra means Mithra God which

— 174 —

exists in the nearest position to the solar light among all solar deities. This is the reason why that codename of Lucifer was given to him.]

Show Taro [I see, it is an intelligent code name. Nancy, is your code name Oro?]

It looked like his question was the correct answer. Her voice tone suddently changed.

Nancy [How come do you know that!]

Show Taro [Those who are not aware of Baron Franchetti's Ca'd'Oro Art Gallery(Ca'd'Oro=golden palace) are not worth to be called art lovers.]

Nancy [That's a brilliant reasoning. I'm much stimulated. By the way, I found something at an antique shop in Hong Kong. Will you care to evaluate it?]

Saying so, Nancy took a small box out and handed it to Show Taro. He opened the box and there found pink color materials for seals. Through a lupe of ten-time magnifications, he checked it through electric light, then opened his mouth.

Show Taro [This is Drunken. Japanese collectors call this stone-made seal as Suifuyo (drunken colored pagodite).]

Show Taro returned the sealing materials back to the box and put the box on the table.

Nancy [Suifuyo⋯What meaning does that word have?]

Show Taro [They call the staying color of the cheek of a young white skinned woman who is intoxicated with liquer Drunken.]

Nancy [What do the curved letters mean?]

Show Taro [Riches, Noble and Long Life.]

— 175 —

Nancy   [That sounds wonderful.]

Show Taro [Everyone wishes to get the three, but if one demands these excessively, that one's life shall be shortened perishing oneself. This word implies in silence the importance of balancing.]

Nancy   [How can you be that clever to have that much knowledge?]

Show Taro [My life is dedicated to solve misteries.]

Nancy   [Let's eat while the dishes are still warm.]

The couple agreed to start taking dinner that had been delivered some time ago.

Show Taro [What did you order?]

Nancy   [To start with, prosciutto and melon, then we go over to grilled scampis.]

Show Taro [I see. These are the produce of Veneto. They look delicious.]

Nancy   [As I thought you must like these much.]

Show Taro [At Venice produce from all corners of the world is arriving altogether.]

Nancy   [And as a matter of course, such products as Murano glass, Venetian lace or Venetian weavings are all available there.]

Show Taro [You are right. Such gourgeous curtains hanging from a high ceiling is well matched to the buildings built in the era before Baroque.]

Nancy   [Talking about something else, while you lived in America did you ever visit Chicago?]

Show Taro [As the streets located inside the Loop are generally

— 176 —

safe and a pleasant place to visit, I have been there quite a few times.]

Nancy [So you must have been there on the weekends.]

Show Taro [In Rivernorth district there were nice jazz clubs. I remember covercharge there was about five dollars.]

Nancy [Outside of that area is a dangerous zone.]

Show Taro [When a relative of my acquaintance visited me from Germany, he was robbed of his video camera somewhere around three blocks to the west from John Hankok Center.]

Nancy [Is that person a German?]

Show Taro [He was a towering tall man but was not chewing a gum and looked apparently like a sightseer.]

Nancy [Was his life saved then?]

Show Taro [What I heard is in the first place he was careless enogh to ask a child to take a photo of him. This was very silly of him.]

Nancy [I see, then the child took the camera away.]

Show Taro [Yah, that seems what happened.]

Nancy [Chicago may have changed since when you were there.]

Show Taro [May I visit your place when next I will be there?]

Nancy [When you come, will you take me to the jazz club?]

Show Taro [Sure. You have my word.]

Nancy [I hope what you have said is not a simple lip service?]

Show Taro [Do you wish a lip service?]

　　Saying so, Show Taro put his lips on those of Nancy.

Nancy [This service is most welcome.]

— 177 —

The two body shades overlapped each other. The night still kept a long balance.

13. Remittance Preparation of the Second Share

The meeting for preparation of the second remittance was held at the casino in Macao. On this meeting Nancy was present as an additional new attendant. Right at the moment Indrajit met Nancy he immediately realized she was Emily's room mate whom he saw at their place several times, however, as he had become a suspicious man as result of working as arms dealer for more than ten years, when he met Nancy he decided right away that he would check Nancy up to ascertain if Nancy meets to what Emily told about her.

At this meeting, the three women of Jinlian and Akemi with Maria added to the two looked to be behaving themselves but it was also a fact that they were suspicious about the relationship between Show Taro and Nancy. One same suite was allocated to Show Taro and Nancy where there was only one queen size bed. Jinlian was thinking if they did not sleep on that one queen size bed, it was extremely odd and strange so the reason must be clarified. Akemi also demanded to find out whether the two would sleep together or not as long as Maria previously asserted that they were not in love relationship. Maria, as long as she is receiving the fee for having Akemi's fortune told, was bound by the duty to answer Akemi's questions, she was then made to stand a difficult position including the hush money she received at the previous time.

At this meeting, Indrajit made it clear that the drawing amount by Hell Computer this time was planned to be 7 million dollars.

Also, at that time, Indrajit told them he was to issue an export letter of credit to Town Street Bank of Chicago and remit the credit amount to Paradise Soft which was owned by Chen Jing Jin. He told them documentation procedures had already been completed. Indrajit had also finished preparing three documents of remittance request to three subcontractors and addressed these documents to this Paradise Soft Organization to be on the safe side.

To one of those three remittees 5.95 million dollars were planned to be remitted and as regards this remittance each remittee's company's delivery notice and related invoice were made out in each company's formal format. As Mao was a man with extremely few words, it was only twice when he opened his mouth. The meeting room was set at the side from where the sea could be viewed so that even if some one might be watching from the side of casino that meeting room was not able to be viewed.

Robert Grant and his members who were standing by in a room of a hotel next to the hotel where the meeting was being held were ready to catch the information which was supposed to be going on there through the wire tapping device that Nancy equipped with her. This second remittance also had a possibility of insurance fraud relating to overseas trading, so, there was a possibility that insurance premium was being paid to a certain other insurance company. However, from the meeting room that was being used this time not a single word was leaking to be heard from there which could very possibly mean that meeting place was wholly covered by electromagnetic shield from the ceiling to the glass windows.

Robert   [Hey, Nancy?]

— 180 —

Nancy 　[…]

He called Nancy many times but no answer came back from Nancy.

While waiting for the meeting to start, Jinlian, Akemi and Maria kept staring at Nancy and talking in whispers. Jinlian told the other two the outcome of wiretapping their behaviours which she obtained from Chen Jing Ji. He was asked by Jinlian to eavesdrop the conversation and sound in the room of Nancy with Show Taro.

Akemi　　　[What happened last night?]

Jinlian　　[They had sex twice on the bed.]

Akemi　　　[That's vexing.]

Jinlian　　[Nancy is totally different from her quiet look…Do you understand what I mean?]

Akemi　　　[Is that all you can say about her?]

Jinlian　　[They took shower together, so, what they talked or did in the shower could not be detected.]

Akemi　　　[She looked like hiding some ulterior motive. What about Nancy's fortune?]

Maria　　　[Did you get what I asked you yesterday to have ready for me today?]

Jinlian　　[This is a color copy of her passport which I obtained from Chen Jing Ji. Will you decipher this in the next room?]

Maria　　　[Understood. Is someone there in the next room?]

Jin Lian　　[My secretary is standing by, making your fortune telling tools ready there.]

Going to the next room which Jinlian made ready, Maria spent about a quarter of an hour and exercised holoscope and Tarot

— 181 —

Cards which was made in the 19th century. When they thought Maria must have finished the telling, they went together into the next room.

Akemi [How did your telling come out?]

Maria [As I thought it would be.]

Jinlian [Would be what?]

Maria [What probably happened in the previous life was Nancy derived Show Taro from Akemi. You were a daughter of a textile goods store. I have seen that he was buying you curtains. At that store, you could have noticed that she was there, the youngest daughter of a noble who is not very wealthy.]

JinLian [So this is said to be a gradge fight. But this time I also am here to join the battle.]

Maria [You have no such need.]

Akemi [You mean as I can no longer win the battle?]

Maria [Because her fate is getting to be sealed,]

Jinlian [Do you mean by that she is going to⋯『die』?]

Akemi [Never say die! I don't expect that way of winning this battle.]

Maria [Ms. Nancy is to come into the worst period of fortune. During this period of time, she will defence a person and face the risk of her life.]

Akemi [And how does it end?]

Maria [⋯I repeated my telling for twice but⋯death comes out at each time.]

Akemi [Thank you. If that's the case, we cannot help watching how the situation moves for some time.]

— 182 —

Jinlian   [I thought you would put a curse on Nancy.]

Akemi   [Even if I may win, I don't wish to have a bad aftertaste.]

Jinlian   [Let's come back to the meeting room. Soon Zedeng Mao will be coming up.]

No response could be obtained for repeated cell phone calls nor any telephone reply, but when the scheduled time came nearby, it was sighted that a cruiser was brought alongside the pier near the hotel. It was reported off from the cruiser ZeDeng Mao wearing a straw hat and sungrasses and Chinese clothes got on the shore. When Mao came into the meeting room, Chen Jin Ji declared the opening of the meeting.

Chen   [Now, as every member is ready, we are now opening the discussion meeting of the phase 2.]

Indrajit   [I do hope that this time, too, every program will smoothly develop.]

Mao   [Which remittee's account on the list will be used this time?]

Indrajit   [We are making consideration of Dubai, Zurich and London in that order .]

Mao   [When will you come to the conclusion to choose one of the three?]

Indrajit   [It will be decided during next week.]

Chen   [Okay, then, let's toast.]

Chen Jin Ji looked to be thinking to give a good service to Indrajit whom Chen thought he did not entertain well enough last time. Whatever is said, this business is quite a profitable business to Chen bringing him quite large sum of money, on the condition, however, he would accept the point of money laundering in the process of the whole flow of this transaction.

According to what Chen understands, Mao was an incarnation of charisma of Hong Kong underground money world dealing with many large-scale customers. One thing, however, that is concerning Chen was that Mao profested self destruction of Chen so that if this prophecy of Mao came true, the code name Shaman Rouge might have turned out to be right. Guided by Chen, they moved to casino except Indrajit, Nancy and Show Taro. Those three took tea at the casino club. One cause for concern was there joined Maria in place of Akemi.

Indrajit [Nancy, How many ten years is this meeting again with you?]

Nancy [Since I saw you several times at that time.]

Indrajit [I used to hear Emily had a man, but that you are meeting Show is a news to me. What a coincidental reunion is it.]

Show Taro [Nancy has a large mole under her shoulder blade and around the left side of the kidney.]

Indrajit [Now I remember, Show is making it a habit to take Nancy's clothes off while kissing the mole!]

To this talk Maria seemed to be showing some reaction.

Nancy [Talking about Emily she is still in Chicago even now.]

Indrajit [Is she single?]

Nancy [She waited for one full year since she came not to receive replies from Indy, but after that she got married twice and in both marrages, she got devorced within three months.]

— 184 —

Indrajit   [What is she doing now?]

Nancy   [She now is an expert realestate dealer. She was eager to meet you again.]

Indrajit   [Oh, how much I do wish to meet her again--]

All of sudden tears flew down from the eyes of Indrajit.

Nancy   [Sure you can meet her.]

Indrajit   [NO! I can never meet her again. How can I tell her I am in such business? She does not like anything unfair. You know that, Nancy!]

Nancy   [The most important thing is, Love.]

Show Taro   [When this business is over, you can take your hands off your present business. This can be a good timing.]

Indrajit   [⋯I will go to bed for tonight. Thank you, Nancy.]

Indrajit stood up and left his seat for his room. When his figure became unseen, Maria looked around and opened her mouth.

Maria   [He killed several people in past.]

Nancy   [What happened to you to say such a blunt thing suddenly? Maria, are you alright?]

Show Taro   [Nancy, she can see what ordinary people cannot see.]

Maria   [I can see he is having machine guns customs-cleared under false declaration as motorcycle supply⋯that he is handing 100 dollars to a soldier who stopped him is seen⋯The auto cannon was disassembled⋯he is recomposing the parts. In truth he is an arms dealer.]

Nancy   [Phew. You've hit it.]

Show Taro   [Do you now believe her?]

Nancy   [I understand she is a psychic.]

Show Taro   [If you have enough budjet and can pay her fortune-telling fee, she will work on your request.]

Nancy   [Who··· is the person that can help Indy?]

Maria   [I am afraid I cannot see that much···but one thing for sure is he is still seeking her.]

Nancy   [Her birth date is different from mine for two months.]

So, Nancy told Maria the birth date of Emily.

Maria   [Wait a second···]

Having said so, she took out Tarot Cards of the 19th century all of the sudden.

Maria   [The magic power of these cards is not very strong, but is still a good one that worked well in Paris in the 1890s. It used to tell the fortune of women of Moulin Rouge.]

Nancy   [I see. This is an antique product.]

Maria   [As I have the information about the birth date of Indrajit from Show Taro before···Well, these two···if they are made to meet again they will return to the original pod.]

Show Taro [Will they be able to reach the stage of marriage?]

Maria   [He would need a special permit of American Government as he already sent an instruction out to kill at least several persons in line with his arms dealing business. Should he fail to get it, it shall not be possible that he escapes from the circle which the magic power of Raja is mastering. My fortune telling shows only with his power of prohibition he shall not be able to break Raja's magic power···]

Nancy   [Does Indrajit also have a magic power?]

— 186 —

Maria [Though he is equipped with natural ancestral power, he has not tried to nourish it seriously ever. That is the reason why he could not grow up to compete with Raja who holds a strong monk soldier group at his side. To overcome Raja, only with such lineage of love between Emily and him even though it is a strong lineage he can not win over Raja since Indrajit's father is practicing some autosuggestion on Indrajit to disable him to return to America. He has to escape from that magic from his father as well.]

Nancy [Thank you.]

She put twenty dollars in silence.

Maria [One important thing. Do act caring about your own safety.]

Nancy [I know⋯Thank you for your words.]

14. Occurrence of Difficulty in making Remittance

Another meeting with all members attended on the day when arrival of remittance into the bank account of Paladice Soft was opened, when a small trouble took place. ZeDeng Mao wearing Chinese clothes and sunglasses as usual whispered in Chinese several words to Jinlian and Chen, then Chen had several of his underlings gathered. Becoming aware that Indrajit and Kubera were nervous, the Japanese people also became to feel uneasy. Then unusually, Mao started to talk in the first place.

Mao　　　　[Mr. Indrajit, Regarding the remittance this time, is it not possible to change the priority order of Dubai?]

Indrajit　　[It was fixed as I told you yesterday. Has there been any problem coming up?]

Mao　　　　[At this ongoing moment, I cannot figure out why but Japanese Ministry of Ficance has intervened to make an inspection.]

Indrajit　　[How does that relate to this case? Please explain.]

Mao　　　　[It is easy to move the money that arrived in Hong Kong to Macao, but after that action is complete, there comes a possibility of an investigation being assessed on that money.]

Indrajit　　[Oh my gosh!]

Mao　　　　[If Mr. Chen's company send remittance to the Dubai branch of the same bank that received the cancelled money of purchase of the painting of Hell Computer,

	they will be sure to watch it.]
Chen	[Which bank is it that is being investigated?]
Mao	[The one of this morning is Trading Swiss.]
Chen	[For what purpose?]
Mao	[It is not known to us as yet as to whether it is a Japanese gangsters' money of circulation or deals of drugs.]
Indrajit	[Is there any countermeasure available? Even if all of us are work together, we cannot afford to combat against the persuaders of Your Highness Rajar.]
Chen	[Here is China.]
Indrajit	[Then, what countermeasure?]
Mao	[Is it possible to change the destination of the remittance either to Zurich or London? As it is, the borner line is shut out.]
Indrajit	[If we go ahead nevertheless?]
Mao	[Gunshot in a square.]
Indrajit	[I understand. Let me make a contact.]
Mao	[Tell us if the amount of money can be split.]

Indrajit left his seat and came back in a few minutes. He was swettng on his forehead but looked he got an answer.

Indrajit	[Remit 5.96 million dollars to Zurich.]
Mao	[What about splitting the fund?]
Indrajit	[No split.]
Mao	[Delivery?]
Indrajit	[Same as usual.]
Mao	[Mr., Indrajit, Can you go to Zurich with Mr. Chen?]
Indrajit	[Why do I have to?]

Mao	[Limit of remittance amount is set as 5 million dollars. The balance of 950,000 dollars have to be hand-carried and put in the bank directly.]
Indrajit	[Understood. What about ticket?]
Chen	[We will arrange.]
Indrajit	[You are to bring the money, aren't you?]
Chen	[No, Jinlian does it.]
Indrajit	[I thought you were going.]
Chen	[She goes only to the airport.]
Indrajjit	[Is she capable enough to do this?]
Chen	[Hong Kong Airport and China Pacific Air is under her control.]
Indrajit	[What about Zurich?]
Chen	[I have done arrangements with my friend.]

Listening to the conversation among the three, Show Taro and Nancy were convinced that 950,000 dollars in cash would be handcarried though the account number for that amount of cash to be deposited in Zurich was not known to them. They however did not have any idea as to how that money could be remitted. Coming back to the hotel room, Nancy went out to the valcony and wrote a mail on her cell phone. Robert was supposed to investigate to grasp the five-million-dollar remittance account details that were to be handled by the Hong Kong bank. However, as they were not sure what might flow to the opposite direction was unknown, she was unable to take the countermeasure of freezing the account using pressure from her insurance company.

Jinlian, Chen and Indrajit went to the airport and was to transit by helicopter, where a man was waiting for their arrival at the airport.

As Jinlian had lovers here and there, she asked the president of
this airline company to have him serve her this time. This president
was a medium built man and had been engaged in emergency
transportation between inland China and Hong Kong as a pirot.
When Hong Kong was returned from U.K. he got funded by a
certain arms dealer and founded the present airline company. As he
knew much about the crues of underground money and also as he
was involved in such illegal business being committed by military
related personnel as to resale the expendables in the armoury to
the third country, there were no worries of public security officials
to search China Pacific Air. He also had an inconspicuous
appearance so he scarcely had a chance to be asked for a business
interview.

That he was nonconspicuous was a secret of his success in his
business. The hidden ability to sniff out the smell of money on him
and to attract and control him was what only the unique charm of
hers could achieve.

Jin Lian   [Sorry to have kept you waiting. These gentlemen are
              Mr. Chen and Mr. Indrajit whom I asked you to take
              care of.]
Zhu   [How do you do, I am Zhu XingMing of China Pacific
              Air.]
Jinlian   [Mr. Chen, Will you pass the bag to Mr. Zhu as is.]
Indrajit [Is it not better for me to keep it?]
Xing Ming [No worries. I will keep the bag where even the
              investigating authorities cannot trace it. When you

arrive at the destination airport, please take an action as described on this piece of paper, Mr. Chen.]

Saying so, Zhu handed over to him a piece of paper which he took out of his pocket.

Chen　　　[I got it.]

Xing Ming　[As regards the plane you are to fly by, as there are empty seats in the business class of the plane which is waiting there, please take one each of these tickets. Talking about passports, I will stamp on them now in here, so just pass your passports to me.]

At Zhu's request, the two showed him their passports. Opening the related page of the passports, Zhu Xing Ming quickly finished stampling using the rubber stamp that he seemingly borrowed from the relative official.

Xing Ming　[Will you get on board from here. I will arrange your baggages loaded immediately.]

Having finished his talk, he swiftly walked away dragging the two baggages.

Jinlian　　[Right, now, have a nice trip!]

Indrajit　　[Thanks!]

In one moment, Chen Jing Ji and Indrajit boarded the airplane.

Indrajit　　[Mr. Chen, That woman Jinlian is a charmer.]

Chen　　　[Why do you say that?]

Indrajit　　[In the first place I thought she was your woman as she is such a good looking woman.]

Chen　　　[Yah, she uses more technics than my wife.]

Indrajit　　[But that man Zhu Xing Ming also seems to be her lover and she is also trying to fall Show Taro down.

	Thinking about all such she is totally different from any other women I have ever met.]
Chen	[She is a very energetic woman. She looks like absorbing all of her men's energy as the staff of her life.]
Indrajit	[We should be careful to deal with her magic power.]
Chen	[Do you mean you can decipher her fortune?]
Indrajit	[I at least am feeling that she had destroyed quite a number of men. Don Juan is said to have destroyed many women. Like him, I cannot stop feeling that she is a type to destroy many men.]
Chen	[Can you handle astrology?]
Indrajit	[Yes, as I am out of the family of Brahmin, I studied that field to some extent.]
Chen	[Okay, then, please tell my fourtune as I am now telling you my birth date.]
Indrajit	[Alright. Shall we do it just to kill time.]

Taking about 20 minutes from then, Indrajit created Chen's holoscope and intended to tell him a simply outlined prophet, however, the result of his telling came out with an astonishing result.

Chen	[How much more shall I be getting successful?]
Indrajit	[So far as I have deciphered your fortune, any more development than at the present stage will depend on the turning point that will come in the coming few months.]
Chen	[I guess that would mean the remittance work this time will go smoothly.]

Indrajit   [Yes, that will go that way. However, you should be careful about investment. My fortune telling is showing an implication which says unconfirmed victory will reverse the result.]

Chen   [I see.]

Though Indrajit dared not to tell Chen, he saw a possibility that means death, but as a usual practice of a prophest, he could not but wrap that word in oblate. But that result of his prophecy made Indrajit a bit nervous so he tried to find out his own astrological fortune and found no death implication but a possibility of a change. He was given a capability to see through his future because he was a family of Brahmin.

At the backside of Zurich Airport, the underlayers of Robert found the baggages of Chen Jing Ji and Indrajit and checked the both baggages through x-ray transmission device but failed to find anything like bundles of notes of $950,000. The baggages were again checked at the customs.

Inspection Officer   [Do you have any article that has to be declared?]

Indrajit   [No.]

Inspection Officer   [Will you cooperate with us to exercise some sampling inspection?]

Indrajit   [Go ahead.]

The officer opened the heavy bag but could not find anything but some clothes for changes and sightseeing guide books of China.]

Inspection Officer   [These are guidebooks of China. What about those of Swittzerland?]

— 194 —

Indrajit   [As this country is not my first visit.]

Inspection Office   [Thank you for your cooperation.]

Finishing the customs clearance, the two killed time at a cafeteria and walked to the reception desk of the designated airline company. There, like reading a manual book which had been handed over to them, very smooth conversation was exchanged. Necessity of time adjustment was necessary in order to kill the waiting time till the baggages were delivered to them and also to make sure that no one was watching them.

Chen   [I am Mao. I received your contact.]

Clerk   [Is your sister well?]

Chen   [Jinlian has a slight cold.]

Clerk   [This bag had been delivered.]

Chen   [Thank you.]

As the clerk sent out a bag which was a familiar bag to him, Chen put it on his shoulder even without checking the inside of the bag.

Indrajit   [Don't you check the inside?]

Chen   [100 dollar notes no doubt. We don't use fake dollar notes.]

Thus, the car riding the two arrived at the bank. There had been Josef and Luise. They were prepared with a well polished Luger P08 in their pockets. They were dressed in businesslike suits and could not but look like an executive of a leading industrial company and his secretary.

Indrajit   [Early arrival, isn't it.]

Louise   [You must be tired.]

Chen   [Shall we put this in bank once?]

Chen passed to Josef the bag that he had been carrying here from the airport, Indrajit added his words to Josef

Indrajit   [Here are 950,000 dollars.]

Josef   [Let's have the bank man put this in the account.]

The bank man received the bag and counted the notes of 950,000 dollars. Indrajit felt relieved. His animal like intuition had been telling him that those two people who had been waiting for him may have had an intention to kill them if the notes were found as fakes. When the checking was finished, Chen sent his declaration to Jinlian and Indrajit to Kubera that the second remittance was completed sugesssfully. By this notice those prisoners held at the casino in Macao were to be released finally.

With this exercise having been safely finished, Chen Jing Ji was to reconfirm the fact that the person of merit was not the master of underground money but Jinlian who had powerful business leaders under her influence. Reason why he thought so was when last night he called her, she must have been with the president of China Pacific Airline. He thought ZeDeng Mao who would not appreciate that body of Jinlian was in a sence a very weird man. He felt if Mao showed a little bit of love to her his business must jump up. He thought the same way with Show Taro, too. But now what he is concerned the most is what sort of amount the next remittance would be.

Chen   [Indy, How much will the next remittance be?]

Indrajit   [I have not heard about it]

Josef   [For next time, we plan   £15,000,000 in the form of letter of credit.]

Then, they parted. Chen chuckled to himself thinking he would be able to make a big jump up with the next income as seed money.

15. Departure for Abalone

It was a warm day but Heinrich got under the car and was just about to finish changing oil seals. And there, Kato of EMM drove his car. The number plate of Kato's car always showed 731 so it was easy to recognize that it was his car. Number 731 sounded ill-omened to many people but for Midori Manji it was a proof of trust of that their products were based on a firm confidence that was gained through many living-body tests. Kato seemed to have an obvious preference to this number even in choosing the room of this number when he stays at a hotel.

Kato   [What do you want me to do for you today?]

Heinrich   [The full restoring of this 1932 model Mercedes that was found in Libya is just about to be finished. Do you want me to give you a ride?]

Kato   [Where did you learn car restoring technics?]

Heinrich   [While I was studying overseas in America. I used to produce a few custom cars and sold them to build up funds.]

Kato was patting the chrome plated mall for a while and opened his mouth.

Kato   [But you're very lucky you could obtain such parts that fit the car you are restoring.]

Heinrich   [Well, I made it up using two parts off the broken car. I used chassis recovered from the car owned by General Rommel. This car of his was bombed after he had ridden it to Germany for the purpose of receiving medical treatment there. It is such a highly luxury 1930th car that is hard to find at any auction nowadays. The engine was of a car left abandoned in the desert nearby Tripoli with the rear seat made like a honeycomb swept by machine guns from air.

This restored car will help you feel like General Rommel did.]

Kato   [I see. Incidentally, I know you have something to talk about with me today which is not like this restoring talk.]

Heinrich rose up from the creeper on the floor, wiping oil attached to his fingers.

Heinrich   [Mr. Kato, Why don't you try sit on the car?]

Kato   [Aha, Okay, Just a bit of observation. To me the scalpel that Leutinant General Ishi used to possess is more interesting to look at, though.]

Heinrich   [General Ronmel may have sat there, too, in addition to the rear seat. He may have taken command sitting in the right front seat perhaps opening the map of Cairo.]

As Kato took the front assistant's seat, Heinrich sat in the driver's seat and tried to put the engine on. With a sound of bomb, the engine started and Heinrich lightly beat the accerelator pedal and everytime of his beating, there pop out white smokes.

Heinrich   [I may perhaps have put too much engine oil.]

As it got a bit smoky, he put the gear at the low position, then the car slowing started moving ahead. While talking to Kato, Heinrich changed the gear to the second position then to the third.

Heinrich   [I am doing various remittance works at the moment on business. I need to use the name of the Indian

	factory of Midori Manji to fill this need.]
Kato	[So, what exactly are you in need?]
Heinrich	[I like a few sheets of writing paper with Midori Manji India letterhead.]
Kato	[I guess you will come to need more due to a chance of the plan or the like, so you can have a whole bunch of the letterheads.]
Heinrich	[But don't cause me any trouble using them, is that what you say now?]
Kato	[As long as you know that, I have no complaint.]
Heinrich	[By the way, what sort of the size of the order of construction of the Indian factory?]
Kato	[How do such information relate to you?]
Heinrich	[If I happen to put a larger sum than what it would possibly be for the construction cost of a factory, there comes a possibility that even the most idle inspector may see through the deception.]
Kato	[Purchase cost of the land may be 2 million dollars, then 4 million for the building and 20 million for a set of equipment for the chemical reaction tower and for other incidental facilities⋯15 million as I remember it, so all these will add up about 41million dollars as a total business scale.]
Heinrich	[I will keep it mind not to exceed that amount as the amount of order.]
Kato	[Okay. Mind you I am supposed not to know the details.]
Heinrich	[It will be helpful if you take it that way.]

加 **Kato**　　　[By the way, we need a few more logs for our research work. Can you make arrangements to get these to us?]

That Kato called the objects for the living-body experiments as logs was a traditional habit ever since the time of 731 Troops.

Heinrich　　[I reckon all what you need is blood only, isn't it?]

Kato　　　　[As we are a blood product manufacturer.]

Heinrich　　[I will arrange to let a killing people contractor in South America. By the way, what level have you reached now?]

Kato　　　　[Taking a monkey as example, only one more step till we could reach the level of making one whole monkey from one drop of blood. But in case of level of your demand is from one concentrated drop which is not an easy target to achieve.]

Talking this way, both finished a run once around a circle. Kato got off the car where Louise came out.

Heinrich　　[Hi, Luise, good timing you came out here. Will you take ten Amazoneses who have been ready in Brasil?]

Louise　　　[When do you wish me to start the work?]

Heinrich　　[Let them be taken into a vessel which I have kept waiting on the Atlantic, after two weeks from now.]

Louise　　　[You mean that old coffin, don't you.]

Heinrich　　[And from there send them to Abalone. I will appoint you as Admiral of SS Indian Sea Fleet.]

Kato　　　　[Won't you send me some abalone as I don't mind them frozen. Abalone in that sea area is good both for sashimi and stake.]

Heinrich　　[You have my promise.]

Finishing saying that, Heinrich turned to Louise.

Heinrich [At the time of your leaving the vessel, send five to six abalone here.]

Then, Louise greeted with German style greetings.

Louise [Siegheil!]

Kato [Thank you. Looking forward to balloon fish.]

Kato returned to his car looking as though nothing had happened. The two saw Kato's back off and resumed their talk.

Heinrigh [Now, talking about something else, in Amazon they are looking forward to the arrival of the brides. How successfully have those amazones been getting refurbished?]

Louise [The ten amazones of this time's selection were chosen through one from eighteen competition rate so to them operation of new type computer is absolutely no problem. They are best suited to handle analysis of wireless communication of American troops in Abalone.]

Heinrich [Okay, I am expecting their superb performance. Rather than selling arms goods, to sell information to the radicalists in Middle East is safer as tracing is much more difficult than the trade of arms. How to get good return safely is important.]

Louise [On a different note, when will the two U-boats of the Indian ocean fleet be changed to a new model?]

Heinrich [We will have to wait till the third world countries would come to order a bit more boats. If more orders come, we will become able to accomplish manufacture

	of parts that can be applied to six boats with the materials for four boats···]
Louise	[What about Russia-made parts?]
Heinrich	[Such parts that are made in Russia have a very high rate of accidents so boats using such parts cannot be used for our important crews.]

There in the contemporary technical level reliability of Nazi German U-boat is still by far the best, therefore, comparing that high level, reliability of Russian Nucrear submarine is much less.

Louise	[Now, I am going with much care.]
Heinrich	[On your return trip to South America, guard the cargo vessel Makara for cargos for the Middle Eastern customers to pick up till Makara arrives at the entrance of Persian Gulf. However, you are to return from Comoros Islands waiting for a vessel that is coming to pick you up. I already told about these arrangements to Josef so before you sally out, get airline tickets from him. End.]
Louise	[Excuse me.]

She went to the desk of Yosef and received the operation manual, a set of airline tickets and the travel allowance. She continued to the airport from there and flew to South America where her cooperator is waiting for her. From the east of Caribbean Sea she rode aboard a cruser which was meant for the night-time fishing. Due to jet lag, she was attacked by a strong sleepiness and seemed to have fallen in sleep for about 30 minutes. When she was shaken to get awake, the joining with the submarine had already been finished so she got aboard on the submarine taking her luggage.

Loise stepped up to the bridge of the submarine, Captain Marlene Castillo received her. Marlene was a passionate daughter between father of mixed blood of a Spanish noble and a native Brazilian mother and a welknown dancer at the Carnival of Rio. Her bewitching figure was too attractrive to be concealed in her uniform, however, as all crew on that submarine were women, her attractiveness did not show up that much.

Marlene [Wellcome to Amazones. To Admiral, Siegheil!]

The crew members standing in line side by side on the deck tapped their heels together to express their welcome.

Louise [This boat is now to take off to the operation seafield. Everyone, Be ready at each position!]

Responding to her order, everyone expeditiously entered inside the boat through the hatch.

Marlene [The crew staff are consisted of women only, but we all are expert soldiers.]

Louise [This boat is a valuable boat having survived WW2, so I rely on your good discresion to keep it and use it to the fullest effect.]

Having said so, Louise sent her hand out to Marlene which she grasped tightly. Around them wet southern sea with pleasant bleeze was spreading. In a-few-minute time, figure of the cruiser was melted into the dark under the cover of night and became invisible.

Marlene [As is, keep forwarding at ten knots!]

Navigation Officer [Aye Aye Sir!]

Louise [Don't you navigate underwater?]

Marlene　[During night sailing, we use a diesel engine. Using this method, we can get a longer sailing distance.

We cruise under water till the sun rising time and switch the cruiser to snorkeling. Our cruiser can get more speed in the sea but this is what the fate of getting old would mean.]

Louise　[Are there any other problems arising from deterioration due to time lapse?]

Marlene　[Type of torpado is oldfashioned. Nowadays the main stream of torpado is homing torpado. We cannot chase our target by ourselves.]

Louise　[Give me the detailed information of Amazones, such as its benchmark.]

Marlene　[U-boatXXI type, 1621 tons, 4000hp, Speed on water 15.6knot, in water 17.2knot, 15,500 nautical miles at 17.2 knot in water and at 10 knot on water, practical depth 150m, maximum depth 350m which is the deepest performance we experimented with it, 6 torpade tubes. This U-boat was removed from German Navy on May 3, 1945 and recorded as scuttling processing but kept being used by SS Atlantic fleet, however, due to long range, it was transferred to Indian Sea Fleet.]

Luise　[As SS was able to expunge the past of Adolf Hitler or Coco Gabrielle Chanel, they had no problem to eraze the past of scuttling process which is fabricated to be added to this U-boat.]

While they were talking that way, the boat was going ahead on the sea continuing radar-monitoring. Before dawn was approaching, the executive officer confirmed the dawn by periscope. After she

— 205 —

confirmed it, the captain let the boat move under the water. From there, the operation of the boat was changed to underwater sailing using a snorkel. After the boat moved into water, the captain and the executive officer came to the office of the admiral and then the order of the operation was unopened.

Louise　　　[I was instructed to open this operation order after we came under water and not right on the departure of the boat. Therefore, here I am opening the order now.]

Marlene　　[This is unusual. I feel thrilled like in a movie.]

Louise　　　[Destination where this operation is practiced is Abalone which has not been changed from previous. The operation consists of two parts.

Operation A　To send replacement personnel to Abalone.

Operation B　To guard the meeting of Cossac, a Russian cargo ship with Makara an Indian cargo ship and to escort Makara to the entrance of Persian Gulf. End.]

Marlene　　[Is that all?]

Louise　　　[It sounds like the cargos aboard those vessels were what was important, but we are not notified about the contents of the cargos.]

Merlene　　[Roger···Looks like cargos are bigger than previous.]

Purpose of the sail this time was for the staff reassignements of ten family members in Abalone. There in Abalone some tens of men were stationed who and whose wives had not started a family as yet, and also those couples whose children were grownup and were living independently elsewhere.

As at that place, Abalone, there was a rule that local fishermen would not touch the ocean area where black skinned natives did fishing, those people selected from the members of SS African troops were saftely stationed for three generations already by then. Many of brides of those stationed members of SS African troops were from South America or from the area of the Carribian. In the day time, those people including the brides were leading everyday life showing naked upper bodies, therefore, even if they happened to be observed with binoculars by Indian fishermen, they were not to invite any suspicion from them.

One other assignment given to those SS African Troops took place when the two vessels of Russian cargo vessel Cosac and of Middle East Terrorists receiving vessel Makara met in the eastern sea area from Abalone and the change over of such arms as missilles between these two vessels.

When this exercise was executed, twelve missilles were taken down of which ten are re-loaded on Makara and the extra two were to be hidden in Abalone. Besides Missilles, Casac was loaded with 500 assault rifles. Nevertheless, the statement on the invoice was written to the effect that those cargoes were of a set of equipments for use at the drug reaction facility of the Midori Manji India chemical factory.

Another point was, though Makara was made as an Indian national vessel, such registered name was a name of a vessel which was already scrapped. This vessel was bluntly made revived to serve their convenience. From the extremist organization of Middle East, General Omar played a role of witness and was quested to stay at that place till he obtained their consent to leave there. The X-day was to be wired at a later date but General Omar was requested to watch after the transaction was complete if there should be any vessel that would chase Makara.

The Russian vessel, Cosac was going down to south as was, aiming at the west coast of Australia, while Makara went to west for Middle East. Amazonese went ahead of Makara and after confirming safety of the waterway at the south side of the island, Makara was to pass the waterway by to west. If in case there should be a vessel pursuing Makara, the operation manual stated that they had all rights and authorities to protect Makara from such pursuing vessel. However, one thing that had to be noted was that those tornadoes which had no chance to be tried for the past several ten years could work well as expected or not was what no one had ever tried as yet.

16. Night before the Third Remittance

Then, sometime later again, this time the remittance arrangements to the account in Hong Kong of Advanced Engineering which holder's name was Chen Jing Ji became ready.

If that timing was missed out and they failed to take Indrajit into their side, it would mean that they should fail to uncover what was flowing behind the funds. Could they succeed in revealing the truth before the last day in Macao? Nancy was saying she had effective means to make it succeed, but she did not reveal any details of the means that she had in her mind. Suppose everything went well, how could they let Indrajit escape successfully⋯

At this meeting, all the members that were present at the second meeting gathered when Nancy said she had an idea. It looked like she did not wish to let Show Taro know about it, but it might be only natural and could not be helped as Show Taro was in fact just an ordinary person of no secret. He never held any special capability or ability. What could be said about him at most was that he was a person who had a little ability regarding art objects and that was just about all.

As everyone has now got used to this transaction system, all handling steps could very easily be finished.

Mao   [The amount of remittance this time is 15 million pounds. In view of substantiality of this amount and also in line with the listing order on the name list, London will be considered.]

Indrajit   [Your assumption is correct.]

Mao   [Regarding the purchase order⋯Hell Computer placed

an order of a chemical reaction test facility with
software adjustment function added⋯Such description
sounds pretty normal so there may be no need to
worry if we have it dealt with in a normal open way.]

Indrajit   [Yes, You may be right.]

Mao   [Well, I think I can accept your opinion.]

Then, Mao must have been convinced that Indrajit will make
remittance to London, he assured Indrajit saying as below.

Mao   [London is open at this moment for receiving
remittance. Rest assured.]

Indrajit   [Understood. I reckon so far we are moving very
smoothly.]

When the meeting was over on that day, Show Taro was to go to
casino taking Akemi and Jinlian. Needless to say, that was not
really what he wanted but he had to give time to Nancy to take
Indrajit out.

However, this action of Show Taro looked to Jinlian and Akemi
nothing but Nancy's retreatment from the competition battle to
acquire Show Taro. Chen Jing Ji had foreseen that Jinlian had not
yet been able to get Show Taro in her hands. Chen therefore
successfully persuaded Jinlian and took her out before roulet was to
begin. He told Jinlian that the aphrodisiac which Jinlian made
prescribed recently was very effective on him so he wished to use
it with her. At that word of Chen, she got on his plan and told him
that she would try it together with him on that night

Mao made an unusual visit to casino. Buying tips worth for one
dollar he showed his one-point betting technic in the sight of Show

Taro, Akemi and Maria. The three and the people around there were excited to sight this betting scene of Mao wondering it was what was called Mao's legendary miraculous technic.

Mao was dressed in his usual Chinese clothes and was wearing sunglasses. He never showed even the slightest movement of his eyes. All what he did was to place the tips in silence and repeated this action for three times. Then, he changed the tips with cash. In the thunderous apprause by all people there, his betting for such a short time thus finished

Akemi   [Why do you stop it so soon?]

Mao   [Never too much of anything.]

Maria   [Are you able to see it?]

Mao   [I am making it a rule to myself that I bet within the sphere of my concentration power only when I feel that at that time zone that number will come up. This is the secret of my undefeated gambling power.]

He took a sip from a glass of Oolong tea which he received from a waiter who was passing by him.

Mao   [At the roulet game at this place, selection of the betting position can be made till the dealer stops betting. Therefore, at a match game the opponent tries to hit the point he aims at after studying the position which this side has selected. Therefore, I can feel the tension of the opponent and can judge the timing, and I make a guess of how many frames will be missed. Doing this way and hitting it is all what I do, so this method of mine is a quite clear deductive reasoning but to those who cannot understand such psycological

— 211 —

method it looks like a mystery. Talking about money speculation facet of economy, it becomes a more difficult deal as extra rich people's expectancy or speculation would be added to it]

Show Taro [According to what you have just talked about, economic investiment measures will come out much more difficult that to win roulet game.]

Mao [You are right. What I know is when monster that takes the lead in the market keeps rushing about widely, you will never be able to win the game unless you follow its will. However, when the time of Apocalypse is filled, such monster will be absorbed into the market principle. And that is the best timing for us to move.]

Show Taro [Your theory is a really interesting philosophy.]

Mao [You are a person that will not be involved in lure by Jinlian. I like it. At some other occasion, I wish to do a different type of business with you.]

Show Taro [That is quite overestimated comments on me. Thank you. But why can you say that?]

Mao [Jinlian was born under the star which attracts nova or supernova. Such critical and dyeing stars will shine once at least, but will end to get exploding under the destiny of never being able to escape from her electromagnetic field, though I don't know whether it is a black hole or a pink hole. But what can be said as a conclusion is among those that could make an escape a true winner is included.]

— 212 —

Show Taro [Do you mean I am that true winner?]

Mao [No, It is a matter of possibility. That you can keep a long life at least means you are a brand stock that could respond to investment, though you may not be able to cope up with Ms. Maria's clairvoyance.]

Being looked at by those men, Akemi and Maria looked at each other.

Show Taro [What you talk about is unusual.]

Mao [Let me excuse myself tonight now.]

Mao vanished away beyond the launge. Seeing him off, Akemi opened her month.

Akemi [What is Mao after all?]

Maria [He is a lonely person. An ascetic of Shugendo is accompanying him. He may be able to make all kinds of anticipation though deductively⋯]

That night, as Nancy was not there, Akemi was in good mood.

Then, at that very time, a couple of aquainted faces passed by. They were Heirich and Josef. They were there in relation to Romano's jazz concert that was going on at the hotel next to this hotel.

Heinrich [We did not expect to see all the three of you at such a place as here.]

Show Taro [Long time since then, Heinrich.]

Josef [By chance, were you able to decipher the poem in Les Centuries that you were studying previously?]

Show Taro [You mean 6-49. If we translate Mammer as the bodyguards who are looking for gold, the meaning will come out as follows. If we take the cane at the third line with curved hook as standarte, the cross is meant as that authority of church will be driven away, therefore the deciphering comes to be the following way:

1st Line　By the party of greedy bodyguards leading by grand Pope

[By the author's reading, Mammer has two meanings. Mammon (greedy) and Mameluk (body guard troops and they were not Christians.)]

2nd Line　They will conquer the Danubean area

3rd Line　By standarte with curved hook, falling cross and authority of church

4th　Line Hostages, Gold and silver treasures and jewelries that exceed 100,000 pieces

This does not necessarily refer to Hitler. It may be related to what is happening now in Eastern Europe.]

Josef　[I was talking about it with Heinrich, too, but tell me if anything else that will be happening from now on is still included in Les Centuries.]

Show Taro [Do you mean that Les Centuries may still include what did happen as stated there but can no way be proven what they are?]

Heinrich　[It will be helpful if we could decipher Les Centuries a little bit more quickly…]

Show Taro [That is more difficult that to clarify enigma.]

Josef　[Do you mean by that if it is enigma there is a possibility to break it?]

Show Taro [All codes can be broken when time comes, but Les

— 214 —

Centuries is difficult as it is a record which was put in letters what a person in 1555 saw as images using the knowledge available then only.]

Heinrich [Please tell me one such example.]

Show Taro [Regarding 5-8, these figures mean the date in 1945 of the following day after Germany surrendered.]

1st Line Those whose death was hidden by living fire will be released

2nd Line Inside of Sphere namely Globe there develops terrible misery

3rd Line At night, a group of aeroplanes changes cities into heaps of wreckages

4th Line Cities are flaming up and advantageous situation is at the side of enemy, namely, allied forces

Just to add some additional remarks to the above translation, the first line implies that Kamikaze corps started their activities covering the fact of its nothing but a suiciding act by emphacizing the honor of its duty. Next, the word Fleet used in this line in Les Centuries is not meant for navy fleet but for air fleet such as No. 5 air fleet that was stationed in Miyakonojo in Kyushu. Then the forth line describes such situation as Germany was to surrender which means tide of the war was in favor of allied forces.]

Heinrich [I feel thirsty···Show Taro, you really have an interesting deciphering ability.]

Saying so, he took a sip of the cocktail in his hand.

Josef [Won't you mind to explain more in detail?]

Show Taro [In an age when there is no word to phrase an aeroplane, and suppose on that aeroplane a symbolized mark of a rising sun was attached, they must have expressed such object as living fire. And to add another fact, though death in the war as a consequence will follow inevitably, this part of the story was never openly reported to the public. Next, talking about the earth, at that time in the whole world, death was shouted in triumph. Both Europe and Japan were filled with dead bodies. And a huge formation of bombers which could be called as air fleet continued to burn out all cities. Suppose Nostradamus had even actually sighted such a scene, more explanation than what he wrote in Les Centuries would have been difficult. He looked to have shown when what he wrote would happen by the number shown on each volume of his books and by the number marked on each psalm. Those marks were not truly put on each happening but some crue in addition to numbers is hidden. But for those who do not have ability to decipher such hints, Nostradamus psalms are a mere meaningless row of words.]

Josef   [Is there any matter that may have any relation with us that is coming to happen?]

Show Taro [Talking about that possibility, I may say that 7-14 could have some relation with us. The following may be of interest to you.]

1st Line Error on maps will be open

2nd Line Medicine box in a pot in the grave is opened

3rd Line denomination of sacred wisdom is growing further and further

4th Line Black taking place of White, New taking place of Old

Josef [As is, these sentences are hard to understand, but does Black mean fascism?]

Show Taro [In the modern world, ethnic radicalism may be more adequate.]

1st Line Due to the fact that the border partition is not based on the ethnic distribution, description on maps is deemed as incorrect.

2nd Line What this line would mean is considered as intimation or ideogram of what was cherished from the ancient times.

3rd Line If sacred wisdom or sect of philosophy is taken as the time when a sect of Isram grows its power,

4th Line Ethnic radicalism taking the place of capitalism but varied to neo and no longer returning to the traditional radicalism.

Josef [That deciphering reminds me of the present world situation.]

Show Taro [I think part of Nostradamus prophecy which is difficult to understand may be better to be treated case by case and delay deciphering separately to a later date. As regards Isram, the oil producing countries are getting powerful so speed of growth is different to each Isramic country and this tendency is also developing inside America.]

Josef [It can certainly be said that they are accepting immigrants can be paraphrased as refugees are encouraging that action.]

Show Taro [Apart from such Isramic countries, Russia also cannot

	stay away from Muslims. Likewise, in China, Muslims in the oil field work away from home to coast eventually expanding Muslim inhabited area.]
Josef	[Well, if that is the case, such situation as described in the forth line will come true, am I right?]
Show Taro	[Taking China as example, there in China while there exist Internationalists, there are Ethnic Radicalists at the other side who try to have Han Chinese monopolize each and every thing. Furthermore, at the side of Muslims there come out Muslims who aim to increase profits for Isram never minding Han Chinese.]
Josef	[Is Isram a threat?]
Show Taro	[No, Not such a thing. In relation to the first line which reads the era when the drawn borderline is wrong regardless of race or people, this modern age is the age mentioned in the first line and in this very age the matters described in the latter lines are to come up. This is the correct translation of this psalm. News about the group of people who greet each other with Nazi salute is reported in Moscow and the image color of this group is black. Likewise, Muslims often raise black flags, like in ancient Rome the color nero (black) was originally meant as a noble color.]
Josef	[Which religion was Nostradams supporting?]
Show Taro	[He was a Catholic but when he saw the future, it is supposed that he was not always bound by that position of his.]

All people listening this conversation between Show Taro and

Josef groaned. Thus, that night was getting late. They expect Show Taro further more studies of Les Centuries.

While in the meantime Romano who finished his piano concert at a hotel next to this hotel was joining them.

Romano [I was listening to you at the back of the people. Do complete deciphering such psalms that are related to Italy and have not been realized while I am still in this world.]

Show Taro [Psalms relating to Rome are not meant for prediction made for ancient Rome. For such matters that can be surely said as these are what already happened, possibility of such matters to happen from now on does remain to exist. There are several psalms in which Rome is involved but I have not been able to deciper these as yet.]

Romano [Can you see when a prophecy comes to loose its efficacy?]

Show Taro [I presume 10-74 has a relation to the time when Nostradamus' prophecies will be ceased to be effective, however, as my deciphering work has not been completed as yet, I am not in a position to tell accurate results of my deciphering. But one thing I can say now is the figure 7 is closely related.]

Romano [Won't 7 be an era number?]

Show Taro [As it is the termination of a term of an extremely big figure 7, what it means is that the term finishes its transiting⋯Suppose we take it as UN statistics of world population prospects showing the figure of some

7 billion level and up, it can be defined that such timing when world population reaches that level will be between around October, 2012 and sometime around 2020. Then, at that time, disaster will be caused both by natural calamity and by wars, consequently the world population will never have a chance to come up to the level of 8 billion so the increasing rotation of population will cease then. If this deciphering is considered as right, what will happen?]

Romano [⋯I have no word to comment⋯]

Heinrich [Do you mean that while we are still in this world⋯ doomsday will come?]

Show Taro [No, I have not yet fully finished my deciphering. But what must be noted is on the second line the psalm states time of huge scale massacre represented by the sacrifice of a hundred bulls will arrive, and on the third line, that will happen at a time near the happiest millennium. And to conclude the psalm, the forth line states the dead will revive from the grave which can be taken as a possibility of the dead to be digged out as food for use by the then alive population.]

Heinrich [If you round off what you have said, ⋯what conclusion do you arrive at?]

Show Taro [The psalm can be read as after a sharp decrease of population takes place by 2020, then for the first time an era of peace will arrive. If my deciphering is correct, the time frame between 2012 and 2020 is a rough identification of such period of time. However,

— 220 —

before an extremely big figure of No.7 is completed, which means right before the world population comes to exceed 7 billion, can be considered as the accurate time when aforementioned disaster will take place.]

Romano   [Well done. Isn't it good enough for you to have deciphered to that much.]

Show Taro   [Les Centuries loses its meaning if it is not deciphered in relation to the two matters. Most translators of Les Centuries read and write better French than I do, however, in order to be good translators, they are apt to pursue a perfected translation as the form of a psalm. If taking the preface addressed to his son Cesar written in 1555 and the letter addressed to Henry II, the King of France written in 1558 as abridgements, what is difficult to decipher is relation of the two in the whole flow of situation.]

Then at that moment, Josef who has drunk up a sip of cocktail opened his mouth.

Josef   [Viewing the situation in the whole flow of the time, the important period of time has been specified as in between 2012 and 2020.]

Show Taro   [You are correct. However, Nostradamus was not revealed in the order of matters as they occurred. He replaced what was shown to him at random and further changed these by numbers and published it as well-shaffled cards.]

Romano   [Is revelation the words of God?]

Show Taro   [It is not God but some spiritual existance. To start with, AD means Anno Domini, namely, God exists with us. Therefore, a human can no way teach his people God's teaching when it has just been born and while it cannot speak a word. When this way of thinking is taken into consideration, the meaning of year 1999 of 10-72 and the seventh month can be overlapped on that period of time.

If this year of 1999 is translated as the year since Jesus Christ started delivering God's words, as Christ was born around AD12 to 8, the words of God should have started being delivered to people about three years before that time which would come to be AD17 to 21. Therefore, with year 1999 added, the period of time would come to be 2016 to 2020. Also, as Roman calendar starts at March so it can be deciphered that the seventh month would mean the present day's September which was to be deemed as the important month. In astrology, the calendar also starts from March.]

Romano [Okay, then what will happen?]

Show Taro [If checking with the letter to Henry II, it comes an unprecedented darkness of the sun.]

Heinrich [Tell me what will come after that.]

Show Taro [Rays of the sun are blocked by something other than a solar ecripse that is caused by the moon overlapping the sun. Something happens and lithometeor or the like hides the sun with a cover.]

— 222 —

Josef   [And how long does it last?]

Show Taro [I guess three days when the sun becomes very dark as never before. There is a prophecy which was told by a German Catholic nun in the 19th Century about those three dark days.]

Josef   [Three days, I see···Incidentally, what is it that you said as 'something'?]

Show Taro [I cannot predicate what it is, but am personally thinking deviation of magnetic pole will arise in autumn and in spring in the following year, the position of magnetic pole will interchange drastically. According to the letter sent to Henry II, there comes a very long and dark solar ecripse, and in October, something will make a large scaled movement. And in spring of the following year, such unusual condition as gravity losing its original function will take place.]

Heinrich   [Tell me if that happens why such occurent results in making the earth dark?]

Show Taro [You know aurora is magnetic dust. As aurora which is created in the northern hemisphere is drawn by the huge size north pole by the name of Arctic. Therefore, if fluctuation of magnetic pole takes place for the running three days, dust thus magnetized will massively wander about in the atmosphere and if Van Allen Belt ceases to function, radioactive rays will shower on the earth and the earth will become a dangerous place.]

Romano   [Interesting···but I don't want to believe it to happen

···]

Show Taro [And, according to Maestro Nostradamus, the magnetic pole which people in the 16th century could not but phrase it as 'something' migrates and in spring on the following year a cataclysm will take place.]

Heinrich [What will happen internationally?]

Show Taro [In the order of sequence, change of the holders of supremacy will take place as a result of a major earthquake.]

Heinrich [You mean Pax Americana will be lost···interesting.]

Romano [To us, Romans, it is a good news if Pax Romana is to be reproduced.]

Heinrich [Romano is interested in ancient Roman's Meditearranean Supremacy.]

Romano [You, too, must have a strong interest in revival of SS of Third Reich.]

Heinrich [Well, well, let's esteem each other's position and toast to it.]

Romano [Agree. Anyway, shall we toast with liquer instead of English tea just to change the mood?]

Heinrich [Since the age of my father, our family keeps no alchohol, no smoking and take fish dishes rather than meat.]

Romano [In that sense, Dry Law is not really working but as regards antismoking is pretty well going under the influence of SS in America, I guess.]

Heinrch [Russia is well aware of the importance of no-smoking

— 224 —

and no-drinking.]

Romano　　[Is Russia under the SS sphere of influence, too?]

Josef　　[Ave Rome and Siegheil.]

In such a way night at the launge of the hotel was passing by. Show Taro was wondering with himself where he did not have to refer to the content of the continuation part of the letter to Henry II was a good thing or otherwise.

The Nostradamus'prophecy largely consists of two parts. The part that was completed by 1555 includes letters addressed to his son Cesar and from the first volume to 7-42, The other part is at a high possibility produced by 1558 which includes letters to Henry II and his writing of volume 8 to 10.

The latter part of preface of each volume is showing the catastrophy that is to happen in future, but for those people who do not have a key to open the hidden meanings Nostradamus' books are totally uncomprehensive. In addition, Volume 7 lacks number of psalms while other volumes are all listing one hundred psalms. This fact remains to be a big mystery and to date the reason has not been clarified. Only it is wondered whether it was due to religious persecution or intentional deletion to protect such printed books from getting lost due to time passage.

Many researchers and decoders of the prophecy of Nostradamus could read and write French far better than Show Taro. But to everyone's surprise, such a person who surely and clearly finished interpretation of the prophecy has not yet come out to the world. Therefore, it could be taken that the reason why this could not happen would be such efforts to try to get a perfect decipherment shown on the French language might have become an obstacle to get the deciphering impossible.

Perfect deciphering means for example, if one French word has five, three, four different meanings, 5x3x4=60 different ways of translation can become possible and of these 60 choices one that has the most puasuasive expression is to be selected. To raise an example, the God's Palace which is shown on his letter to his son Cesar and his statement of the decline of the earthbound palace can easily be understood by any of the modern people as loss of prestige of Church and decline of Mornarchy. On the otherhand, if the reader is a Catholic and the deeper his faith is the more difficult for such a person to find the contents of Nostradamus prophecy. And suppose this kind of situation developed in that era, such translation would automatically be removed.

The deciphering method of prophecy is similar to that of decryption of encrypted messages, once the situation changes, excepting what could definitely be said as have been completed till then, all decipherings must be considered as objects of devalidation over again. It has to be a basic routine that roll-over works must be repeated in case a world-size calamity takes place.

It also can be thought about that Nostradamus who had an expert knowledge of Latin besides French must have naturally been aware of the fact that the other languages were also available. Therefore, it is only natural to think that he must put such expression that is understandable to people in the English speaking hemisphere when he wrotes such part of statements in his book that he wished those people to decipher by reading such part in the way of reading English or French words that were replaceable to English and when this replacement is done, what he truly meant in his historical position may come to be able to be understood by those people. With his superb talent, he must have forseen that after WW1 English will completely overtake the position of French language.

Acrtual fact is, as the computerized era has come, all the programs stored in the computer are written in English. Taken it for granted that Nostradamus did now it already, it is understandable that French alone even with a perfect ability together cannot read out the modern world. Rather, those psalms that have not yet been successfully deciphered may have to be reviewed over again using languages other than French as a key for deciphering. If we presume that the research of Nostradamus and his books will develop further, it will not happen before the 21st century.

Les Centuries 3-94

The first line　People shall come to be aware after 500 years that it relates to that person

The second line　Existence of that person who was made the symbol of that era

The third line　Then what comes with a big shock is, silver lining is published and put on the screen (donrra).

The forth line　That will recover people's satisfaction of that century

Suppose this psalm is meant for Nostradamus himself, as he was born on December 14, 1503, the applicable date of the x-day can be calculated from the year 2004 onwards. In other words, whatever publicized in the form of books or played in the form of dramas will make a big hit in the world. That movies produced these days often hold the element of Nostradamus may not be unrelated to this probability. To add more, buried in the enormous uproar that arose at the end of the 20th century in line with the millennium commemoration such evaluation as that prophecy of Nostradamus does not always come true spread quite widely. For the purpose of offsetting the dissatisfaction that the supporters of Nostradamus had to experience, the forth line may have been meant for.

On that night, Nancy showed Indrajit to a hotel nearby. She took him to a suite at that hotel, and Indrajit who was seldom perturbed showed a truly surprised look. There waiting for him was a little aged Emily Brown. The two stood still for about ten seconds looking at each face as if they were confirming the time flown since they were together last time.

Indrajit   [Am I deaming!]

Emily   [Indy! I have been missing you so much!]

The two tightly embraced each other. Both of them could not stop their tear so they left it dropping down. Did God finally accept them?

Emily   [Nancy told me your whereabouts.]

Indrajijt   [Thank you, Nancy.]

Emily   [If you choose to return to America, she may help you.]

Indrajit   [What, what does she mean?]

Nancy   [I need the information that is to be exchanged with money at the back of this time's remittance program.]

Indrajit   [I can't escape from pursuit of Raja Mitra.]

Emily   [I have a program ready for your use which is you to change name and make it possible to live in America.]

Indrajit [Are you serious?]

Nancy [Sure yes, but to make this plan successful you need to cheat Kubera and Shiaku and Suzuki altogether.]

Indradit [Okay, What am I supposed to do?]

Nancy [To be honest, I am an FBI investigator. I also let Show Taro believe I am a researcher of an art insurance company.]

Indrajit [Is it true? Isn't he your man?]

Nancy [Not my man in the past though he may be my man at this moment.]

Indrajit [Women are fearful···]

He looked down but Nancy held him at his both shoulders and shook him up.

Nancy [Okay? If you will cooperate with me, you can defect to America covered by the program of American Government and live in America with a different name, with Emily.]

He looked at Emily's face and saw tears shining on Emily's cheeks.

Indrajit [So, what do I have to do?]

Then, at that time, Robert came in from the next room. Negotiation of winning Indrajit around had just begun.

Nancy [This is Robert.]

Robert [Hello, I am Robert.]

Indrajit [Thanks for meeting me.]

Robert [We are now making an investigation about the

— 229 —

remittance of a huge amount of money by the means of a check issued by Hell Computer. If you will tender your cooperation with us in this regard, American Government will be in a position to assure you of safety of you and her. This offer of ours is being made based on our confidence that a flow of something illegal exists at the back of this issue.]

Indrajit [I admit that could be the case, as we are arms dealers.]

Robert [With your admittance, may we understand you will please speak out?]

Indrajit [I am afraid there will be no way for me to escape from the pursuit by Raja Mitra.]

Nancy [If we are able to seize a physical evidence we can not only put out an interpol notice but also become able to make wholesale arrests of the instruments of Raja in America.]

indrajit [I agree···Then what can America guarantee for us?]

Nancy [America will guarantee lending of a social security number so you can live in America with a different name and safety of Emily and yourself.]

Indrajit [···I wish a little more time for me to think about your offer.]

The night was still very early and just about started.

17. Mafia's Hunch

That day started with a very fine morning. Chen and Indrajit finished the procedure for money transfer of 12.75million pounds to the European industry which is the subcontractor for processing, out of 15 million pounds that had arrived at Advanced Engineering. In compliance to the request of the bank, they attached with the remittance a purchase order issued by Hell Computer and a statement for a chemical processing equipment from the processing subcontractor. As the branch manager of the bank saw the figure of ZeDeng Mao at the back of them, he did not make any more question so the transaction at the bank was finished without any more question from the branch manager.

On the smooth completion of all such procedures Indrajit contacted Raja Mitra. There were other men who were reported in the office of the branch manager that the transaction was smoothly progressing. They were Heinrich and Josef who had come to Macao for some unknown reasons.

A few days afterwords, when the fund was being drawn out in London, there was a figure of a Chinese transport ship on the Yellow Sea.

On the shade of this ship, another shade of a ship that came from the east overlapped. This shade was the shade of steeltubes which were delivered from North Korea. There on the ocean, twelve steel tubes were transferred between the two ships. When the transfer was finished a whistle was blown and the man on the bridge was waving his arm. That man on the bridge was a man called Wang

Chao who was an instructor of the captain of that ship as well.

He was a big and fat man and looked like a hard drinker who seemed not to be able to bear the cold without taking whisky all the time. Wind was strong on the ship on the sea and the fall season was changing into winter, so it looked he could not go without taking whisky. Transaction he was to do must have finished already but he seemed to be waiting for another man whom he was expecting on the ship that was to go down to the south from then. In thirty-minute time, a white dot on the ocean appeared which came nearer and was getting bigger. When that white dot came much nearer, he confirmed an Italian flag swinging at the stern of the ship. When the ship came nearer, the name of the ship that was shown on the top of the ship could be read through a large size binocular so Wang Chao recognized it as Santa Rosalia. As it proceeded further ahead so as to be able to see the face of the person on that ship, a man came out to the bridge taking binoculars in his hand. Wang Chao confirmed him once again using his binocular and understood that was nobody but Bernard Gambino.

Wang Chao thought it was worth for him standing outside the bridge and waiting for him.

Putting Santa Rosalia alongside his ship, the two ships were sailing side by side to the south to Shanghai. Since Gambino was taken back by his companions Bernard made it his assignment to work outside Italy visiting around Mafia-related clients. There was a merit of him sailing alongside Chinese warships in order to enter the port of Shanghai, as in such case no one will have a chance to condemn entrance of his ship.

Bernard stayed at a vacation home of his acquaintance which had a yard where a yatcht could be stationed sideways for a few weeks but he could not stay there for ever as a guest. Kobe consists of towns with lots of slopes and those towns were developing on the area where the mountain skirts were joining the sea. Start of development of this area is made by Taira-no-Kiyomori who opened a port for the purpose of starting trading with China when it was called Song Dynasty. In the last days of Tokugawa Shogunate, a western style Navy Traning Center was stationed there which directly contributed to found the base of prosperity of the modern age.

As it is a usual practice of a seaport, loading and unloading works of cargos to and from a large size vessel was relying on the labor supplied by Mafia organizing system and in line with this, bars or red-light districts started development there.

As this town is where foreigners from overseas countries used to live from an early age, it is a good method of exercising to walk around old western style residences built in the era of Meiji. In addition, those visiting foreigners used to visit Kyoto guided by Japan's Yakuza (Mafia) related sightshowers and if such foreigners wished to purchase a knife such as a Japanese sword such guide used to take them to sight the manufacturing process of kitchen knives that was popularly being done in the place called Sakai.

There came a wire from Santa Rosalia to Wang Chao. It was a request for him to obtain a port entrance permit to Port of Shanghai.

As long as the promise he made with Bernard to let him eat Shanghai crab, he could not but get an extrance permit to Port of

Shanghai. He thought out a plan and succeeded in getting a special entrance permit under the name of the mayor of the City of Shanghai. He got that permit contacting the city government telling them he happened to find an Italian cruiser which was undergoing some repair work on the sea. Consequently, the cruiser was towed by a Chinese Navy warship and came alongside the birth of Shanghai.

Consequently, Bernard came to stay with Wang Chao's for some time. On that night Bernard and the other people with him was shown a mountainful Shanghai clabs which were still alive.

Wang Chao [I never thought you were truly coming only for eating Shanghai clabs.]

Bernard [But I never expected so many clabs that are good enough for all members of Santa Rosalia. Grazie.]

Wang Chao [Remember you prepared good enough quantity of grilled scampi using freshly harvested scampis to let all my fellows enjoy them? This is just a small return to your treatment then.]

Bernard [Talking about something else, what is that tower like tube which is aboard your ship?]

Wang Chao [That is a reflecton tower for a chemical factory.]

Wang Chao was trying to conceal the other business he is handling. Mafia as a business is dangerous enough by itself but on the other hand arms business with the middle east armed organization is an equally dangerous business.

Bernard [What kind of abracadabra is that swastika?]

On the tube which is disguised in a shape of refection tower the

— 234 —

trade mark of Midori Manji is marked in a big shape.

Wang Chao [In the eastern countries, manji is a pattern that espresses lucky omen.]

Bernard [Is that right?]

Wang Chao [Tommorrow, when we do a bit of sight seeing, I will show you a temple. In Asia, that mark is noting unusual at Buddism temples.]

Bernard [In Europe it is a mark of problem.]

Wang Chao [Have you been aware that Manji in Europe is written in reverse direction?]

Bernard [Oh, I see⋯]

Bernard was once convinced half way hearing this explanation, but was still wondering as he was feeling he had seen this Midori Manji that he saw that day but could not readily recall where he saw it before. He then asked the captain of Santa Rosalia but he did not know it either. However, there was one person who was the ship doctor of Santa Rosalia who did remember that mark.

Ship Doctor [When I saw it for the first time, I remember I thought it was a strange shape of trade mark. I saw it on blood preparations.]

Bernard [What is the name of that maker of which country?]

Ship Doctor [It is a Japanese company named Midori Manji.]

Bernard [Check what kind of company is that company.]

Wang Chao [Wait a second, Bernard. What of that company do you wish to know?]

Bernard [History of that company.]

Wang Chao [What for?]

— 235 —

Bernard [As I simply felt I saw that mark somewhere before.]

Wang Chao ordered his subordinate to take to him downloaded materials of Midori Manji. Looking at these materials he read part of it to Bernard.

Wang Chao [Midori Manji is one of the major blood preparations manufacturers which was established by ex-members of Specific Bacteria Operation Unit which was the former Unit 731 in WW2. The establishment fund for this company was diverted from the special accounts of American Government in order to prevent information from flowing out to Soviet.]

Bernard [What was that Unit 731 doing?]

Wang Chao [Living body testings.]

Bernard [Bacteriogical warfare···dysentery bacillus or plague bacillus?]

Wang Chao [Not those only. They used to study lethal dose of poison gas. There may have been such gas chamber as Nazi but no evidence is left whatsoever. All evidences and proofs have been taken away by American troops.]

Bernard [! ! ···I may have seen at Café Sforza? I have a feeling somebody's business card fallen on the floor or am I wrong···]

He kept thinking for a while and hit upon an idea that when those disgusting fellows wearing SS uniforms forced him to get a shot of truth drug, the label pasted on the ampule containing the drug clearly read Midori Manji. Bernard felt that Wang was trying to hide information he had of his customers and at the same time

— 236 —

instinctly felt the whole scheme of this story smells something smoldering. This feeling of his was alike the instinct of a beast to chase its game. As a boss of Mafia and also as an owner of a yachet name of which is after the patron saint of Palermo, Sicily, he was interested in this regard.

In the streets of Shanghai Wang's underlyings took around Wang and the crew of his boat for sightseeing. Wang found the same mark for sure at Buddhism temples and also at such antique shops that were selling old furniture made before WW2. At one of such antique shops, he saw a Manji mark on a peach shape food basket, so he asked the shop.

Bernard [Please tell me something.]

Shop assistant [What is it, sir?]

Bernard [Isn't this mark Swastica of Nazi?]

Shop assistant [Direction of this is the other way round. This is Manji.]

Bernard [What does Manji mean?]

Shop Assistant [Some people say it is a sign of long life and good luck motif and with Lamaism, it is meant for the virtue of the sun.]

Bernard [What does virture of the sun mean?]

Shop assistant [The sun gives warmness which is just good for one person regardless of whether that person is rich or poor. In other words, it means fairness.]

Bernard [And the reverse of that is Nazi⋯I see. Very educational information. Thank you.]

Shop assistant [You are welcome.]

Bernard thought he had heard a very interesting talk. In Europe they never teach the original meaning of such word so people cannot but come to conclude it as something like a taboo to touch. They are not really wanting to know about it and no one will teach people what it really means. Secret why Bernard made a success in the world of Mafia is because he was of a character to show interest in whatever minor things that seem not to count much. After all, what makes difference between life and death can be just a very slight difference.

Thus, that day ended but he was still attracted by the tube shape chemical reflection tower which was unloaded onto the quay. He had his underlings make investigation and obtained a copy of the invoice that was attached to the tower. He felt a bit quilty to Wang but he proceeded his own investigation about this matter. Besides the invoice, he also obtained information of arrival of China made equipment of a similar device

18. Birthing Cargo Ship Cossak

The cargo ship Cossak finally arrived from Nakhodka. Bernard had been reported by his underlings that this cargo ship was to go to Perth In Australia via Singapore. The ship owner was Vladimir Molotov, a Russian. Bernard thought Nicola would be quicker to gather information about this man so he placed a call to Nicola Zamir in New York.

Bernard	[Long time no see, Nicola, This is Bernard.]
Nicola	[I see you have made a escape safely. By the way, don't tell me you are still not in Italy?]
Bernard	[No, I'm in China. By the way, I need information about Vladimir Molotov. Will you please tell me all what you know about him?]
Nicola	[He is working as political merchant with regards army related goods and automobile components.]
Bernard	[What of those is he dealing?]
Nicola	[Just as what I just told you. That is all he handles.]
Bernard	[Selling on Black Market of the equipment of Army's possession, I see.]
Nicola	[Well, that is possible, too. It was he who used to export Russian icons to Europe for one period from the 1990s to the 2000s.]
Bernard	[Did he capture icons from churches?]
Nicola	[There were captured goods as results of religious oppression. He captured such goods with an excuse that the churches who were the original possossors of

— 239 —

	the icons were gone and sold them through illegal routes.]
Bernard	[Were there any other obvious movements?]
Nicola	[He sold a military helicopter to a Japanese religious cult. He is also rumored to be involved in selling negotiation of submarine which was scheduled to be dismantled.
Bernard	[He certainly doesn't seem to be an ordinary guy.]
Nicola	[His work behaviors are not so rough. He would rather be an intellectual crime.]
Bernard	[Any other information about him?]
Nicola	[That is all.]
Bernard	[Grazie.]

As might be expected, at the hand of Nicola, information on the international underground organizations are well accumulated, however, under the present circumstances the information Bernard gathered from Nicola could not be taken as something that has any incidentality.

Export procedures had already been in progress. Bernard made an investivation of this sample case, camouflaging it as a field visit, to examine what was being done there. If quality of the export control being done by China, it could work as a hint for a smooth smuggling. Even if he may be professional as regards smuggling, it was absolutely necessary that he prepares a manual so all of his underlyers must be trained to bring out the same successful result, otherwise nothing will grow to a big business. By putting a big container on the fluoroscopic apparatus, inside of the container can be examined saving to open up the cartons stored in the container.

The relative documents stated that the contents of the container was parts of autobikes. In line with the statement on the documents, being put in the fluoroscopic apparatus, there were vaguely recognized silensers or such parts as exhaust pipes. Bernard reckoned it was what it should be. To the countries which are equipped with such device, it is impossible to export living humans packed in a container, but as he recalls it, Chen Jin Ji was making export of women from inland China his main export item, which may mean that somewhere at some ports such equipment had not been prepared as yet.

The next container was attached with an invoice addressed to Midori Manji India. Confirming the contents through X-ray, a few corn shaped objects and some objects that were covered by comlecatedly netted tubes. Bernard was looking at these with interest wondering if those were the device to accerelate the reaction of chemical products.

Bernard [This one is for the factory of the world's know chemical manufacturer's, isn't it.]

Officer [These days, even the top class companies are ordering from China regardless of the kind.]

Bernard [What exactly do you mean by that?]

Officer [Things that we have never seen before are passing through the customs.]

All of sudden he seemd to have lost interest in his present assignment and turned round to Bernard.

Officer [As regards things that no one ever has seen, if you are told this is what this is, that's the end of the discussion.]

— 241 —

Bernard	[Tell me a bit more about what you mean.]
Officer	[For instance, if something with a shape of a tank is seen, any one that saw it would become aware that it would be arms products. However, if those are a new weapon it can happen they are apt to overlook it. I understand you are dealing import and export of art objects. In your art business, you may be cheated with a fake of a type that you have never seen before, but after a while it became popular on the market, then no one will be cheated again. This case is the same as what is going on here at the moment.]
Bernard	[Do you have any example that happened recently?]
Officer	[Do you know Meissen Pagoda doll made in China?]
Bernard	[Yes, I have seen such.]
Officer	[That was developed by a certain dealer in Jingdezhen for the purpose of selling it on Japanese antique markets. To explain, they create mold from the real doll and use the mold till it is used out and broken which means production of about 200 and a few more dolls. And when they finish selling all the quantity produced, that's it and they end the sale.]
Bernard	[Then, what will happen?]
Officer	[At the beginning all are easily cheated, as the price is even less than $10,000 which if bought at the auction in Europe it would be as much as $20,000. And after a while the buyer remembers he saw the same doll at that place, too, etc. If this is rumored, careful buyers stop touching it. Then the dealer drops the price down

— 242 —

	to about $6,000 and so on and to close the sale they clear the stock selling them at about $1,000.]
Bernard	[Is that still a profitable business to the dealer?]
Officer	[Annual income of a Chinese is only a few thousand dollars. If several hundred dollars can be earned per doll, that money will be good enough to lead a do-nothing easy life for a while. If the business meets the targeted balance, it can be a paying business.]
Bernard	[Have any other fakes gone through this port?]
Officer	[It was several years ago. Fake Antique Baccarat was shipped out of this port for France.]
Bernard	[Was that meant for a sale in France?]
Officer	[I guess so.]
Bernard	[Neatly gift-packed?]
Officer	[Those were packed in China made box printed made in China.]
Bernard	[Didn't Baccarat France make a fuss about those?]
Officer	[As those fakes were sold at flea markets to antique dealers coming from overseas, it seems to have escaped the eye of French Authorities.]
Bernard	[How could it happen?]
Officer	[Fledgling and simple Japanese or American antique dealers must have bought those fakes easily trusting as offered by French dealers so no one that bought the fakes ever filed a police report. This means the fakes were made at the level that professionals could not easily distinguish the difference. Or saying more about it, even with fakes, if number of people start copying

— 243 —

and reproducing those fakes it can ultimately happen that fakes takes the place of authentic glasses.]

Bernard [How could such a thing come to be possible?]

Officer [Especially of Japanese antique dealers, there are young dealers who scarcely exercise such work as to purchase and face a book and spend their efforts to study such materials. Few young Japanese dealers possess French dictionary.]

Bernard [Wow, your talk was very interesting. Thanks a lot.]

The officer who was deep in talk with Bernard turned around to him and stamped the inspection stamp on the documents nearby him in a very casual manner. Observing that the officer did not even check the documents and put the stamp only because the documents were carrying the name of a major welknown company, Bernard thought that for such large and trustworthy company, customs clearance is very easy at all times, though this is also the same in Italy. When in Italy Bernard tries to make export declaration as an owner of a small enterprise, the officer in charge of him gets very meticulous about his documentations and any other related things but once the officer comes to notice he is a Mafia, he changes his attitude and issues the permit obediently. Large beings always seize more advantageous position.

A few days later, the Russian cargo boat Cossac entered the port. In an effort not to waste the fee for rent of the berth, unloading and onloading works were handled efficiently in a short time. In only a few hours time, the work was complete and Cossac sailed out for the next destination, Singapore.

19. Chasing by Santa Rosalia

Wondering where to go to seek something interesting to do there, Bernard was checking the information about Phuket in Thailand for his potential next visiting place. He was feeling awkward to continue to be the guest of Wang Chao. China was a place where it might shut its border line out in accordance with the convenience of the Government's spec. In this regard, that he had as his own transportation means the large cruiser Santa Rosalia worked as a handy means to sail out anytime he wished to move. He sailed to south alongside the coast and was then passing by the open sea of Hue in Vietnam. Bernard fixed a large binocular on the deck and was enjoying tropical cocktail. The moisture-laden wind blowing in the southern country gave such sticky feeling just being there, but slight intoxication could help him forget that discomfortable feeling.

There in Ho Chi Minh before Bernard reached Phuket in Thailand there was casino which was operated by a Mafia family with whom Bernard had been dealing with before Vetinum War. As the head of that family once came to Sicily in the past, Bernard started thinking to stay there a while and play casino. He was thinking women in Vietnam might be as cute and nice as those in Hong Kong.

While he was meditating such this and that, his cell phone rang. Amount of information that could be obtained while sailing alongside the coast was definitely more than when sailing offshore.

The caller was Nicola Zamir, his customer in New York. Bernard kept giving him a suggestion to change a direction of his business

— 245 —

and start sales of drugs but those days since sales of stolen paintings drastically decreased their association was getting scarce in comparison to the past. As Nicola and his group were transacting diamond, they might not be too keen to start anything new which had its own risk.

Bernard   [Ciao! How many kilos do you want?]

Nicola   [Reason of this call is not for that. Bernard, I have a request.]

Bernard   [What is it? Tell me the details.]

Nicola   [I want you to chase the Russian cargo ship, Cossac.]

Bernard   [What for?]

Nicola   [That ship left Singapore a few hours ago but the strange thing about it is Cossac did not discharge one of their container loads that hold cargos addressed to Midori Manji and parts of automobiles.]

Bernard   [What does that mean?]

Nicola   [That vessel was schedulled to stop at Perth after Singapore, but I found out those cargos I mentioned was not listed on cargo booking at the port of Perth.]

Bernard   [Such is a daily occurance in Italy.]

Nicola   [Don't get crossed. Who knows your first impression of some smouldering smell could be to the point.]

Bernard   [In Ho Chi Minh City of Vietnam there is a casino which used to be meant for use by American troops. I was planning to gain a sum   ···Are you ready to fill what I may fail to gain by gambling there?]

Nicola   [What you mean is as in any case you will loose there so you will remit the money lost to me with your

— 246 —

gratitude?]

Bernard [HaHaHa···You have never changed. I will contact you later.]

Nicola [I will make fuel and food ready for you, so load these in Singapore.]

Bernard [Roger.]

Finishing the talk, Bernard told the captain to change the destination.

Bernard [Hi, I have cancelled the Cashino visit. Change to steer for Singapore!]

Captain [Okay.]

Santa Rosalia chased the cargo ship straight, but the delay which was aleady produced is quite much. However, as Nicola relayed part of information gained by the military reconnaissance satellight, this pursuit drama could be well performed. The cargo vessel was passing by Malacca Strait with a slow speed. Speed of Bernard's pleasure boat was getting over the waves at 25 knots.

From then onward low-pressure area moves on Indian Ocean. This change of weather condition became the reason of delaying the originally expected time lapse from when the meeting was open till when on and off loading works were executed, however, Bernard and his people were not aware of this developing weather situation.

When they arrived in Singapore, Santa Rosalia received a contact from a pilot boat to the effect that the onloading work of the necessary supplies was to be done without letting Santa Rosalia arrive at the Singapore port. What does Cossac relate to after all? Sometimes Zamir became enthusiastic about matters of no

— 247 —

significance. Bernard used to this habit of Zamir but that was creating some dissatisfaction in his mind. Therefore, that he who was still being seeked by Italian Government on the interpole notice then changed from being chased to chase gave him a half-way satisfaction.

Accorditing to weather forecast, Indian Ocean was to expect rough weather. This is bad news as following the season of Shanghai crabs, season in Singapore was just about to go into the season when the winter cuisine sautéed mud crab came to approach the high time of the best seasonal dish. MuLoLood crab is one kind of blue crabs. The cuisine guide book Bernard was reading told him Japanese enjoy this crab by taking it from the pan on the fire but Bernard wished to take it as sateed with strong fire with vegetables in the Chinese cooking style. Imagining this cooking style, Bernard was driveling.

Bernard thought it was about time to let Nicola owe him something. With this thought, he rang Nicola up.

Bernard　　[As someone uses me like his slave, I missed out the chance of having mad crab.]

Nicola　　[What at all do you mean by that?]

Bernard　　[I am talking about a crab which is harvested in the sea near Singapore. If it is sateed it produces juice and changes to a very delicious cuisine.]

Nicola　　[You can eat such a food any time no probem?]

Bernard　　[Nicola, you never know what I mean. Epiculeans close their shops just for going out to get it.]

Nicola　　[Sounds crazy.]

— 248 —

Bernard	[Epicurism is it.]
Nicola	[What do you want.]
Bernard	[When this is done, you are to prepare for me permit for birthing at casino and the best room at the casino hotel.]
Nicola	[Okay.]
Bernard	[Understandable, aren't you. You're what you should be.]

When the line was cut, Bernard prepared a few of lures. Going through Maracca, Indian Ocean would be just in front of him.

Perhaps at this chance he might wish to fish marlin and have it cooked in Carpaccio. He might be able to have it cooked into Sushi which as he heard was the most favourite food of Japanese. Taking this chance, why not enjoy food materials other than what he had took into the boat, otherwise purpose of leading a happy life would be lost. Bernard is a man that knows how to enjoy his life.

20. Double Cross

Indrajit confirmed arrival of remittance and then started contacting Wang Chao for delivery arrangements. The hotel he regularly stayed was an Singaporian hotel 『Santa Lucia』. Kubera had a need to patrol the jewelry shops he operates so he had flown to America already being absent from Santa Lucia, which was convenient for Indrajit.

Though the majority of shares of this Santa Lucia Hotel was held by India, Raja Mitra was also a large share holder. Santa Lucia which is used as the name of this hotel came after the name of a saint in Catholicism. This name is also sung in Naples folk song, Santa Lucia. Raja Mitra was not making Santa Lucia as his patron saint, but as said as 『See Naples and then die』 , he was wishing to own his summer house in Naples some day and to enjoy yatching there from time to time.

He was naming himself as Mitra which originally was the name of the principal image of Mithraism and was the object of veneration. Mitra knew well that Mithra means light, therefore, he had a special feeling towards Naples where Santa Lucia which also means light was made Naples' patron saint.

At the façade of the hotel, white marble pillars were making a row which reminded ancient Roman temple. The concept of the construction of that hotel was fusion of Pompeii, the paradise of ancient Roman city, with an elegant winter resort of 19th century's lives of nobles. One thing Singapore was missing was a scenic and slightly elevated peninsula from where view of setting sun could be enjoyed. However, the orange orchard was giving out a strong aroma as if it were the model of Paradise on Earth.

And at this hotel one automobile was parked sideways, and Nancy got off escorted by a doorboy. Off from the front assistant's seat Robert came out and after looking around showed an okay sign, then Emily came out. They moved to the lobby and told respective names to the front desk and checked in the hotel.

At around the same time, a taxicab which was taking Show Taro and Maria arrived and finished check-in. However, those who were to be staying at that hotel were Show Taro, Maria and Nancy only and Robert was carefully going to stay at a different hotel. If something should happen, he thought this hotel might not be safe for him to stay.

This party had selected junior suite respectively so each suite had a small salon. Robert entered the room where Nancy and Emily were seizing and was receiving an explanation as to how Nancy was negotiating.

Nancy   [I have briefly finishied preparation work for presentation of the information to American Embassy.]

Robert   [By what you say preparaton work do you mean the contrivance to help Emily and Indrajit out from this environment provided the arrangement you are making works satisfactorily?]

Nancy   [Yes, exactly.]

Robert   [Do you think Indrajit will take our offer on presentation of our conditions?]

Nancy   [That's why I took Emily with me. She is our ace up our sleeve.]

— 251 —

Robert   [Okay, then won't you show me copy of the documents that are to be sent out from American Embassy.]

Nancy   [Here it is.]

Robert took a look at the documents that Nancy was fabricating. Those documents were such as follows.

The addressee of the documents is made as FBI Secretary.

According to Indrajit, the remitter this time was an armed organization in Middle East and complying to their request, twelve antiship missiles were scheduled to be produced for the purpose of occupying the entrance of Persian Gulf. Regarding the supply of warheads, it was to come from a trading firm that was owned by a Russian businessman, Vladimir Molotov. Those warheads were re-birth goods changing part of the Soviet's old-fashioned warhead. Profit that will be gained from this deal is planned to be used as contribution money for use of a candidate of the next president of Russia, but whether this news is true or not was unknown at that stage.

Then, those 12 warheads were to be loaded on the cargo ship Cossac from Nakhodka. A Shanghai person by the name of Wang Chao was to purchase the main body of missiles made in North Korea and at the arms factory of Chinese People's Revelation Army, propulsion mechanisms were to be manufactured. These when completed were to be loaded on Cossac at Shanghai Port and the final destination on the invoice was to Midori Manji India Factory in Mumbai, India. Mistery there was that Cossac did not discharge one container out of several containers that contained automotive parts. They did not discharge another container that contained missile related goods, either. In truth, contents of this undischarged container which was supposed to contain automotive parts contained disassembled parts of assault rifles.

On the way to Perth, Australia, that cargo vessel was to meet up at Macara on which General Omar who was a leader of the disguised armed organization was riding. And there, two Missiles were taken by the side of Indrajit and transferred the two to SS African Troops. The balance of ten missiles and assault rifles were to be transferred to General Omar on Macara. When this meeting was over, Cossac was sailing down to the south for Perth, but whether Macara might sail to Pakistan or to Iran was unknown. Only what was known about Macara was it was a disguised cargo ship and armed.

Missiles of that time were reported with normal warheads, however, all depended on how many weapons could be gathered from over the world. It was also possible that nuclear warheads might be disguised as normal. Reason of this suspicion was the declared price was extraordinarily high and if in case what was called by the name of Gorgon, possibly, would meet description of those warheads. Also, there might be such purpose as to prevent possible resale by betrayers. It was said that suppose Gorgon was meant for the code number of V5 or V6, it was a missile that could mount nuclear warhead and such warhead could be detached and used as a nuclear bomb.

Also, that meeting point was exactly the same sea area that was called Navarone as the code used by Japanese Navy. In the history, it was the spot where Subhas Chandra Bose who was sent by U180 of Nazi Germany changed the vessel to Submarine I-29 of Japanese

Navy. He participated in WW2 in Battle of Imphalas taking several thousand Indian soldiers as the supreme commander of Indian National Army at the side of Axis powers. At that time, the grandfather of Indrajit also joined this war as an officer.

After the war was over, he was tortured as a partner of Japan, but after India made its independence in 1947, soldiers of Indian National Army received kind treatment and made an object of national pension system. As regards Sushas Chandra Bose, he was reported dead at the crush of the plane he was riding that fell down and fired on Songhan Airport in Taiwan, however, his grandfather told Indrajit he met Bose in person at least several times after the war was over.

To add more, that ocean area was where Indian Navy independently set up a regulation as no trespassing area so that no visa were to be issued. The original inhabitants there would never approach that ocean area either, believing that area was a place of African earlier settlers. For this reason, Indrajit himself had not been there at all.

The boss of Indrajit was a person called Raja Mitra. With him Indrajit got aquainted at the race of Indy500. This boss was a member of Hell Computer working team and was in charge of accounting. His grandfather came from a family of a feudal lord and for this reason he studied in U.K. but later he joined Nazi in France. After that, this grandfather of his never returned to India nor becoming an officer of Indian Colonial Army but joined Nazi SS Free Indian Legion as an officer there.

As the above was what Indrajit told when he was intoxicatd, it might not be too reliable.

He was a favorite of Himmler so was sent to the utmost front of the war at the invation of Normandy which is his first experience to be stationed at the utmost front. This SS Free Indian Region consisting of 2000 soldiers fought protecting Hitler Youth which was called by The Allied Forces Baby Region and as a result it is said some 600 could safely escape. Among those 600, there was the grandfather of Raja Mitra.

By change, Mitra is meant for Mithraism which was worshipped in ancient Rome. This religion worships light. It is also called as Mithra and this is the reason why he was called Lucifer (a bringer of light) by Christians. Indrajit had heard Raja Mitra had some connection with SS Free Indian Region in India and had understood from the butler that he had received for several times people who were wearing the SS uniform. He was also taught that the original model of medium-range nuclear missile which India was developing came from the SS developing weapon called V6.

Regarding Hell Computer, in the past, Indrajit was participating as a mechanic in the racing team that belonged to Hell Computer. CFO at that time of Hell Computer who was in charge of the racing team and who happened to come from Toronto in Canada so Indrajit could gain the job with them by this CFO's favor. Since then relationship with this CFO with Indrajit kept continuing such as borrowing his sleeping bank account. Indrajit was just borrowing his account and nothing more, but whether Hell Computer itself knew about it or not was totally out of Indrajit's knowledge.

Regarding Emily, she happened to stay at a room next to his at the hotel when she was there as a campagne girl of a promotion program.

Emily Brown then was one of the successful realtors in Chicago but agreed to get married with Indrajit abandoning her ongoing business if he could naturalize himself in America.

Indrajit and Emily were in the process of applying for an extradition of refugee in exchange of tendering their cooperation to American Government.

FBI Investigater Nancy Franchetti

To Robert who was reading the documents besides Nancy, she cracked a smile.

Robert   [Will America move with this information only?]

Nancy   [I am now doing an adjusting work with American Embassy.]

Robert   [How do you feel about possibility of their acceptance?]

Nancy   [If we can stop Maccara and can make an inspection of it, they will clearly know what we say is a real fact.]

Robert   [And what will happen?]

Nancy   [I think American Government will move to accept asylum application. We hold the information which includes what even the U.K. intelligence could not dig out. Or, do you choose to send an enquiry to Scotland Yard?]

Robert   [No, no, That's good enough. In addition, Emily is an American and you both want to live in mid-west which is good. As many Indians are involved in IT related industries, there may be a risk of Raja Mitra comes to find them, but dressing-up of hot-rod will be a safe business, I believe.]

Indrajit   [Thank you.]

| Emily | [I am so glad that he has a marketable skill. We should be alright even if I give my realtor business up forgetting about the annual income of $300,000.] |

While they were talking that way, they realized some people were coming to them. Robert opened the door and let two men come in.

| Robert | [Welcome. We are expecting you here.] |

| Nancy | [Indy, These gentlemen are Joe, American Ambassador and Henry, the military attache.] |

| Joe | [I'm advising you that acceptance of the Secretary of the State was obtained subject to the conditions that there is no lie in the Duty of Disclosure and you must not leak even a word of this agreement for the coming twenty years. And, at this time you ought to cooperate with American Navy. If you agree to these conditions, we will proceed to get this asylum program applied.] |

| Indrajit | [Yes, I will cooperate but please tell us how.] |

| Henry | [You are to come with us. After one hour from now, you are to ride on a helicopter at American Embassy.] |

| Indrajit | [Me alone?] |

| Henry | [Till this strategy is completed, we ask Nancy to guard Emily.] |

| Nancy | [Okay. Incidentally, Robert goes together this time, doesn't he. Only he can get information through Nicola.] |

| Henry | [Robert, please come with us.] |

| Robert | [My pleasure.] |

| Indrajit | [Please take care of Emily.] |

Nancy   [I'm not the only one. You don't have to worry as Show Taro and Maria are also watching her staying at the same hotel. Maria is a medium and Show Taro can also tell what's going to happen by his own deductive method.]

Emily   [Please take care. I am waiting with my fingers crossed.]

Nancy rang Show Taro and Maria and they came out from respective rooms they were staying.

Show Taro [get a grip. Good luck.]

Indrajit, who had Show Taro's tap on the shoulder, nodded.

Robert   [Okay, Now I am borrowing your fiancé, Miss Emily.]

Emily   [Do watch yourself.]

Indrajit [For sure I will come back to you.]

Joe   [Now, shall we leave.]

Henry   [Mr. Indrajit, Is this all the luggage you take?]

Emily   [Yes, it is.]

Henry, the resident military officer, received one suitcase and dragging it he showed the party to the embassy car. While they were shifting by that car Robert threw a question to Indrajit.

Robert   [Mr. Indrajit, I have a question.]

Indrajit [What is it?]

Robert   [According to what I gathered from Nancy, Subas Chandra Bose did not die in Japan. Is it true?]

Indrajit [According to what I heard from my grandfather, he fabricated a story as if he were returning to his country from Japan via Soviet, but in realty, he seems to have gone to China by a fishing boat.]

— 258 —

Robert	[According to my grandfather's interview with American Army, he understood Bose died by plane crush in Taiwan and was cremated there. Was it not the case?]
Indrajit	[That person who died was a different Indian. Japanese Press did not confirm it by photos, or, more exactly, did not let it confirmed by photos.]
Robert	[Yah, That's what happened.]
Indrajit	[Talking about Yoshiko Kawashima, the Manchuria Royalty, the only evidence of her death was a photo taken by a western cameraman which was showing her damaged face that was unable to be discriminated as hers or else as the damage was so much.]
Robert	[And in realty, she was alive with a different name.]
Indrajit	[Half of the ashes of Bose which had been kept in Japan was sent to a grandson of Bose who was a professor of an American university. The grandson had the ashes put through a DNA test but the result of test could not evidence the ashes were his. Look, what was the reason why the body must have been cremated using a substantial fire power when there were scarcely no such strategic materials as petroleum in Japan at that time?]
Robert	[In order to make verification impossible of that was truly his body?]
Indrajit	[Exactly. In addition, people who could verify at that time that Indrajit died by accident was officers only of Japanese Imperial Army. Army officers cannot say

— 259 —

	anything but Yes if ordered by their superiors. Isn't it right, Henry?]
Henry	[Yes.]
Indrajit	[To add more, After WW2 America used to have expectations to let U.K. release their colonies as markets for use of America. Therefore, even if America should know this fact, there was a big possibility of America keeping silence to U.K. You know America itself was originally a colony of U.K. before its independence.]
Robert	[You are quite right.]
Indrajit	[And, That America itself is going to get polarized against communists' Soviet after WW2 as the leader of liberal countries is a clearly logical situation to come.]
Robert	[That fact had already been recognized by American soldiers.]
Indrajit	[And that was the reason why General Patton offered his opinion reorganizing the surrendered Nazi German Troops and letting them attack Soviet further up to Moscow, am I right?]
Robert	[I have heard about that story before.]
Indrajit	[Regarding the plan to have the U.K. colony released as markets for use of America , as long as America knew how much natural resources U.K. procured from India during WW2, it is a quite natural consequence.]
Robert	[Nevertheless, America may not be happy if India becomes communized.]
Indrajit	[What Subas Chandra Bose aimed at was Indian

— 260 —

independence from U.K. and to achieve this aim, they had to convene remnants of Indian National Army that was cooperating with SS Inida Brigade or Japan. Fundamentally, they were not communists of Soviet or China. Talking about the color of their politics, color of the axis powers is black and not red. The historical significance of WW2 is the fall of world empires such as U.K. or France that used to master the seven seas and the fact that the two super powerful countries of America and Soviet were changed from inward countries to outward countries. Along with this change, colonies were opened to America for its market.]

Robert [I quite agree with you, but that was not the matter which I could judge.]

After this conversation, Robert and Indrajit went to American Embassy and from there they were carried by helicopter and landed on the American Navy destroyer called Sharon.

There, they were taken to the bridge where they greeted Richard Halison, the captain. They were his one more work on his way back from Persian Gulf.

Captain [This vessel is pretty old but that much more machine guns are loaded so it is highly suited for inspection and seizure. I would expect your cooperation.]

The man of the sea extended his big palm and shook hands with the two who came aboard his destroyer.

Captain [Will you determine the present position of a cruiser which is pursuing the cargo vessel?]

Robert　　[Yes, I will contact Nicola right away.]

While they were talking, Indrajit was shown to an officer's cabin guided by a sailor.

Dawson　　[I am told by the captain to take care of you. Please call me Dawson.]

Indrajit　　[Okay, then please give me some water. And, can you tell me the birth date of the captain?]

Dawson　　[Just a moment. I will bring water for you. By the way, may I ask you why you ask such a question?]

Indrajit　　[As I have ample time to kill, I think I may use my Tarot Cards. If you like, shall I tell your fortunre?]

Dawson　　[Well, if you say so⋯]

Saying so, he wrote his birth date and the birth date of Captain Harrison which he remembered as a birthday party for Captain was held on the vessel

Dawson　　[I'm now getting water for you.]

As the sailor left him, he took the tarot cards out. While he was creating holoscope, Dawson came back with water.

Dawson　　[Excuse me.]

Indrajit　　[Do you wish to stay here and watch what I do?]

Dawson　　[Don't you mind if I stay here?]

Indrajit　　[I will firstly tell your fortune.]

Having said so, he started to try to tell his fortune. Result came out after about ten minutes.

Indrajit　　[As the fortune of you, Mr. Dowson is not good from now for about a month, but if you surpass this bad period, your married life will go well again⋯but one thing I can see is you will have a baby before your wedding day.]

Dawson [Yeah! As you say, we have had a baby so we plan to hold a wedding celemony when I return on the land home at this time. What a surprise that you can tell such matter!]

Indrajit [At present I have the cards of the 20th century only so with these cards I cannot tell you any more details, but I did tell fortunes of several Indy500 racers using these cards. In any case, your fortune is told on those cards especially for the first one week from today, therefore, you should refrain from taking the first move even if you receive an order to do so⋯if it is a fire alert, you had beter not go up to the deck.]

Dawson [Thank you for your advise. By the way what about the fortune of Captain Harrison?]

Indrajit [That I will do from now on, but I will tell the result directly to Captain in person.]

Then, Indrajit started to tell Captain Harrison's fortune and got a result which told him Captain's fortune would be the worst during the coming month which would be even worse than that of Dawson. Indrajit prior to boading this vessel had known that a change of his fortune would be coming and also his intuition had told him that several people whom he first met on Sharon were haunted by black shadow. That was the reason why he decided to tell Captain Harrison's fortune. Looking at the groomy look of Indrajit, Dawson asked him timidly.

Dawson [Will anything bad happen?]

Indrajit [Have you ever joined a sea battle?]

— 263 —

Dawson	[Not yet, but my skill of handling machine gun is outstanding.]
Indrajit	[The coming battle will be a battle of ancient Rome.]
Dawson	[Of ancient Rome? What type of war is it?]
Indrajit	[Do you know about the war tactics used when the navy troops of ancient Rome conquered the sea troops of Carthago?]
Dawson	[No, Not really.]
Indrajit	[They fought by striking the body of the enemy galley with the prow of their vessel or while sailing in parallel they throw a bridge over to the enemy's vessel through which warriors rode on the enemy's vessel and fought there.]
Dawson	[That is a scene of a historical spectacle.]
Indrajit	[You should not apply for the storming members.]
Dawson	[Why not?]
Indrajit	[I can see the result. Even if the battle would end with victory at our side, Sharon shall not perfectly survice the enemy's attack.]
Dawn	[You must be saying a fire will take place on Sharon.]
Indrajit	[As the enemy is also disguised. They are also on a cargo vessel so it is not very clear to me but they are armed people···and···you will see a ghost.]
Dawson	[Ghost? We are now in the 21st century, aren't we.]
Indrajit	[My Tarrot Cards tell me Captain Harrison shall be finished off by a ghost···Keep it very sure in your mind that the enemy is invisible but close in on you people excerting a magic power.]

— 264 —

Dawson [So, is the enemy something not of this world?]

Indrajit [You will encounter an enemy that is protected by something that is not of this world.]

Indrajit realized what he felt about Captain Richard Harrison who was standing on the bridge when Indrajit got aboard the ship. Therefore he became quiet. He then understood the fortune of several sailors and that groomy thought became overwhelming him.

This is what can be said about intuitive people. Such people when they are aboard a ship which is going to sink often see week fortune on many people on that ship. It goes without saying that those who go out of such a ship before it sails out shall not loose their lives. This is the same for travels by airplane. However, what often happens is people whose lifelights are about to vanish will gladly take a cancelled seat and think they are lucky enough to be able to get that seat and then end to be killed by an accident never knowing it is a ticket to go to the hell. Similar cases keep happening in the modern world so that here the author wishes to add a true story that he knows about.

This case took place several ten years ago. A man who was working at a major company got appendicitis and became impossible to make a scheduled business trip to Europe. His superior took his place and flew to Europe and on his way back to Japan he encountered Korean Airlines Flight 902. This case was the Korean jet passengers flight which mistakenly deviated from the set air route was shot by a Soviet battle plane and was forced to land. At that time, that subsidiary man who happened to be seated at that particular seat was shot and the one bullet of the machine gun penetrated him from the upper side of his back down to his abdomen which killed him instantly.

This case was a sudden change decided close to the departure date so the same ticket was used only by rewriting the passenger name. In other words, that particular seat was the place of death and as a consequent the man who got appendicitis could escape from the hand of the reaper and his superior who substituted him was caught by the reaper.

Should the subsidiary man have had some good fortune, he might have gone to the men's room in the plane and might have been chatting with a cabin attendant, then his life might have been saved. Human fortune can largely change with a slight change of chances. In addition, no one can see what can be called lucky till the result of such course of action becomes complete.

At Nancy's request, Maria and Show Taro kept being at the side of Emily and in the meantime, Maria was asked to tell the fortune of Emily and Indrajit. As Show Taro could not join Maria, he kept silence and just kept watching but he was strongly interested in what Maria would see in their fortunre. Nancy was on the other hand interested in watching how Show Taro would react to what Maria would see.

Maria [Indrajit will face a big difficulty.]

Emily [What can you see?]

Maria [The original meaning of Macara is a mysterious fish which is used as a symbol of Kama's flag.]

Show Taro [My understanding is Kama is God of Love in the Indian mythology⋯]

Maria [Macara is to sink with the battle with Sharon or even if it can barely escape it cannot escape from the

	storm.]
Emily	[Indy is coming back, isn't he.]
Maria	[Well⋯]
Emily	[What can you see?]
Maria	[The eyes of the ocean⋯Amazones?]
Show Taro	[She looks like seeing something.]
Maria	[Sharon will send as its name many things⋯]

And then, Maria fainted. Nancy brushing her chestnut hair upward and looked at Show Taro.

Nancy	[What is it all about?]
Show Taro	[In Greek mythology, Sharon is the ferryman of the river Acheron which flows between this world and that world.]
Nancy	[And that means?]
Show Taro	[Means damage will be caused to Sharon, too, ⋯ Amazones means woman warrior, but why eyes of the sea, I wonder.]
Emily	[Will he come back?]
Show Taro	[I am not too sure, but I can see Macara is not a common cargo vessel⋯]
Nancy	[So it would mean the one vessel Sharon would not be enough. I will contact Henry at the embassy.]

Show Taro instinctly felt that Maria saw something not good so he sunk in thought.

21. Reloading on the Ocean

At the meeting point called Abalon the cargo vessel Cossac had already been mooring, however, as the sea was raging the transferring vessel Macara did not yet arrive there. Macara was struggling to proceed against a storm in a raging sea. The crests of waves were continuously breaking against Macara as if they were trying their utmost to swallow the monstrous fish Macara.

In the Abalon ocean area, SS African troops put a boat on the ocean before the cyclone grew bigger and by that boat several technical officers boarded Cossac. They took out the designated warhead checking against the technical documents which they received from the admiral and shifted it into the specially devised container and joined it to the main body. The cylindrical body marked by the company emblem of Midori Manji was new to them so some of them mistook it as Harken Kreuz for a second.

Military Engineer A [From when did Harken Kreuz become green color?]

Technical Officer [Take a good look at it. This is Manji and is the trade mark of a pharmaceutical company called Midori Manji.]

Military Engineer A [Sorry, As I have read only historical magazines⋯]

Military Engineer B [This size is for sure not the anti-ship missile of 200 km range.]

Technical Officer [Complete setting as per procedure manual and drop it on the sea.]

— 268 —

Military Engineer B [Roger.]

The overcasting way of the cloud was just right so they could proceed the work without caring about the military reconnaissance satellite of the major countries.

In this way, the container which contained two missailles was made floating on the sea, but as they started water injection, soon from one side first the container began to sink and gradually kept sinking in vertical way deeper and deeper.

Military Engineer A [The container reached the bottom of the sea.]

Technical Officer [Record by GPS the exact position. What depth?]

Military Engineer A [Depth of the upper edge of the hangar is 120m as scheduled.]

Technical Officer [Okay, now two warhead-equipped barrels have been set.]

Military Engineer B [Are you sure we do not have to land these onto the island? You know well what remain on the island are only the old gun barrels used during WW2.]

Technical Officer [These are SLBM (Submarine launched ballistic missiles). In the warhead container, several Russian dismantled nuclear warheads are filled. Setting these deep in the sea, the shell can be thrown regardless stormy weather. These are superb weapon that can be drawn by U-boat keeping the depth of 100m on a command.]

Military Engineer B [So this is Gorgon, isn't it.]

Technical Officer [Yes, Code name V6 Gorgon.]

— 269 —

Military Engineer B [What about the balance ten barrels?]

Technical Officer [Those are what was ordered by General Omar of Middle East and are Code V6 for use of ground launching.]

Military Engineer B [I see.]

Military Engineer A [What is the difference?]

Technical Officer [V6 if one extra step is added can hit New York from Persian Gulf.]

Military Engineer A [Is that much impact really necessary?]

Technical Officer [This type we are now handling can be good enough if it can reach Israel from Pergian Gulf.]

Military Engineer B [What confidential level is this on?]

Technical Officer [The highest. In any case, Israel does possess nuclear weapon but is treated as non-nuclear possessing country. The confidential level of this is just about the same level of Israel.]

Military Engineer A [What is the reason why the fact that Israel possesses nuclear weapon is openly known?]

Technical Officer [People who believe to possess nuclear weapon is evil are leaking such information. Human has what is called conscience. After all, even though there may have been lots of confrontations between Israel and Palestine 2,000 years ago, Palestine was Israel's neighbor since such a long time ago and there may have been considered such relationship as marital relations regarding the lineage. Well, It may be said that they are too close to go well along.]

Military Engineer A [Use of nuclear weapon may only result in

— 270 —

calling for the enemy's nuclear weapon. Isn't it no good?]

Technical Officer [That's why nuclear weapon takes away the significance of the broadness of all countries. If what is wanted is to terminate other countries, the best way to do so successfully is to nuclear-bomb all countries. If this is done, there will be no winner. There is no country that has a defense system with which it can intercept a nuclear missile attack against any country other than its own country. And that is the very reason why such idea as to guard one's country exerting right of collective self defence is born.]

Military Engineer A [What you are saying is what America is trying to construct against China, isn't it.]

Technical Officer [Such a system as nuclear weapon interception to detect and intercept on adjacent waters near Okinawa ICBM that was launched in China while it is still at the stage of rising process. Speed of all missiles on their rising stage is slow enough to be able to be destroyed quite easily.]

Military Engineer A [Does China have any countermeasure for that?]

Technical Officer [If China succeeds in concluding a treaty with Russia for Russia's automatic participation, China will be safe but Russia would not agree. Reason why is Russia is already a country operated by multi-party system. If a country's congress is split into many different parties, basically speaking a preemptive attack itself will be exposed to the criticism by the congress. In this meaning, China may be the only country that can use nucear weapon on their own will for the first time. Still it will be impossible that will happen if China becomes multi-partilized as the multi-party system will lead to easy leaking of information. Even Israel cannot protect to hold information to itself that they are armed with nuclear weapon.]

Military Engineer A [Is nuclear weapon that Israel holds can be really enabled for use?]

Technical Officer [When no country is attacking Israel, it will be difficult for Israel to use its nuclear weapon, as there exists international public opinion.]

Military Engineer A [By holding nuclear weapon, Israel is raising the risk of its being attached?]

Technical Officer [Such risk of Israel being attacked with nuclear weapon will be small while the president of America has his interest in peace of Middle East.]

Military Engineer A [It is a wasteful exercise to themselves that Israel or North Korea keeps nuclear weapon.]

Technical Officer [Well, you may not really be right. As Beijing is unable to intercept nuclear missile that may come from North Korea, North Korea can continuously keep the population of a big city of China in hostage, isn't it right?]

Military Engineer A [So you mean North Korea is not really aiming at Beijing as its military target?]

Technical Officer [If not for military victory, North Korea will

— 272 —

be quite satisfied if it can destroy the luck of the core of the administration of China.]

Military Engineer   [Shall we return to the land. Waves are getting high.]

In fact, waves were still calm there as that area was a corner of the ocean hedged by an island. However, the sea roaring was telling that a storm was passing by the side of this ocean area. It was imperative they hide their boat in a cave on the island before the military satellite was to pass by. They could not leave an engine equipped boat outside on the island where the habitants there were believing that African ingenous people were residing. Number of islands where fresh water was available was limited so that they could not be too careful when hiding the boat.

U2552Anazones continued patrolling under the water at the southern side of the waterway running on the south of the island waiting for Macara which was supposed to come from the west. From the high ground of the island, by a signal of twittering light it was being transmitted that the shade of a ship was visible and in the meanwhile a watchman confirmed he somehow found a vessel out there. Three hours after that confirmation by the watchman, the vessel passed through the waterway.

When the vessel was passing by, Marlene was comparing the photograph on the military instructions with the target vessel. Carefully reading the twittering light that was jumping into the periscope, she opened her mouth.

Marlene   [Admiral, That is Macara. Will you identify it by yourself?]

She passed the periscope to Louise.

Louise	[Certainly. I have identified the target.]
Marlene	[Are we to go surfacing now?]
Louise	[We are to wait a while. Now is a lead time till we receive the sign of completion of cargo reshipment labor. Don't miss wireless communication.]
Radio Communication Operator	[Aye aye ma'am.]
Marlene	[Rogh waves. Already twelve-hour delay.]
Louise	[If the meeting had been finished in the yesterday evening, the transshipment had been finished in the early evening regardless of the change of weather.]

When such transaction was to take place, in view of the necessity of patrolling, related submarine could not moor in the base built in a bored cave. A regulation had been set for submarine to stand by under the water of the ocean in order to keep war preparedness. Macara passed at a point of 1,500m from Amazones at 10 knots. A flag on the must was showing General Omar was on board. Macara passed through the water way and entered the Abalon sea area then came alongside Cossac but that scene could not be observed from Amazones.

The observer stationed on the island kept observing this scene while confirming no other ships were sailing in the near sea area. Looking at a nautical chart Louise was comparing the position of Amazones with that of the water way. Till that day, similar transactions had been exercised without problem but she was wondering whether this one could be finished as safely as before.

And after a while, Marlene who was looking at the observatory on the island through periscope started taking notes using alphabets while staring at the outside scene. Finishing taking the notes, she handed the notes over to louise in silence.

[From the direction of one o'clock, a pleasure boat is approaching. Distance 10 nautical miles. Speed 25 knots or thereabouts.]

Some bad vibes prevailed there. Why did a pleasure boat of the rich wander into there?

However, as she wrote it as a pleasure boat, it was not a warship, which was a good news any way. It also noted that this boat actually kept changing its speed from slow to fast and vice versa.

Bernard   [Look, For sure I will catch one this time. Captain, won't you watch the distance of marlin and the position of the fishing line so that the line is not to be cut by the fish.]

Captain   [That is not so easy.]

Bernard   [Just try a bit harder.]

Cook   [Can I help?]

Bernard   [Scoop it with net!]

In that way they somehow succeeded in catching a speardfish in the sea several miles ahead Cossac.

Bernard   [Cook it in carpaccio, won't you.]

Cook   [Bernard, why don't you let me try to cook it into Sushi?]

Bernard   [Can you cook Sushi?]

Cook   [When I landed on Kobe, I bought a Sakai cooking knife. It is a knife of rare beauty which is as good as Japanese Samurai sword into which soul of Japanese bladesmith was thrown in, Don.]

Bernard   [Is sharpness of your Japan-made knife that much superior to that of Henkel ?]

Cook   [Most of surgical sculpels are made in Japan, Don.]

Bernard   [Okay, cook as you like it. I will leave it to you. By the way, isn't the American destroyer getting late.]

Around at that time, the cargo vessel Cossac, having finished unloading work and weigning the anchor, quietly started for the south. Fairly big delay had arisen already to sail for the next port Perth. Macara that was loaded now was busy to fix the loaded cargos not to shift. Observing this view, Omar was satisfied. The ten Gorgons had too big destruction power to be used under common situation but the China-made assault rifles were indispensable weapons for Guerilla warfare. Half of the loads are useful weapons for strengthening arms of his soldiers and the other half was to be sent to the armed organizations at the utmost front. To report the end of the deal, he wired to SS a code which means the completion of the deal. This notice was deviced to be received at Omar's country at the same time.

Communicator   [Captain, Message stating the transaction was safely completed was received.]

Marlene   [Shall we emerge and see General Omar off?]

Louise   [No. There is a pleasure boat which nationality is unknown. Just wait this time.]

Marlene   [Roger.]

Louise   [Guard Macara keeping the distance of 2000 to 3000 at 10knots per hour.]

Marlene   [Roger.]

As it would be known later, this carefulness came to save the fate of this submarine, but at that point of time no one was aware of what would be happening since then.

From Santa Rosalia, Bernard was trying to catch Robert via satellite phone but could not connect the line successfully. Reason why he was trying to contact Robert was because the American destroyer Sharon was chasing Santa Rosalia just at the back of it and the boat was floating in the midst of roaring waves fighting against those waves which was caused by the tropical squall. Leaving on the deck the marlin he had fished, he was ordering several underlings of his to get ready for a fight.

Bernard　　[I bet there would be no cargos loaded on Cossac.]

Captain　　[What do you wish me to do?]

Bernard　　[Look at that deck of the cargo vessel Macara.]

Both Bernard and the captain looked through binoculars.

Bernard　　[Don't you think you have seen that red container in Shanghai?]

Captain　　[Sure, That container is the one we saw on Never Green in Shanghai.]

Bernard　　[Wait a second. I took a photo by my digital camera just for sure.]

Captain　　[What are we supposed to look?]

Bernard looked at the image data on his digital camera and read aloud a number there.

Bernard　　[Number of the container is…is Container number 582264 there?]

The captain repeated the number in the mouth and was looking through binoculars and suddenly shouted.

Captain　　[Aha! Yes, there is.]

Bernard　　[We will receive that.]

Underling　[Are we going to pirate that?]

Bernard	[That is just a shabby old cargo ship anyhow. Macara ···What does Macara mean?]
Underling	[IDK, Don.]
Bernard	[Take the machine guns out! If it lost sight of U.S. Navy, let's palm that off to Nicola!]
Underling	[Okie-dokie!]
Bernard	[Lock and load Jolly Roger and Red Flag.]
Underling	[BTW, what for Red Flag is used?]
Captain	[You didn't learn history, did you.]
Undering	[I have been to primary school only.]
Captain	[Jolly Roger was originally meant for an amusing agreements and understandings. This tradition was firstly started when Rhodes Knights attacked a vessel of Muslims on Rhodes Island.]
Underling	[Then, what kind of tradition was it?]
Captain	[Design of the badge that is worn by cavalries shows a skull and crossbones. When a ship with such mark approaches, if the approached vessel was willing to pay for the toll fee, the vessel raised a white flag on the mast. Then pirates are boarding on the vessel and collect the toll fee but guaranteed safety of major cargos and crew's lives.]
Underling	[What will happen if the white flag is not raised on the mast?]
Captain	[If no white flag is to be raised, then it is brought down and raise a red flag instead. Red flag is meant for battle flag, therefore, what next will happen is bombardment, then a further approach and aboardage

— 278 —

followed by a close combat inside the vessel.]

Underlying [And during the close combat, we can seize whatever spoils of the war.]

Bernard [Yes, That will give you a chance to get a memento for you to hand over to Rosanna.]

Underling [Will anything good can be found?]

Bernard [The main cargos are mine but whatever you take from the enemy you fall down is yours.]

Underling [Understood. Now you're talking!]

Chaptain [They may be heavily armed. Beware!]

Underling [Roger.]

Captain [This is the key of the armoury! Take it!]

Underling [Which key?]

Captain [You will find machine guns and pistols. Bullets are in the other armoury. Open them all and take a look.]

Underling [Are there enough weapons for five people at least?]

Captain [One dozen (for twelve people's use) are there at least. Wear a bulletproof vest. Be sure to take Beretta pistols and knives as well.]

Ship's Doctor [My goodness, I must prepare anticeptic solutions. Before you go, take lard oil out from the kitchen and put it on the face, neck and wherever exposed part of arms!]

Underling [Roger.]

The underling stepped downstairs. Bernard calculated that it would be sold at a good price to Jewish and this way of thinking of Bernard was the cause of his avouching himself as guardian deity for the Sicilians. his mercenary motives and power to make prompt

— 279 —

decisions were also the driving force that enabled him to expand his sphere of influence.

22. the Waves on Indian Ocean are High

The transaction finished as planned, but General Omar kept staying alert against the approaching unidentified vessel.

He ordered to heave up the anker and told his underlings to take everyone's battle position.

Autocannons had been covered by canvas cloth but the cover was being removed and autocannons were gradually showing up. On the bridge, there observed were large binoculars which had more than several higher resolution degree than that of normal binoculars and through the large binoculars the scene of a marlin being fished. The marlin kept shaking as the boat rode over large waves. It looked like a fish that must be quite tasteful.

While General Omar had been wondering if the boat was of Italian nationality, he saw a tropical zone special scquall was closing in on that pleasure boat. He thought he would have that scquall in no time.

The pleasure boat came further close and the Jolly Roger was observed, so General Omar ordered his underlings to depart as soon as possible. Ahead of the vessel a narrow water way was waiting for the vessel to go through so it is not possible to sail at the utmost speed and in addition, Macara was an old- style steel vessel which could not make even the speed of ten knots. Though it was narrowly carrying the auto cannon, Macara was a reformed vessel not equipped with armored shield and bridge was just substituted by thick steel sheet for footholding use of the height of only 1.2m.

The 1000-ton class huge body of Macara started to move forward

— 281 —

to west slowly. In order not to damage the cargos it slowly proceeded at 8 knots. Thus, the vessel went through the rain croud just about half of it, in order to save the fuel for the return sailing home, it was necessary not to sail in high speed. However, when the distance to Santa Rosalia was further shortened, Macara came to find that Mafias came to represent their true intention, namely, they looked like preparing something like machine guns on the deck. General Omar, while confirming preparation for fight was getting ready at his side, too, had a fight flag raised on the main mast. Now, General Omar and his underlings clearly understood that the pleasure boat never raised Jolly Roger just as a joke. General Omar made a broardcase onboard of his vessel.

General Omar [Attention, All hands. The approaching pleasure boat is a pirate boat. Number of the attacking pirates seems to be a few. Firstly, make their bridge as target for shooting. As we will see how they react wait for next broadcasting.]

Just then, the destroyer of American Navy appeared its brave figure over the high waves through the squall. The observatory of SS Africa Troops had of course grasped this situation, so they also were preparing for a fight but according to their regulation unless the enemy became aware of the existence of the SS force no attack was to be started from the side of the island.

Reason for this regulation was, to maintain the secret in Abarone sea area keeping in confidence the fact that that island was under the seize of SS. Until the order for start an attack was wired from the submarine, their guns were ordered to keep silence. In any case, only with four 20mm cannons they would have no chance to win the battle against the destroyer, though SS held in its possession small size surface-to-ship missile or portable anti-aircraft missile.

At the bridge of Sharon, Captain Richard Harrison was taking command. Indrajit also came back from the cabin. Robert was using binoculars as well.

Captain Harrison   [Hey, Robert, Is that boat which is raising Jolly Roger really Santa Rosalia?]

Robert   [Judging from the receiving longitude and latitude, that is Santa Rosalia no doubt.]

Captain Harrison   [According to International Law, pirate ship is the object of attack order regardless of its nationality…Why does American Navy have to support pirate ship…Unless there is a request from the embassy, it is beyond comprehension.]

Robert   [Since the Allied Invasion of Sicily during WW2, Mafias and American Troops must have been in friendly terms…]

Captain Harrison   [Is what you said an irony of a British guy?]

Robert   [Look, The boat put Jolly Roger down and raised Red Flag. Battle looks like to be started.]

Captain Harrison   [Attention, All hands. The pleasure boat of Italian nationality at front entered a state of war against the smuggling vessel. We are now to battle against the smuggling vessel avoiding the Italian boat!]

Indrajit   [The fatal day has come. Only God knows to be or not to be.]

Robert   [Cargos on the vessel looks like missiles]

Indrajit   [You are right. But I do not know specs of the missiles.]

Robert   [Judging from the size of the cargos in question, those cannot just be anti-ship missiles. These may be able to target at Israel from Persian Gulf.]

Captain Harrison   [I understand···For that size, it may come to be necessary even to support Mafias.]

Hearing this conversation, Robert called Nicola.

Robert   [Nicola! The missile in question probably is such a size as to be able to target at Israel from Persian Gulf! Can you hear me?]

Nicora   [Ensure to make an official inspection and capture those cargos! Please!]

Robert   [Roger!]

Indrajit   [The Jewish, Mafia and American Navy···We are to witness the reincarnation of Operation Husky of WW2.]

Robert   [Here is an Indian. In addition to an English person.]

Indrajit   [Though I am not a member colonial army, isn't it an irony of the history.]

Those people who happened to gather on the bridge of Sharon keenly sense the word of history repeats itself over again.

On the other hand, in the vessel Macara, rightfully, tension was going to be risen.

General Omar   [A destroyer of unknown nationality is also approaching. This destroyer may be chasing the pirate boat, therefore, keep on the watch for this as well.]

While Marlene was watching out through the periscope, she

— 284 —

caught in her sight twittering light at the observatory on the island. Again, she started taking notes using alphabet. Louise standing next to her observed what she was writing and read the notes Marlene was writing.

[War preparation by Pleasure Boat is now under way. Enemy newly added to its force a destroyer which is also ready for the battle. Macara kept raising red battle flag.]

Time for Louise to make a final decision did come.

Louise [Marlene, Hereby I give the command to attack.]

Marlene [Roger. All hands, Battle Station!]

First Mate [Roger! All hands, Battle Station!]

Marlene [Load torpedos!]

First Mate [Load torpedos!]

Louise [Is warhead of torpedo not marked?]

First Mate [No, it is still marked Harken Kreuz.]

Louise [It will be a problem if those torpedoes won't fire.]

Tension ran high in the submarine all in one gulp. They were then going to do tornade attack with tornados that had not been used for more than sixty years. In addition, Amaszones was being operated by women only, which is a change from the past tornade attacks. In this tension prevailing in the submarine, Marlene was patiently waiting to see a vessel going through the strait through a periscope. Talking about Louise, she was sitting looking at the nautical chart and looked like pondering something. In the era of homing torpedo, such action as to set the sights by periscope became out of date, however, till they finish the stock they had, there was no other way for them but to put up with the old-fashioned torpedos. Through the water way, two vessels were seen

— 285 —

to be coming.

Marlene [Confirmed two vessels coming out of the water way.]

Sonar Attendant [Three, judging from the screw sounds]

Marlene [What is it all about?]

Sonar Attendant [The one over there looks like an American destroyer but it looks like there is a flat bottom pleasure boat between the two destroyers and that boat is an Italian boat.]

Marlene [Are you sure that the one at the furthermost is an American destroyer?]

Sonar Attendant [No way to misheard that screw sound! The bottom of destroyer is the deepest of all!]

Marlene [No.1, No.2,No.3,No.4 Start injecting water.]

The executive officer [No1,No.2,No.3,No.4, Start injecting water.]

Tension ran high at once.

Marlene was pasted to periscope killing her breath and Louise did not move an inch glaring at the nautical chart.

Just before the boart was to pass the water way, Bernard sent out an instruction.

Bernard [Take Jolly Roger down!]

Captain [Now to attack?]

Bernard [Macara looks like passing the water way as is, so that our Jolly Roger will be disturbing to the American destroyer. Raise the red flag (battle flag) on the mast.]

Underling [Roger!]

— 286 —

When they changed the flag to the red flag, at the side of General Omar start of war order was issued.

General Omar　　　[Open war battle. Machine guns are to be set to the bridge of the pirate boat. Autocannons. Keep the state of setting the sights on the American destroyer and stand by!]

Then the machine guns resounded. Bra-ta-ta-t··· And as a natural result, there came the sound of glasses broken down at the bridge of Santa Rosalia and all members were in the state of laying on the face down. On the surface of the bridge the popping sound of bullets of machine guns striking the deck continued.

Captain　　[Don, We may have done wrong.]

Bernard　　[Damn! ! Didn't know they're armed···]

Underling　　[Joe was killed!]

He raised his face half way and said so.

Captain　　[···..]

Bernard　　[We may have been at stake unless we had not been armored···]

Captain　　[Don, Look at that.]

Bernard looked and saw that great marline which had been hanged was completely smashed up leaving the head only.

Bernard never gave up surviving even if he was put in the Boca do Inferno, so he was thinking that dinner that night would be soup and grilled headbones cooked from the head that was the only leftover of the big marlin that he caught earlier that day. On the other hand, he regretted he should have played with the other woman of his favor while he was in Shanghai. Santa Rosalia was sailing at the back of the starboard of Macara.

That scene happening on Santa Rosalia was fully observed by General Omar who was staying at the bridge of Macara, however, to him an enemy that was much more fearful than Mafia who was playing a roll of an intermittent pirate was drawing near. That was the destroyer Sharon. Both of the two 20mm autocannons equipped on Macara were forcusing at Sharon. Omar was feeling thirsty. If he surrendered in accordance with the progress of the situation and was seized, the enemy would come to know what the cargos were. Should he resist to the bitter end and die in battle…

Omar   [Send a wire.]

Telegraphist [How?]

Omar   [We are in battle against an American destroyer. Inshalla!]

Tension was all there on the bridge of Macara.

Telegraphist [Here came the reply. Defend Gorgon to the death. This is Jihad. Loyal brothers, your canonization is celebrated. Allah akbar!]

This telegram was read out and all members aboard the vessel prepared for dealth.

Omar   [Start preparation to scuttle the vessel. Do your best if the bridge falls down!]

Underlings [Roger!!]

Some three underlings ran down to the bottom of the vessel to install detonator. When the vessel was seized by the American Navy, this vessel must immediately be scuttled.

In the same time zone, on the bridge of Sharon, there were men who were counting the timing observing the scene on Macara.

— 288 —

Richard	[Drop the speed to 10 knots!]
First Officer	[Roger!]
Richard	[When Macara comes out of the water way, we issue order to stop.]
First Officer	[Roger!]
Robert	[What is that cargo?]
Indrajit	[The specially big size red container of Never Green is the hanger of warhead of missile.]
Robert	[What is that ordinary look container?]
Indrajit	[that contains firearms.]
Robertg	[And the white tube marked with Harken Kreuz?]
Indrajit	[That is the reversed mark and reads Manji. It is the main body of disguised Misille!]
Robert	[Big, isn't it.]
Richard	[Judging from the size, that cannot be an anti-ship missile.]
Indrajit	[That must be Gorgon.]
Robert	[Nuclear warhead must be collected.]
Richard	[Those will line up after coming out from the water way. We will seize them soon.]

Robert and Indrajit stepped down to the deck in order to join the recapture unit which was organized by Captain Richard Harrison. Distance between Sharon and Macara was about 800m but in between the two, Santa Rosalia was still sailing disturbingly. Indrajit encountered on the deck that sailor he had talked with.

Dawson	[Are you making an assault on Macara?]
Indrajit	[After attacking there, we will at least have the warhead collected for sure. Are you joining the assault

corps?]

Dawson   [I will believe your prophecy so will stay at the cannon platform.]

Indrajit   [Good choice. My regards to your baby and fiancé!]

Dawson looked like having accepted Indrajit's advice. It seemed that he still had a chance to survive this crisis and could resist against destiny. On the deck, the ship inspection members who did not know yet what would be waiting in their destiny were standing by and at the end of this group, Robert and Richard joined.

At Amazones, all crews were surpressing their breathing and neuvously watching Marlene looking through the peliscope and the behaviors of the sonar attendant. Louise was looking at the position of the submarine and the water depth.

Louise   [Hasn't the island reported the position of Destroyer?]

Marlene   [It is at the moment moving 1000m behind Macara and now is further approaching it.]

Louise   [Is Pleasure Boat in the way of torpado?]

Marlene   [If the bottom of the boat is flat, torpado can go through as is.]

Louise   [What about homing?]

Marlene   [What are here are all old models which have high possibility of misfiring.]

Louise   [⋯God knows.]

Then, next, Marlene saw white smoke rose up from Macara but it was flown by wind and was not working as smoke screen. Battle was starting between Macara and Destroyer. Machine guns of Macara exploded at the section where the assault troops to seize the container were lining up. With a roaring sound, sailors were rowed away with some ended in lump of meat.

Robert protected Indrajit and turned down over Indrajit. Indrajit was a living witness so Robert must keep Indrajit alive. When Indrajit raised his face, some fluid came into his eyes.

Indrajit　　[Some fragments are stinging you. You're bleeding.]

Robert　　[Indy, are you alright?]

Indrajit　　[Not really. Something is stinging my foot.]

Saying so, he frowned his face.

Indrajit　　[Anyway, won't you take that arm of yours away as it is heavy on me.]

Robert　　[Don't say such strange thing.]

Hearing this word, Indrajit grasped that arm and found it was the cut out upper arm flying from nowhere. On the wrist of the upper arm a wrist watch was ticking time hollowly. The Dad ring on the ring finger was barely showing that the upper arm was a part of a man's body who used to have children. Human can continue to live without one of the arms, but if he becomes to be just that single upper arm, does that upper arm have no individuality any longer?

Around that time, people on the bridge had already grasped the ongoing situation. In the storm of busy telephone conversation, Richard was thinking about the fact that nuclear weapon was included in the arms of the enemy. The highest concern of him is if the vessel could endure to keep nuclear weapon safely in case fire took place on Macara.

Richard　　[Can't but accept seizing the vessel would be difficult under this situation. Shut the noise of the autocannons out!]

The Captain at the bridge also decided to go into war. Destiny of the disguised cargo vessel Macara had already been set.

Warheads of the two vessels were flying about over Santa Rosalia which was sailing straight forward by automatic operation. Bernard and all the others could not move an inch lying on the floor with the face down crossing themselves.

There eyes from the sea were watching such battle scene on Santa Rosalia. Amazones had one more advantage which was a pair of good ears. How good they were could be explained that only if she heard the noise of fish swimming, her ears could tell the size of the school of fish and also the species of fish such as tuna from skipjack. This skill of hers had been improved to match the needs and was a quite necessary technic by which the ship cook had been helped many times in past and Marlene were also well aware of this fact, too.

Sonnar Attendant   [Captain, Just now, to the two o'clock direction, three sound sources were overlapped.]

If two vessels were sailing at approximately same speed, when the two came to the twelve o'clock direction, the vessel which ran outside of the other would come to be getting just slightly late. The state of the two vessels was trying to line up little by little. The loaded torpedo was an old type so it could only proceed to the twelve o'clock direction. Marlene was adjusting the timing looking through the peliscope.

Marlene   [Put the helm starboard at 3 degrees. Slow forward.]

Steerswoman [Roger]

With all her nurves stretched, she was concentrating on the scene caught in the peliscope. Macara might be surmurged due to trival damage. It looked to start curving to the other side.

Marlene   [No. 1, No. 2, Fire!]

Then Marlene started watching her wrist watch and when 30 seconds passed, two more were additionally fired.

The first two torpedos passed and gone very near the backside of Macaca. Bernard on Santa Rosalia who could finally manage to lift his face up then saw the white trace line of a torpedo was rushing to Santa Rosalia and he got fainted. In time for the arrival of the reaper but in a small voice not to be heard by the captain, he made the sign of the cross.

Bernard   [I was a bad boy not to listen to you Mom. Amen.]

But the captain heard it and he, too, prayed in a small voice.

Captain   [I will never again steal others' goods. Amen.]

They came back to little boys when they used to belive God or Santa Claus and were waiting faithfully for the guide to the hell to come.

However, the thud of explosion did not sound. The torpedos passed through the underneath of the boat. When they got relieved, there rose a loud sound and a water column on the opposite side. Kaboon! It was a sound to affect the stomach.

Bernard   [Turn around and leave here, Captain! If only we can
keep our lives, we can come back to that life of
debauchery!]

Forgetting all what they prayed, the nature of Mafia again came back to dominate Santa Rosalia. The Captain fully turned the rudder anticrockwise to avoid Sharon and left the battle sea area.

Bernard   [Nicola, Can you hear me? Macara is soon to sink and
Sharon is also severely wrecked. Santa Rosalia is also

in the condition almost beyond repair. As we are calling at the port of Singapore for repairing, please make arrangements. I will set the price of the drug that I obtained in Shanghai at two million dollars! Please have the money ready.]

Nicola　　[What I will buy regardless of reason why you sell are diamonds and paintings only, but for this time only, I will cooperate with you and act as broker. Then, to whom am I supposed to wholesale the lot?]

Bernard　　[You tell a pizza house the topping of Marugarita is Rosalia, then your talk will be linked.]

Nicola　　[Which pizza house do you mean?]

Bermard　　[Any pizza house in the Italian streets will do.]

Should Archangel Michael hear their talks, he would have wished to slap down the ultimate weapon onto them. They came back to such accursed daily conversation shamelessly.

At the bridge of Sharon, the crews were confirming that they succeeded in silencing the two autocannons, when suddenly an explosion took place which reduced the sailing speed of Macara down to half. And all of sudden, Sonar Attendant screamed out.

Sonar Attendant　　[Two torpedos are approaching coming through the pleasure boat!]

Captain Richard Harrison instantly looked around there, but as they were at the exist of the water way, the sea bottom was shallow so it was not possible to turn to right to avoid the torpedos without avoiding the possibility of going onto rocks.

Richard　　[Port the helm! Use noisemaker!]

Helmsman　　[Port!]

Fire Controller   [Use noisemaker.]

Then, after several ten seconds later, Sonar Attendant cried.

Sonar Attendant   [Noisemaker is not working.]

And at the next moment, the vessel was shaken with a loud sound. Bam! With the big dull sound, both documents and coffee cups were blown away. In the vessel, emergency bells rang all at once and on the board per area outbreak of a fire was shown. Captain struggled to his feet but at that moment the next two torpedos hit the vessel furthermore and one of the two exploded. Explosion that time took place near the power storage.

Richard   [I cannot believe why the noisemaker did not work. It was the newest model which was exchanged with the old one only last year.]

And, telephone rang.

Richard   [Richard.]

Sailor   [Captain, This is information about the unfired torpedo.]

Richard   [Is it made in Russia or China?]

Sailor   [No, neither one.]

Richard   [I understand noicemaker did not work.]

Sailor   [It is a matter of course that it didn't.]

Richard   [You mean the newest model?]

Sailor   [If we were in 1940.]

Richard   [What do you mean by that?]

Sailor   [⋯]

Beyond the telephone line there was a sound of explosion. It seems fire caught something but no reply came back any more.

Captain's wrinkles between the eyeblows became deeper.

— 295 —

Rihard [⋯!??]

Inclimination of the vessel became bigger. The extension of the firing compartment could not possibly be stopped.

The executive officer [Captain, Please issue Evacuation Order. Let's limit it to ourselves only to chase the escaping Macara.]

Richard [This is Evacuation Order! Five military policemen are to remain as captors. Those five are to seize the sinking Macara!]

In the Submarine Amazones, the members were listening the sound calmly. At the arrival time of torpedo, the sonar attendant took the headphone off from her ears. Sound of dull but with striking power resounded.

Sonar Attendant [Destroyer was hit.]

Marlene [I took photos but only one water column was observed. Didn't the other torpedo explode?]

After this, the next two torpedos reached but water column observed was only one as well.

Marlene [Destroyer was severely damaged! Two torpedos exploded. Destroyer started to lean to left by 30 degrees.]

Louise [How is Macara getting?]

Marlene [As sea weaves are reaching one meter below the deck, the vessel is flooded considerably much. Speed is as slow as 4 knots.]

Louise [Can we be observed by Destroyer?]

Marlene [You're right.]

Louise folded her arms, wondered for a few seconds and closed

— 296 —

her eyes. Then she issued her voice.

Louise   [Can't be helped, Turn around and go down to south.]

Marlene   [Roger!]

Louise   [Send telegram to Heinrich.]

Marlene   [Please tell me the content.]

Louise   [Delivery of Gorgon to Macara was complete, but Macara and Destroyer had a fight. Macara is expected to sin Enemy Destroyer was hit twice by torpedo and was severely broken. Destroyer was led by Pleasure Boat. Please confirm no information has been leaked. Sieg Heil!]

U2552 sent telegraph in eniguma and turned around and sailed down to the south and quietly submerged down to depth 120m.

Pandemonium reigned the sinking destroyer and in the midst of that situation life boats were lowering down on the sea. Among them, Indrajit and Robert could slip themselves in. Sharon looked like keeping chasing Macara at the speed of 5 knots or thereabouts trying to seize Macara.

At the port of the bow, it was observed that some five sailors holding submachine were standing by. After a while, Sharon seized Macara which deck was being washed by waves and at that same moment General Omar issued the scuttling command and took off the sheath of his scimitar. There was no bullet left then. He put a pistol at his belt.

As his last resort, he swore to himself to finish that battle by one-on-one flight and hid himself in the shade.

When American soldiers transferred to Macara, explosive for self-sink exploded and the vessel shook violently and reacting this explosion one unexploded torpedo of Sharon came to explode. The two vessels were entangled to each other and were sinking further. Kicking open the cabin door behind which Omar was hiding, one soldier jumped in. Omar cut off the soldier's wrist instantly, but another soldier who heard the screaming of the hurt soldier shot Omar several times. Omar tried to say Allah but he could not even issue any word. There, the brave worrier used up all his strength.

At the same time when Omar died, at the bridge of Sharon, those members aboard Sharon caught in their eye sight destroyers coming through the storm in the west which had been reinforced at Nancy's request. Richard did not leave Sharon which received its last moment. Macara sank a little earlier than Sharon, but the vessel Sharon also became the ferryman of Acheron (the river which devides this world and the other world in Greek Mythology) for Richard.

Richard sent a telegram in plain text which read [For Justice of God, I am in persuit of Macara.] It seemed fire shifted into munisions bunker. When the last energy was released, the huge lump of iron with bodies of men on board was being swallowd into the realm of the dead.

— 298 —

23. Hunting for Escapees

When Heinrich Hizinger woke up, the butler brought about breakfast and the translated Enigma.

After viewing the contents of the Enigma, he rang President of America.

Heinrich [Why did you send a destroyer out of my knowledge?]

President [As that was not National Defence Project, it came to me in the form of after-the-fact notice as result of agreement between FBI and the Navy Force. And why did you have torpedos with the mark of Swastika? There was a need to let the seamen who saw this mark die with burns all over the body.]

Heinrich [If you say so, I will reconsider whom I will fund at the next election of president.]

President [Wait. I will promise not to raise the sunken ship if you can assure me for sure that America is out of firing range.]

Heinrich [You have my word for that United States of America is out of firing range. Two conditions. One; American warships will not enter the sea area of 10 nautical miles around Navalon, Two; America will not fail to prenotice capturing operation.]

President [I will make that promise. One condition from my side. Are you willing to admit our carrier task police is to anchor in the sea area of east of Andaman Islands.]

Heinrich [I will admit that as same as in the past.]

— 299 —

President	[Then, will you dispose favors in funding our party's candidates?]
Heinrich	[I will. By the way, as regards reflow of funds of American industries, please keep accounts of our nomination out of your survey subjects.]
President	[You have my word for that, too.]
Heinrich	[You are an understanding person. You will be remembered in the history as a great president. Enjoy turkey dinner at the weekend party. Bye!]

When the world leaders try to divert their peoples' attention to foreign countries, it is often the time when their domestic administration is not going well. At this present time when the world's major countries are taking aim at each other's heart with missiles, and squeezing each other's stomach with currency measures, world strategy relying on war is getting to be a thing of the past. The president of United States does know such commonsensible understanding. No country can make war against SS which does not have any territory. It has a similar meaning of inability to surgically remove a cancer that has metastasized all over the other sovereign states or the home country.

What Heinrich did, following the conversation with the president, was to send his instruction to Josef who happned to be visiting India then. Heinrich was to go back to South America on the following day.

Later on, two Mercedes arrived at the palace of Raja Mitra. Guards of the palace graciously opened the doors of the two cars and received the party on the cars. Further from the scarlet color carpet the butler led them to the salon. As a usual practice, the guards at the Raja's study which was located at the bottom of the palace gave Roman salute greetings to receive the party.

Raja Mitra [What is what you say an urger matter? Mr. Josef.]

Josef [Today I came here taking people whom I wish you to meet.]

The several people who were standing beside Josef took a bow.

Josef [These are Vayu Vanara, leader of SS Free Indian Region, and his subordinate, Onkot Langur. And this beautiful lady is Druj Nasu.]

Mitra who put a parrot on his shoulder not surprisingly walked near to the beautiful woman. Any man who is not attracted by her large eyes and ample bosom is not worth being called a man. Mitra kissed her on her hand. She wore a pendant with a large opal of the prismatic colors on her chest. The green based mysterious colors shined changing the shade of the colors from time to time.

Raja Mitra [How do you do, Madam Druj. I am Mitra. Pleased to make your acquaintance.]

Josef [Reason why we came here is none other than to ask you to punish Indrajit. Let me explain cause of this request. For the transaction in Abalone, chasing Cossack the pleasure boat Santa Rosalia went there and the point is Santa Rosalia took Sharon the American Navy destroyer into that ongoing situation. Result of our investigation of this situation came to prove such leak of information happened under your jurisdiction. I wish you to execute Indrajit but from Singapore, I reckon you wouldn't be able to handle it.

Cooperate with them to have it done.]

Raja Mitra [I understood. Indrajit's regular hotel is Hotel Santa Lucia. But according to what the front desk told us Indrajit had been lost right before the Abalone naval battle, however, in the rooms reserved under his name one man and three women seem to be staying.]

Josef [Will you relay these people to the manager of that hotel for him to give these people whatever assistance necessary.]

Vayu [Shall we finish him by our hands?]

Raja Mitra [I will have a man by the name of Kubera to show you.]

Vayu [I will let Onkot and Madame Druj go there. Onkot has his underlings there and she is an expert hand of daggers and Indian dancing]

Hearing this explanation, Rajer asked Vayu in a whispering voice.

Raja Mitra [Incidentally, what is madame's real name?]

Vayu [Her name is Druj Nasu.]

Raja Mitra [Won't it no way mean a bluebottle fly?]

Vayu [She uses magical beings.]

Raja Mitra [And then?]

Vayu [In order not to be haunted by demon, she never tells her real name.]

Raja Mitra [That is regretful. But she is a beauty.]

Vayu [Roses are beautiful but they have thrones. That's why men are attracted even though they smell dangerous.]

Raja Mitra [She is certainly beautiful with that smile and full bosom though she is about 30 years old.]

— 302 —

Vayu   [Leave this case to us. Primarily, palace is the place where blood is loathed. Your Excellency must not take a wife whose hands are blood-smeared nor make such woman as your second wife.]

Raja Mitra [I know it. But men are such beings.]

Vayu   [Let me keep this case only in my mind.]

Thus, Vayu bowed once deeply and made his exit and thugs to kill were released.

On that same day, Show Taro and the other two were invited by Chen Jing Ji and Jinlian Pan and joined a luncheon party with them at Mandarin Palace nearby the hotel.

Guided by Kubera, Onkot met the manager of Hotel Santa Lucia and got the key from him. Using that key, Onkot had conspicuously positioned six underlings in that room. But he was not aware he broke boundaries that Maria had established in that room.

Chen Jin Ji was waiting for them to come at the Chinese restaurant Southern Cross which he was running. Indrajit who was finally able to come had not been back to his hotel yet so was wearing dirty clothes and what was more was one of his legs was supported by a crutch.

Chen   [Indy, What happened to your leg?]

Indrajit [While I was patrolling a construction site, some construction materials dropped down and hit my leg so I got a hairline fracture.]

Jinlian   [Sorry to hear that.]

Chen   [By the way, I am also going to obtain a bankloan and planning to have a shopping mall constructed in Singapore. I will reserve space for a jewelry shop of

Kubera and also a shop of Indy there.]

Indrajit [Sorry to say, that idea is not really materialized.]

Chen [Don't you like my idea?]

Indrajit [No, no, what I mean is this time for personal reasons Emily and I are to return to America so the remittance business has come to the end.]

Chen [What!]

Chen suddenly made a helpless look.

Show Taro [What happened?]

Chen [I thought I could get money easily for two to three times more, so I had already completed a contract to order the shopping mall construction.]

Show Taro [Before you receive the fund, did you do a potential ordering?]

Chen [Shortage of the fund will total to about 20 million dollars.]

Show Taro [Mao's prophecy came true.]

Chen [I planned to have the fund of Hong Kong Development Bank diverted as unsecured loan and to kick back at least 10% of the fund to the political world. As compensation of this deal, I was planning to let farmers' daughters in inland China work at that mall.]

Show Taro [And in addition you let them do prostitution.]

Chen [You know well as you are really a world business man.]

Show Taro [People who are to be remembered in the history will not do such a thing.]

— 304 —

Chen   [In the history even rascals can mark their names.]

Show Taro   [Such arch villain that killed some million people will mark his name in the history, but such level as cheating young girls and forcing them to prostitute will never be allowed by Heaven.]

Chen   [You said Heaven, didn't you.]

Chen seemed to be a bit irritated being told Heaven by a person who was not even a Chinise.

Show Taro   [Yes, In Japan, Japanese say Heaven, Earth, God, Deity that means all Gods in the world. What is against law of all things in creation is to receive divine punishment without fail. An arch villain will be changed to a hero in the history if what he did meets the law of the next era.]

Chen   [Do you mean I can't be the law of the next era?]

Show Taro   [The law of the era is meant for social system. It never is crime system. Merchants who aim at pursuit of profits only cannot leave their names in history. Waitresses working here are prostituting during their free hours, aren't they? I heard so just now. Taking job seeking young girls coming out from the inland China luring them saying if they work overseas they can get a handsome income and lending them travel expenses at an interest rate that is so high that they cannot but get money by prostitution to pay for that interest⋯such a deed is not supposed to be done by decent people. The way you came must have been similar but you seem not to understand that now is no

— 305 —

longer that kind of era you have been through.]

Chen [What's wrong if a girl coming out from inland China pennilessly borrows money at a set interest rate from the person who helps her and pays her debt back to him? I did similarly and endured such a life as hell on earth till I got married to a daughter of a financial combine.]

Show Taro [I admit you may have got the success you were targeting at by using your handsome appearance, but in the international society, such culture as to get a success by using the means of corruption and prostitution which are widely going on in China will not work. The Japanese phrase 「shame on you」 is a word that is to be used for such cases. Cultures of Tang or Sung were respected in Asia was not only they were powerful dynasties. Actually, Tang was defeated by Isram at Talas riverside and Sung could not win over Jin but was esteemed for its culture and kept the position of the monarch of Eastern Asia.

From now on, if you do not act understanding the world's ethics of business, you will be recorded as a blot in the history.]

Having heard this much, Chen became to look thoughtful and turned to be silent.

On the otherhand, at that time Maria talked to Nancy in a small voice.

Maria [Someone broke my boundary.]

Nancy [What are we to do?]

— 306 —

Maria   [We cannot return to the hotel tonight.]

Nancy   [Let's consult with Robert.]

After much consideration, Robert arranged to send a dealer to gather their buggages and finished necessary check-out procedures. However, it was revealed to the chasers that the destination of the buggages was Mandarine Palace. Onkot and his underlings and Vayu devised a plot.

Mandarine Palace was a hotel where no Indian capital was invested. At the both sides of the entrance a big Chinese lion was sitting pushing down a globe with one paw and a celestial glove with another. The eabes above the entrance was yellow color tile-roofed and only that part of the building was showing the appearance of Chinese palace construction. The off-white marble floor was polished to shine reflecting the lights on the ceiling. Such metal parts as handrails on the doors were gold plated enrivening a gourgeous feeling.

The doorman at the entrance was not dressed in Qing Dynasty style, but was dressed in a full-sleeved attire of Ming Dynasty. The capital of China Pacific Airline was also invested in this palace, but that part of inner decoration seemed to be showing the taste of Zhu Xing Ming. As shown by the name Mandarin, the hotel was filled with the scent of mandarin orange.

In the early evening, Show Taro and his party checked in Mandarin Palace as per Rogert's arrangements. They gathered in the lobby and on that way, they went to the dinner show place. It was Robert's deliveration that all those arrangements had been done, however, no one was yet aware that they had been under surveillance of Onkot since from Hotel Santa Lucia.

What made this surveillance possible was that the front manager of Hotel Santa Lucia firmly remembered the name of the company of the van which carried their luggages.

That day's program was a magic show at 7 o'clock and then Indian dancing at 7:30 and from 8 o'clock a live performance of a jazz band.

They sat on the seats which were comparably near to the stage, in the clock-wise order of Show Taro, Nancy, Indrajit, Emily, Robert and Maria. All of them selebrated the safe return of the members and toasted with beer. At the end of the show, there was a figure that was peeping them from the backstage, but no one of the Show Taro group took notice of it.

Kubera [The one with a crutch is our target Indrajit, then clock-wise beyond two persons there is Maria the medium, and next to her is Show Taro, an antique dealer and next is Nancy in that row, but I am a bit concerned about the two whose names are unknown to us, especially that European with a band-aid on his forehead.]

Druj [Of the three men, which one is the titter?]

She tried to find out a target to whom she could cast a flirtatious glance while she was dancing.

Kubera [No one there that can understand your charm.]

Replying so, Kubera sneaked a look at Druj's full bosom but got an instant blush-off.

Onkot [Go and sound the atmosphere. Don't do too much.]

Druj [Leave it to me.]

As there seemed to be no man that was knocked down by her

glamorous body, Druj was a bit crossed. As a reflection, she for the first time thought Kubera who obviously looked bawdy was much better than the other men and this thought of hers became clear after a short while.

Time came for the Indian dancing. Druj had got concent from the originally appointed dancer for the change and appeared on the stage waving her body which was unsuccessfully hiding her perky breasts. To her great disappointment, she felt those men at that table were scarcely reacting to her body. Only Maria reacted Druj's eyes and secretly pulled the right sleeve of Show Taro's shirt. In recent days she had been aware of what would happen under Nancy's influence, but she was adamant that time to let Show Taro listen to her.

Maria   [That dancer, she is observing us.]

Show Taro [You are getting too neuvous, I guess.]

Maria   [No, You are wrong. She is waiting for an unguarded moment of us.]

Show Taro [Do you mean here is a man whom she is interested in?]

Maria   [No, what I mean is she is observing how much we are getting drunk.]

Show Taro [What makes you to feel so?]

Maria   [I feel her murderous intent.]

After the curtain fell, Show Taro went to the men's room and on the way back he hit that dancer in the collider.

Show Taro [Oh, Excuse me! As I am a bit intoxicated.]

Druj   [No, Never mind.]

Show Taro [You were dancing then.]

— 309 —

Druj   [Yes.]

Show Taro [You looked nice and charming.]

Druj   [Thank you.]

Show Taro [Excuse me, Madam.]

Druj   [No, I am Mademoiselle Druj.]

Show Taro [Sorry I am late to intrduce myself. Show Taro, I am Show Taro Hayashi.]

Druj   [It is some kind of fate that I met you today.]

Show Taro [Oh⋯If you do not mind, when you have a stage in Japan, I will go and see you.]

Druj   [Okay, Then will you spare me one of your business card?]

She received his card in a polite way and bowing deeply she put the card in her cleavage to invite his eyes there. Observing his reaction secretly, she was thinking this man might be of use.

Druj   [When I have a stage in Tokyo, I will contact you. You are an antique dealer, aren't you. When I go to Japan, let me take a look at your shop.]

Show Taro [With my pleasure⋯I wish to see your stage again, Mademoiselle. Have a good evening.]

If he were an Italian, he would have lured her even if he were with his wife. He really didn't have an eye to such a beautiful woman like me⋯Thinking this way, she was a little crossed. But one thing she could confirm was judjing from the feeling when he hit her, he was not armed and that he was certainly intoxicated.

After Show Taro, she purposely hit Robert when he was on the way to the men's room. With this try, she realized he was hiding a pistol under his jacket. Normal passengers come by aeroplane so it

— 310 —

is not possible to bring any firearms into the country. She thought he might have received such pistol at the embassy. He was completely sober and he also was a man who did not show any interest in her.

Druj   [Ah! I am sorry.]

Robert   [Excuse me, Madam.]

Druj   [No, I'm Mademoiselle Druj.]

Robert   [Excuse me, Mademoiselle.]

Druj   [I am···]

Robert   [EX-CU-SE-ME, Mademoiselle!]

Finising saying so, Robert went away still keeping a polite way. He looked entirely work-oriented and did not show any interest in her. Robert really burned her up.

The last one left was Indrajit but around him Nancy and Emily were always there so there was no chance for her to hit him anywhere. Therefore, she could not find out whether he was armed or not but she understood watching him while on the stage that he had few alchophol drinks. Under the circumstantial evidence, Druj had a need to assum that he must be armed as same as Robert.

When Druj returned to the backstage, Onkot, who had been impatiently waiting for her, hurriedly asked.

Onkot   [How is your feeling about them?]

Druj   [That Asian originated man seems to be a Japanese antique dealer. He might work as a springboard for us.]

Onkot   [What about that European look man?]

Druj   [His accent sounds like an British accent. In any case he is no American.]

Onkot	[He won't be a resident in Singapore.]
Druj	[But he is armed with a pistol. This would mean he is not a normal businessman.]
Onkot	[Suppose he came from overseas, such a weapon as pistole would have been seized at the airport.]
Druji	[So that the conclusion will be he got it at the embassy or such.]
Onkot	[A spy, or a military man?]
Druj	[For those professions, I guess he cannot look that much slightly-built?]
Onkot	[You're right. He looks much more intelligent than a military man.]
Druj	[Do you know his name?]
Onkot	[According to the information from the waiter only his first name Robert is known.]
Druj	[Did you check the hotel register book for tonight stayers?]
Onkot	[Manager of this hotel did'nt tell me.]
Druj	[Hopeless, isn't he.]
Onkot	[It is not known as yet which ones and how many are going to stay tonight at Mandarine Palace.]
Druj	[As I couldn't have a chance to hit any one of them accidentally on purpose, I am no way sure but most probably they may be armed.]
Onkot	[They looked to be taking non-alchoholic beer only.]
Druj	[They were talking like Americans.]
Onkot	[Will they be multinational Mafias?]
Druj	[What can be said at least is Indrajit must be Raja's

— 312 —

underling.]

Onkot [I have heard together with the American vessels a Mafia's pleasure boat was raising Jolly Rogers. Does that mean that Mafia was working as the instrument of American Navy?]

Druj [The pleasure boat looks like Italian National.]

Onkot [I wonder what kind of group we are dealing with?]

Druj [One thing clear is to dispose Indrajit.]

Onkot [Well, you're quite right.]

Onkot was waiting for the jazz performance to be finished and to return to his room. It was unknown at that big hotel whether he was staying at the top floor or at a separate cottage. As Raja Mitra did not make an equity participation in that hotel, there were few Indian employees so they were rather eye-catching being Indians which was the most difficult point that they were facing in acting this hotel. To combat with this problem, Onkot stole hotel boy uniforms from the linen closet and let one of the underlings wear it. At a big hotel as that one it was rather easy to commit such risky deeds which would not easily be questioned as the hotel was always busy.

Onkot [This uniform has an ample space at the sleeve openings so the wearer can hide something there. A couple of you, wear these uniforms and go out to observe the situation inside the hotel.]

Having said so, he gave a sign to another underling to go as well.

When the jazz live performance fnishied, Indrajit and his party slowly moved out from the hall. As Indrajit could not walk fast, they waited till other people came out first. When the collidor

— 313 —

became less busy, they stood up and started moving.

As they passed by the elevators, they seemed to be staying at cottages. With a sudden booking and arrival of quite a few people as a group, it was a fact that cottage stay was the only choice. While they were slowly moving, the boy they saw previously came and spoke to Indrajit.

Hotel Boy [Let me lend my shoulder, Sir. Please cling to me.]

Indrajit [Thank you.]

Hotel Boy [Which room is yours?]

Indrajit [The one at the bottom.]

As Emily thought the boy was kind, she secretly handed over to him one ten-dollar note which the boy thankfully received.

Hotel Boy [Shall I have some drinks sent?]

Emily [No, thank you. Good night.]

She sent him back and the boy went away. After the boy was gone, Maria spoke up.

Maria [Look, This room will become dangerous tonight.]

Emily [Could you see anything?]

Maria [That man is not the boy at this hotel.]

Emily [How did you know that?]

Maria [That hotel boy secretly checked and confirmed Indrajit had a gun.]

Nancy [I see. Let's move to Robert's room and wait and see.]

Then all of them shifted two cottages away from Indrajit's cottage and waited holding their breaths and caught a sound that moved toward the bottom of the collidor.

Stealthy steps together with a metallic sound were quietly passing by through the collidor, and after a while a blunt sound of

— 314 —

breaking glass facing towards the garden was heard which meant that instead of breaking through the door, they came around to the garden to invade into the cottage from the garden side. Probably they firstly taped the glass window and crushed it. Those people sounded to invade into the room where Show Taro and Nancy were supposed to stay. Those people hiding themselves in the third cottage from the bottom of the collidor felt that the invaders would come there in no time so their tension was all the more running high.

In that tensed situation, they finally invaded into the room where each of the members laid themselves down on the floor holding their breath and trying to feel the moving shades of the invaders. Suddenly the light was put on which caught that hotel boy holding a gun to whom Nancy's gun fired. He was shot at the wrist of his hand and blood spattered. Robert seized the other one alive and wrested his gun away.

Robert   [Nancy, seize that one you shot and get all he knows out of him.]

Nancy   [Okay.]

Right before Nancy seized him, a knife was flying in and that boy groaned small and leaned against her. On his back, a knife was stug precisely at the back of his heart. While Robert's eyes were captivated by that scene, the other man who was being held by his arms by Robert was led to dealth. Knife again. It was definitely not the work by an amateur killer.

Nancy   [Henry, This is Nancy. We have just been assaulted. Send an armoured Cadillac.

I understand Joe's Cadillac is armoured, isn't it?]

— 315 —

Henry	[I will go right away. Where are you?]
Nancy	[At the cottage of Mandarine Palace. The third cottage from the back. We seem to be surrounded.]
Henry	[Hang in there for fifteen minutes.]
Nancy	[Roger!]

To dodge the enemy's attack Nancy switched her cellphone off and at that moment Show Taro heard her moaning and sound of her falling down. He crawled to the direction of the sound where he thought Nancy was falling down on the floor, but that was not Nancy but that hotel boy. Show Taro further crawled passing over a pool of blood and there he found Nancy fell down breathing hard.

Show Taro [Nancy, Are you okay?]

Nancy [Tom, Thank you.]

He came around the side of her and tried to raise her in his arms and found that a big knife was stabbing on her back. Blood was gushing out from there. Show Taro could not judge whether he should pull the knife out or not. Besides them Robert was in the midst of gun fighting against the enemy that were not in Robert's sight. The enemy looked like thinking the fighting power of Robert's side decreased from 2 persons to one.

Nancy [Tom, turn down.]

Show Taro laid on the floor with his face down and over the laying Show Taro she fired the gun. A shade by the window fell down which was known to them by the sound.

Show Taro [Nancy, Thank you.]

Nancy [Tom, I am cold.]

That she was saying cold in this tropical heat was a proof of her loosing blood quite much. Show Taro moved around the side of her and saw a pool of blood there. Unless she was taken to hospital right away, it was a matter of time for her to lose her life. At the outside of the cottage, it seemed that help hands from the embassy arrived and a new gunfight was being developed. By this arrival of help, Robert was saved. In the cottage it was felt that the shades outside were running away from the attack surrounding them.

Show Taro   [Nancy, I am here.]

Nancy   [Tom, I am cold.]

Show Taro hugged Nancy tightly. Robert switch the light on.

Nancy   [Promise, Re..men..ber?]

Show Taro   [We are visiting the grave of your grandmother together, putting on a gondra a mountainful roses. Venice will surely surely show its beautiful face.]

Nancy   [And then?]

Show Taro   [Then we will run an antique dealing business in your hometown Chicago, even though the shop may be very small.]

Nancy   [Ca..n..w.e..d..o..so..?]

Show Taro   [Don't talk any more, Nancy.]

Nancy   [Kiss me, not..to..forget⋯me.]

Show Taro kissed Nancy.

Nancy   [Once..more..more..p..l..e⋯a⋯s⋯e.]

What a pity! Her voice was getting thinner and thinner. Show Taro continued to kiss her.

Nancy   [M..o..r..e⋯]

Show Taro was kissing her with no thought for the people around them but he could no way prevent her seoul from going off her body. Emily, Maria, and Robert and Indrajit, not to talk about

Show Taro, could never look squarely at Nancy without tears.

Show Taro [Nancy!]

She was no longer moving. She was getting cold.

For the safety sake, they shifted to another hotel for that night under arrangement by the embassy. In the car heading to the new hotel there a radio music program was going on. All people was keeping silence but when that program started by chance 「Besame Mucho」 ,there was no one that was not moved to be tears.

24. Funeral and New Beginning

At a later date, at a Catholic church in the suburbs of Chicago, the funeral of Nancy Franchetti was held.

Show Taro and Maria were there and Nancy's parents and brothers also attended. Emily and Indrajit were there, too.

That funeral day was a cold day with the sky covered with low-hanging clouds. Autumn sunlight was gone and leaves of the trees of the forest were all off the trees. The big size coffin was filled by rose bouquets and Nancy was made up beautifully.

Suppose she were a bride, how beautiful she would have been, in her next life nothing more tragic happening could ever happen···All attendants at the funeral thought that way and teared. According to what her younger sister Sarah told them, at the night when Nancy passed away, the Teddy Bear named Monica in the room of Nancy was found to be fallen on the bed with the face down. Both in the East or the West, it is believed dolls may get the seoul of the owner of the dolls. All people at that funeral wondered that the bear who had the Christian name of Nancy might offer to sacrifice itself for Nancy.

Indrajit [I am awfully sorry for your loss, Show.]

Emily [Nancy was telling me that you were true lovers···I have no word to comfort you.]

Maria [When I saw the destiny of Sharon of getting sunken, I happened to sight the scene of Nancy passing away.]

Emily [I now see. That is why you fainted at that time.]

Maria [I could not say it even after I came back to myself. I

— 319 —

cannot possibly tell the death of my customer and also the the last scene of Nancy with Show was seen then ···]

Indrajit   [You are engaged in a torturing business.]

Maria   [Even out of the business, the future is always visible to me. But I am···]

Emily   [But..?]

Maria   [I am..trying not to sight them.]

Emily   [As I will pay you, won't you tell our fortune as well?]

Maria   [If you can wait till the funeral is over.]

At the later hour after the funeral was over, taking Maria, Show Taro visited Emily and Indrajit.

Maria   [What do you wish to let me see?]

Emily   [What will happen hereafter.]

Maria   [Understood.]

Maria opend her eyes wide and gazed Emily and started talking.

Maria   [Defection of Indrajit will be granted and you are to live under a different name. You will not be able to find a suitable realestate in Indiana, I see another state towards east from Indiana. You are to start running a shop of custom cars. Name of the shop···to me it looks like Indy Custom. There the painting of the 1950's can be done. Regarding pearl painting there, I see you are putting powder of real Mother of Pearl and repeating spray painting for as many as twenty times. You are explaining to your customer that his pearl painting is different from the modern time's pearl painting so that even if the bonnet looks like whity, seeing through the

|Indrajit|side of the bonnet from the top, the color looks bluish.]
[Oh, You are great, Without having any professional knowledge, you are really seeing it!]

Hearing this convincing explanation from Maria, Indrajit coud not but believe Maria's psychic power giving detailed explanation regarding the painting of customs cars.

Maria   [I wish to give you one advice.]

Emily   [What is it?]

Maria   [You know computer technology is needed for exercising custom tuneup of an engine. Don't let Indy to do this work and you are to talk with the technician. Mind you, never let Indy talk to the technician.]

Emily   [But why?]

Maria   [I understand programers of computors are oftentimes Indians. If there should be Raja Mitra related person, you would be ended.]

Emily   [Any other points for us to be careful about?]

Maria   [Computers and computer-related goods are to be dealt with by Emily. What Raja Mitra means is; Raja is a king and Mitra is light so it has the same meaning as Lucifer. Raja has many underlings who are faithful to him. And I see in his future he is coming to sight Indy500. He is ordering Kubera to seek Indy out there.]

Emily   [I undertand. Any other points?]

Maria   [Don't purchase jewelries or the like from Indians. Kubera also has some Indian blood and he is collecting information of people who buy jewelries. Therefore, you must seal your new name to such people.]

Emily [I guess what you said now has not much relation to me.]

Maria [You buy gifts for Thanksgiving Day, Christmas, Wedding Anniversary, and Birthday, don't you? As such times, if you should make a mistake of writing your original name, with no exception Kubera will chase you.]

Emily [What about our children?]

Maria [You wish a gir and a boy, don't you?]

Emily [You won.]

Maria [A girl is already in your tummy and will be named as Nancy.]

Emily [Wow, Do you already know it!?]

Indrajit [So I am soon be a dad!]

Maria [The baby is only on one month stage. I can see every night since you met again.]

Saying so, Maria blushed up a little.

Hearing this conversation, Indrajit looked a bit embarrassed and asked Maria.

Indrajit [I guess you cannot see if we use a canopy bed.]

Maria [Voice can be heard.]

At that time, showing a little shocked look, Show Taro joined the conversation.

Show Taro [Was the scene of Nancy and me seen?]

Maria [So, I am trying not to see.]

Show Taro [Were you a peeping Betty?]

— 322 —

Maria   [Absolutely not! Can't believe plural times per night!]

In a bit distructive manner, Maria blushed up all the more.

Emily   [Let's trust what she said.]

Show Taro [Okay, okay, I will. By the way has your new name been set?]

Emily   [Yes⋯But because of the promise made with the Government, we are prohibited to tell it to any one.]

Indrajit   [We have to keep our past for at least twenty years, on behalf of this child, too.]

Saying so, Indrajit rubbed Emily's inside.

Show Taro [Let's stop to be voyeurs. What new business have you chosen?]

Indrajit   [Exactly as Maria's oracle.]

Show Taro [Then, you mean you will run the custom car business, do you?]

Having said so, and posed a moment to chew over what Maria said, then Show Taro continued.

Show Taro [So, the name of the store you are going to start will be Indy Custom. Is this part of her oracle coming true though whatever extra words may be attached before or after this naming?]

Indrajit   [You may be right.]

He replied with a grin.

Show Taro [If my rent-a-car break down in a state at the east side of Indiana, I will ring you.]

Indrajit   [Yes, Do that please, though I cannot tell you anything further in accordance with the program set by the Government.]

Maria　　　[As Raja will use the force who has a power to see through the futuristic vision, you had better stretch a barrier around the work place and home.]

Emily　　　[How can we do it?]

Maria　　　[He has that ability to some extent. His first name of Dvija is Baramon which means regeneration. But just to make sure of your safety, I will give you eight pieces of this amulet which I expect you to past at the four corners of the working place and also at the four corners of your home. You must do this in order not to be found out.]

　Saying so, Maria took out the amulets and gave these to Emily. Indrajit, covering Emily's tummy, received those amulets, leaning forward to Maria.

Indrajit　　[Thank you.]

Maria　　　[I wish you to be happy.]

Show Taro [Congratulations for your marriage.]

　Then, Show Taro took Maria on his car and left the hotel. On the way back, Show Taro raised a question to Maria in a casual manner.

Show Taro [Since you were talking about the phase of women's troubles, did you already see through this ending?]

Maria　　　[No, what I saw first was the furious attack of Ms. Jinlian only. Ms. Akemi is a woman that has never been defeated by any one, but Ms. Jinlian took several men into her hand before Ms. Akemi beat them to the draw.

　Her previous life was also the same way. Jinlian and Mr. Chen

— 324 —

were lovers some hundred years ago.]

Show Taro [Was Jinlian already behaving in that same manner in her previous life?]

Maria [She is shouldering deep karma. She will continue to make it the object of her life to have men kneel down before her. Her heart will never be able to be cured, though for the reason that she can never meet a man who will truly love her seoul even though there are many who love her body. If she fails to meet such a man, she will continue to seek him forever.]

Show Taro [Since when did you able to see through Nancy's fate?]

Maria [When I met her for the first time, I saw she was your lover in the previous life, in Lombardy in the middle ages.]

Show Taro [And how our relationship ended in our previous life?]

Maria [Since you met her in your previous life, you devoted yourself to various studies. You also achieved some success in your business. So, you bought a mansion alongside the canal in Venice and found Nancy who was a daughter of poor aristcrat's. You received her having georgeously decorated the windows of your mansion with curtains of her favorite color. But one thing you did is that for her you left another woman. Your happiness in your previous life may have not been broken down, but this time the turn may be given to that woman you left. As I am not God, I cannot say anything definite, but as I am not Demon either, I cannot transact life with you. In your previous

— 325 —

life, she ended her life due to tubaculousis or some illness like that leaving three children, and you, too, must have passed away around the age of fifty due to aggravated flu.]

Show Taro [By chance, who will be that woman who has a turn in this world?]

Maria [I wish to let you chose your destiny by yourself. Therefore, I won't tell you from my mouth whatever I see. If I see anything bad, I am willing to tell you how to avoid that bad fate, but even in that case, I cannot tell the person death of whom I forsee. Your life will continue for a long while, so, this I can tell you. That one can see the other's fate may mean, as you said it before to me, to lose something.]

Show Taro [Taking what you have said as a fact, does it mean that you were perfectly aware how the destiny of Nancy Monica Franchetti would end up and nevertheless you could not advise her at all? Was it seen by you what would end her fate?]

Maria [Sharon is literally the ferryman of the Styx.]

Show Taro [When Sharon the destroyer came out, you knew her fate would end…]

From the car radio which happened to be turned on, the melody of 『Smoke gets in your eyes』 streamed out.

That standard number of Jazz made the two quiet.

25. Another Destruction

On Show Taro's return to Japan, he found a message from Akemi who wanted him to come to her company which was an unusual request. He visited her at the president's office in her building in Ginza. After her secretary went out, she put on the cable TV which was placed in front of the sofa. He smelled stronger scent of perfume from Akemi than previous. Also, he felt her a bit sexier than before.

Akemi [Why didn't you see me the first thing on your return? Don't let me worry about you.]

Show Taro [Well, but I just felt uneasy to meet you.]

Akemi [That's not on. You know I have never avoided you in past.]

Show Taro [Well, that's true···but why did you send me an e-mail for the first thing this morning?]

Akemi [Did you see the news?]

Show Taro [What news?]

Akemi [It is on from this morning on cable TV.]

Having said so, she put the television switch on. The news of cable TV was reporting that Chen Jin Ji who was the owner of a hotel and a casino in Macao was missing for some unknown reason. According to the news, his overloan status was disclosed and a run on the bank seemed to have occurred.

Akemi [See, if you had been Jinlian's man, you would have been chased by mass communications.]

Show Taro [···So it looks like.]

Akemi   [May I ask you a bit queer question?]

Show Taro [What is it?]

She moved next to him on the sofa to see his reaction closely.

Akemi   [For some time recently, I don't see Ms. Maria. Do you know anything?]

Show Taro [I don't.]

Akemi   [Even if you think with your hands on your chest?]

Having said so, she took Show Taro's hand to her full bosom. She continued to try to put her lips on his, then at that moment he saw a scene familiar to him and issued to voice in spite of himself and pointed the TV screen.

Show Taro [⋯nnn!]

Akemi   [Show, What happened?]

What Akemi saw was the entrance which was also familiar to her.

Reporter   [I am standing at the entrance of 「Perfect Beauty」 in Ginza. This is the place where Ms. Jinlian seems to visit frequently. We obtained an information from Hong Kong Dashing Coverage of Ms. Jinlian visiting this place today. According to Hong Kong News, Ms. Jinlian is yearning for the president of this company like her real sister.]

Akemi   [Oh, I'm stumped. Why could this informatin leak?]

Show Taro [Is Jinlian scheduled to come today?]

Akemi   [She firstly said she would come the first thing in the morning but later she was saying she would be a bit delayed⋯]

Show Taro [I guess Ms Jinlian's secetary or the like may have told

— 328 —

them?]

Akemi　　[Oh, I hate this peeping business. Why does our building have to be filmed?]

The angle of the camera was changed. That time was from the opposite side building.

Desk　　[Situation in the president's office cannot be seen clearly disturbed by the curtain. Could the person whom the secretary of Perfect Beauty said as a visitor be Ms. Jinlian?]

Reporter　　[Mr. Itoh, According to the secretary, the visitor seems to be a man.]

Desk　　[Could it be Mr. Chen Jing Ji?]

Reporter　　[I cannot tell it but according to an employee of the store in the opposite side of the street, the visitor looks like a man of Ms. Jinlian's favorite though this information is unconfirmed.]

Desk　　[Please continue to cover the proceedings.]

Reporter　　[Yes, I will return the management of this scene back to the studio for the prsent.]

The two looked at each other and kept gazing at the details of the news.

Show Taro　[Is Jinlian coming now?]

Akemi　　[She should be here soon.]

Show Taro　[Is Ms. Jinlian trying to help Mr. Chen out from the pinch he is in?]

Akemi　　[Has such situation as this been profested?]

At her question, Show Taro picked up some possibly applicable parts from his memo.

— 329 —

Show Taro [Les Centuries (The hundred psalms) 8-28

1st Line Fake gold and silver make expenditure greater

2nd Line Then will have a hard time for paying at the fire-like reminders

3rd Line All become unstable and are going to be lost

4th Line Bond on printer, namely corporate debenture becomes overdue

If I translate it just roughly, the expense which was paid for by borrowing in exchange of bonds became unable to be reimbursed due to credit uncertainty, which will eventually develop into default of corporate bonds on financial obligations. Though there is no mention of when it will happen, it is to come in the era when printed bonds are issued as corporate bonds or Government bonds. In this meaning, that era will mean the fall of bubbles economy that happened in Japan at the end of the 20th century or such of American in the 21st century.

The statement of 'feu furent' on the second line can be translated as to fall the trees and fire them, which will reminiscent us of deforestation and of residential development. Therefore, talking about economy of China, while consumer price level keeps rising in the absence of actual demand by prospective residents, such phenomenon is pulling the growth of China up is problematical.]

Akemi   [Chinese economy is also a bubbles economy, I see.]

Show Taro [Such means as to find out the value of the land other than the value of actually existing demand and, making it as mortgage, to issue bonds and keep developing the land is as itself where the sprout of bubbles is hidden. Bubbles will be risen based on that action by excessive credit creation being practiced. I think Nostradamus may be bespeaking that this situation will take place in every country over the world. I am of course no prophet nor a medium so I can no way be sure about what I have said. One thing I feel sure about is to decipher 『Les Centuries』, that the decoder must not be too professional with French language is important. In actual practice, such translation as sticking too much to the details is, even if it is correct in view of grammer, it may look to have missed the true meaning written there.]

Akemi [So, there will be more falls of bubbles economy other than that of China.]

Show Taro [If such economy is based on the actually exisiting demand, it will be okay⋯but sometimes and often times human desire gets inflated beyond the actual demand. And that is expressed by the last word of the first line, 'enflez', which has the meaning of 'to swell' or 'expense increases'. Therefore, that economy is swelling more than necessary and that expenses will increase may be foreseen by Nostradamus.]

Akemi [Conclusion is Mr. Chen crossed the red line.]

According to the television report, Chen Jing Ji used to be the adapted son in law till last week when their divorce was finalized and one of the reasons of this divorcement is rumored to be his extravagance to satisfy demands by Jinlian Pan. He continued to create gourgenous casino and commercial facility without enough preparation of the necessary fund to curry favor of Jinlian which seemed to cornor him to bankruptcy. And what was reported in addition was he was making a political contribution of a huge amount of money. Human desire seems to have a tendency of running out of control in any country. It was a long time ago when a politician called Ghan Zhong said that the destinaton where desire would find its way was self-destruction. His words are still a truth after 2,500 years.

Show Taro [By the way, does this building have a back door?]

Akemi [You can use my car. Won't you make a run away getting down to the basement by fire escape stairs?]

Show Taro [I will.]

He received a key that was given to him.

Show Taro [Which car?]

Akemi [Today's car is a light green Alfa Romeo.]

Show Taro [That's pretty noticiable.]

Saying so, Show Taro casually raised his hand and said bye to Akemi and from the side which was out of the reach of the cameras of the press went by the fire escape down to the parking area in the basement floor.

When he came out from the parking area he was caught up by the press. In a panic, he pushed a wrong switch which was to open the top. Rent-a-car specifications in Italy is different from Japan. The positions of winker and wiper are set in a reverse way against steering wheel on Italian rent-a-cars. It looked while Show Taro was touching here and there he mistakenly opened the electric hood.

Reporter [Mr. Ito, Mr. Chen looks like on this car. As the hood was opened, he seems to accept our interview.]

— 332 —

Desk　　　[Do make a dash.]

Reportger　[Hi, Mr. Chen, are you. Since when have you been associated with President Kitsuregawa?]

An interpreter next to the reporter started to talk to him in Cantonese.

Show Taro　[⋯..]

Show Taro was adamant to keep ignoring them, but the enlarged screen was clearly catching his cheek marked by rouge of Akemi.

Reporter　[Wow, From the morning, such a fresh hicky mark!]

Show Taro　[!!!]

In spite of himself, Show Taro stepped on accelerator to make a jump start and with that high speed, he escaped through the streets of Tokyo.

Reporter　[We will wait a while till Ms. Jinlian arrives here.]

Assistant　[It looks this issue is turning into a new phase. A new mistery involving Mr. Chen Jing Ji, Ms. Jinlian Pan and Ms. Akemi Kitsuregawa.]

Desk　　　[Flaudulent loans and suspect of diversion which have a possibility to affect the political world of Hong Kong and Macao are now expected to show a new development in Japan.]

Announcer bowed once and changed the subject to the next one.

This scene was reported all over the world. Akemi was brushing up in the president office but on the other hand she thought this happening could let her make Jinlian owe her. On the other side, Jinlian was still unable to go out from the suite of the hotel she was staying and just caught the news and was looking at it. Until short time before, she was with Chen Jing Ji in that suite on the top floor of Shinkoku Hotel. Due to a long story, she could not leave there till the morning. She had an interest free debt of 3 million dollars from Chen so that then she was wondering worried about this debt if Chen would hard-press her for repayment. At that very moment, Jinlian was also watching this same TV program.

Jinlian   [Akemi got ahead of me--]

Clenching her hands, she burst out crying without herself. Their fight was temporarily ceased after the dealth of Nancy, which was then relapsing. Jinlian who needs to have as many men as possible who obey and follow her was feeling that Chen Jing Ji was going to his fate, therefore for her a man who would replace Chen Jing Ji was a necessity.

Shinkoku Hotel where Jinlian and Chen Jing Ji spent over night was a prominent hotel in Tokyo. The chic outlook of the hotel was the performance of an American architect of the long past and the floor of this hotel where big figures of Japan's political and financial world were frequently coming in and out was made of Oya stone while other big hotels were using marble stone, and that Oya stone inner decoration was accepted favorably as Oya stone paved floor was not slippery while Japan is a rainy country and this built up a good reputation of that hotel. The construction which was based on safety of the guests rather than the superficial gourgeous look of the building. There were many customers who support this principle of the hotel.

The top floor of that hotel had the best quality rooms called divine suite. Yesterday, too, Chen was meeting several presidents of Japan's leading banks in order to negotiate with them trying to get new financing for a commercial facility which was newly under construction. However, the Japanese banks were exercising credit granting investigation cooperating with banks in Singapore or Hong Kong, so they were naturally suspecting why he could not get funded by banks such as Hong Kong banks if such business of his was so very profitable as he was highlighting. In addition, in spite of the fact that the slow movement of decision-making of Japanese financial institutions is well known, so that the reason why Chen dared to come to Japan was clearly showing to the Japanese banks that he was that much cornored.

Japanese financial facilities aggressively exercised credit granting investigation and contributed to industrial development in the pioneer days of modern Japan. However, after WW2, the age of the long upward slope ended and was replaced with the age when cost increase of pledged assets could not be expected, therefore, the financial world of Japan was put into confusion where no one knows what to do as no precedent was available.

In such situation there took place unprecedented wage increases and the Japanese financial world fell in such situation as called the lost ten years or twenty years. The biggest problem of Japan was as a result of its concentration to grow up employees obedient to the industries, it came to hold no capability to esteem the personnel who were full of American styled spirits of challenge for aggressive and capable students to try to establish companies on their own by their own power.

Most of the Japanese bankers may not be able to be interested in the new type industries. Like computer scored answer sheet, this established tendency eliminates such creative attitude to esteem some new industries that are different from the already existing type of industries. Japanese Government is also emphacizing the policy of people being employed by some other people and Japanese economy world will not raise any objection to that. Such uncomprehensive country is what Japan is. The spirits of Meiji Restration must have been based on the attitude such as if no one won't do it, I will do it. We cannot but wonder where those spirits were gone.

That day was over and Jinlian Pan came to visit Chen.

Jinlian   [How did it go?]

Chen   [I failed.]

Jinlian   [Why don't you forget everything?]

Chen   [I can be in that mood.]

Jinlian   [But let's change the mood! Having some delicious food.]

She took up the telephone next to the sofa. The call was immediately connected.

Chen   [Front desk? Arrange to prepare two servings of the best quality Sushi and one bottle of Tokai wine. Have those brought here as room service of course.]

Jinlian   [Wow, That's wonderful. The best of Tsukiji.]

Chen   [Means left is limited. Though I have loans collectable from you⋯]

Needless to say, as things developed to this worst extreme, the three million dollars which Chen lent to Jinlian without interst and without any written evidence was only a drop in the bucket so he didn't rely on such small money from the beginning. Yes, that loan is nothing to help this overall situation. Unless the loss of 20 million

— 336 —

dollars is covered, destruction will be sure to come as a matter of time.

Jinlian   [Let's forget all about that and enjoy the dinner together?]

Chen   [By chance, can I book a reservation with your recommending Ms. Maria ?]

Jinlian   [She is Akemi's favorite medium. Did you ask Zedeng Mao?]

Chen   [Mao told me last week to find out my savior in a week's time.]

Jinlian   [What more did he tell you?]

Chen   [Well, he said a divination sign which was telling something like a hole is open in my fortune so that what is hidden will altogether be exposed.]

Jinlian   [If you survive that crisis?]

Chen   [I can make a leap forward again.]

As a matter of fact, Jinlian also knew that ZeDeng Mao told the fortune of Chen to Show Taro, she was trying to buck herself up and behaving in a bright way. She was also feeling on skin that the man who loved her was just about to leave her.

Jinlian   [I will go and see a moment. It sounds like the room service has come.]

An employee of that hotel came in pushing a wagon. He gave a polite bow once and said.

Employee   [Excuse me This is room service.]

Chen   [Receive this platinum card for payment.]

He took out a silver color card and hand it to him and the hotel man politely received it.

Employee   [Certainly.]

He bowed politely again and went out.

Jinlian [Now, cheer yourself up!]

Chen   [Always cheerful, aren't you.]

In response to her encouragement, Chen regained a bit of vigor, however that Chen was meeting Jinlian this way was found out by his wife and was given over by the father-in-law, Xi Men Qing. He tendered his agreement to divorcement but on the other hand he knew more than anyone else that Jinlian could not be of his help. At that night, the two talked the night away forgetting all other things.

When he awoke on the following morning, Jinlian was no longer there so he bathed alone. In the bathtub in which he bathed with Jinlian on the previous night, there left a few strings of long hair entangling to each other which to him looked like the vestige of this world. Drinking orange juice on the tray of breakfast which was delivered by room service, he put on the switch of TV. Watching the screen, he came to learn that news reporters and crime investigators had landed in Japan to chase him. Together with the orange juice on the breakfast tray he took two tablets of the synthetic drug, MDMA, which he had taken only half of a tablet last night. He then sank himself in the bath again. Through the skylight of the penthouse, the blue sky of Tokyo at already after ten o'clock was seen. After a while he felt painful, then he was caught by generalized seizure and soon he came to float on the surface of that big bathtub. Since from ancient era, it was a virture in China that King would not be killed by the enemy's sword.

Put your palms together.

THE END of canon Ⅱ. Abalon

Published List

SS 影の帝国（正典 No.1）日本語版　PASSO　ROMANO
ISBN 978-4-7876-0071-4　　　　　April 2011
SS 影の帝国（正典 No.2）日本語版　ABALON
ISBN 978-4-7876-0072-1　　　　　June 2011
SS 影の帝国（外典 No.1）日本語版　Queen's Books
ISBN 978-4-7876-0097-4　　　　　September 2016
SS SHADOW EMPIRE English Edition
　Canon 1　Passo Romano
　ISBN 978-4-7876-0108-7　　　　December 2019
　Canon 2　Abalon
　ISBN 978-4-7876-0109-4　　　　December 2019
　Apocrypha 1　Queen's Books
　ISBN 978-4-7876-0110-0　　　　December 2019

ISBN978-4-7876-0109-4

SS SHADOW EMPIRE Canon Ⅱ English Edition
SS影の帝国　正典Ⅱ　英語版

令和元年 12 月 7 日　第 1 刷発行
Dec/7/2019　1st edition issued
著　者　author　　Tycoon SAITO
翻　訳　translator　Yoshie HIYAMA
発行者　publisher　Yasushi ITO　伊藤泰士
発行所　株式会社創樹社美術出版

（乱丁・落丁はお取り替えいたします）
©Tycoon SAITO 2019 Printed in Japan